The Right Choice

★ ★ ★ ★ ★

Sandra Robbins

Published by Larkspur Lane Press
120 Vancleave Road
Martin, TN 38237
http://sandrarobbins.net

Printed in the United States of America

Cover design by Diane Turpin, http:/dianeturpindesign.com

ISBN 978-0-9968918-5-1

Dedication

Dedicated to the memory of all the women who worked without giving up to see that women in America would gain the right to vote.

Chapter 1

June, 1916
Richland Creek, Tennessee

None of the Saturday afternoon customers noticed when Sarah Jordan slipped out the front door of Weston's General Store. That suited her just fine. If one more of the people inside asked her how she liked living in Richland Creek, she might very well forgo her resolve to endure her present situation and tell them what she really thought.

Thankful to be free of the buzz of activity inside, she let out a relieved sigh, leaned on the railing around the front porch of the white clapboard building, and closed her eyes. It wasn't that she had anything against the people she'd met since coming here, but it was different from the city where she'd grown up. What she wouldn't give to be sitting in the shade of the big trees in their backyard in Memphis. There was probably a cool breeze rustling the leaves right now as it rolled up the bluff from the Mississippi River.

Arching an eyebrow, Sarah glanced up and down the dirt street that ran the length of the small settlement. Her mother called it a town, but to her way of thinking there wasn't much here to qualify it as such. She let her gaze travel over what the locals considered the rural community's center of activity.

Across the road from the store, smoke curled upward from a fire at the blacksmith shop, and next to it three men sat on a bench whittling wood in front of Thompson's Grain and Farm Supplies. Three whitewashed houses and the Richland Creek Bible Church completed the settlement. Not only had she traveled a long distance from where she'd grown up, but she felt as if she had traveled back in time.

Of course she'd visited her grandparents here when she was growing up, but it had usually been for only a few days. Now it was going to be for the whole summer, and she didn't know how she was going to survive in this remote farming community. Her mother said she'd adjust, and she'd promised she would try. But how could anybody enjoy living in a place where the main topics of conversation centered on the summer heat and the lack of rain on the crops?

The store's door opened, and her mother stepped onto the porch. Her blue eyes lit with a smile when she spied Sarah. "Here you are. I wondered where you'd gone."

"I needed some air. It was getting stuffy in there."

Her mother frowned and pressed her hand to Sarah's forehead. "I know you didn't sleep well last night. Maybe you're coming down with something."

Sarah chuckled and reached up to grasp her mother's hand. "I'm not getting sick, Mama. I only wanted some fresh air." A mosquito bite on her arm itched, and she scratched it. "As for not sleeping last night, it was the mosquitoes. They buzzed through my window all night. I must have a hundred bites today."

Her mother's frown deepened. "Are you sure it's not something else?"

Sarah squeezed her mother's hand before she released it. "I'm fine, Mama."

Her mother's face paled, and she swallowed hard. "I know it's been hard since your father died, but we'll get through this time. Before you know it, the summer will be over. I'll be settled here, and you can return to Memphis and the job waiting for you."

Sarah's heart pricked at how selfish her thoughts of a moment ago had been. Instead of feeling sorry for herself, she needed to concentrate on making life easier for her mother. "I know, but I wish you had wanted to settle in Memphis instead of here. I'll miss you when I go back."

Sadness flickered in her mother's eyes. "My life in Memphis came to an end when your father died. I just want to live out the rest of my life here where I grew up and where old friends live. I know it's different for you. You're barely twenty years old, and you have your own life to live. I want you to be as happy with yours as I have been with mine."

Sarah covered her mother's hand with hers and pressed her lips into her mother's palm. "It's just that I hate the idea of leaving you by yourself even though you have Uncle Charlie and Aunt Clara here. Are you sure this is what you want?"

Her mother smiled. "Yes."

Sarah inhaled a deep breath. "Then let's concentrate on having a wonderful summer together."

"I like that idea. We'll enjoy being together. Then when fall comes, you can go back to Memphis and your job at Mrs. Tipton's school." She paused, glanced over her shoulder as if making sure they were alone, and lowered her voice. "And I want you to continue working for our cause even though I won't be there."

"I will, Mama. You know how I feel about the suffrage movement."

Her mother cast another nervous glance over her shoulder before she continued. "Let me remind you to be careful while you're in Richland Creek. Don't talk about suffrage to anyone. The people here are good, but most of them don't con-

7

cern themselves with issues in the outside world. And most of the men are very opposed to women being allowed to vote."

"I know."

Her mother's chin quivered, and she bit down on her lip. "Every time I think we're close to getting the vote, something happens to set us back. I'm getting too old to fight now, but you're not. My hope was that it would happen in my lifetime, but now I doubt it. I don't want you to ever give up fighting for what we believe in so I must pass my dream onto you."

"It's my dream, too, Mama." She smiled and squeezed her mother's hand.

Before her mother could respond, the front door of the store opened, and a man stepped onto the porch. Dark brown juice trickled from the corner of his mouth. He nodded, walked to the edge of the porch, and spit a wad of tobacco to the ground below.

Sarah's stomach rumbled and her chest heaved from a suppressed gag. Would she ever get used to the way of life around here? She waited for the man to reenter the store before she spoke.

"We'll discuss this later. Right now I think you should go back inside and talk with your friends. The ballgame is going to start before long."

"I'm tired. I don't think I'm going to the game." Her mother pulled a handkerchief from her pocket and mopped at her forehead. "Clara said I could lie down in their spare bedroom upstairs."

Sarah frowned as she let her gaze drift over her mother's face. She seemed to be tired a lot lately, but that could be the stress of the move. "Are you okay, Mama?"

Her mother smiled. "I'm fine. Don't worry about me. It's a beautiful day, and you look lovely in your new dress. Put a smile on your face and go to the ballgame. Maybe you can make some new friends."

She had hoped that she might meet at least one person today that she could enjoy getting to know, and she glanced down at the straight skirt of her white cotton summer dress with its eyelet over-skirt. "Of all the new dresses Miss Adele made for me before we left Memphis, I like this one best. Except for one thing."

Her mother's mouth curled into a smile, and she glanced down at the long skirt. "The hem?"

"Maybe we should have had her make it shorter." Sarah darted a playful grin at her mother. "You know it is the twentieth century, and hems have gone up two or three inches."

Her mother sighed, and her eyebrows arched. "We'll make the next one shorter. In fact maybe we can have a new dress made for you soon. It's about time for another check to arrive from your father's estate, isn't it?"

Sarah's stomach clenched at her mother's question, and she swallowed hard. "I think so."

Her mother turned to reenter the store but stopped at the door. "Did you give Charlie the list of supplies we need?"

"I did."

"Have you paid him yet?"

Sarah's hand trembled, and she shrugged. "I asked him to charge it today. I'll pay him when the next check arrives."

"Be sure that you do. You know I don't like to charge anything."

She walked over and kissed her mother on the cheek before she could detect Sarah's concern. "I love you, Mama."

"Don't worry. Everything's going to work out the way God wants."

Her mother's words, meant to console, ignited a smoldering fire that had burned inside her for months. She bit down on her lip and waited until her mother disappeared into the store before she stumbled to the porch railing and wrapped her fingers around it. She wanted to throw her head back and scream out her frustration, but she didn't dare. Not here.

It was all so unfair. First her father who she adored had died, and now the money from his estate had suddenly quit arriving. She pounded the railing with her fists. She had to find out what was wrong before she left her mother here, but she had no idea how to do it. Her letters to her father's cousin who was the executor of the estate had gone unanswered, and her inquiry to the bank had been met with a reply that since she was a woman with no legal rights to the money, they couldn't tell her anything.

Laughter drifted from the direction of the baseball diamond in the pasture next to the store, and she jerked upright. With trembling fingers, she wiped her eyes. Someone might come out of the store any minute on their way to the game and see her crying. She needed to find a quiet spot to calm her emotions.

She hurried down the porch steps and around the corner of the building but slowed her steps as she spied the small creek past the tall oaks at the back of the property. Her parents had met one summer at a picnic on the banks of that creek and fallen in love at first sight. As a child she dreamed of the same thing happening to her when she was grown, just like in the fairy tales her father told. But she'd learned one thing in the last few years—fairy tales didn't always have happy endings.

She trudged to the pump behind the store, grasped the handle, and cranked it up and down. The water flowed into her cupped hand, and she lifted it to her lips. As she stepped back, her foot splashed a small puddle of water that had dripped from the spout to the ground. She glanced down to see if she'd gotten mud on her shoe, but something else caught her eye, the hem of her dress. Her shoes forgotten, she stared down at the bottom of her dress and shook her head.

"It needs to be shorter."

She grabbed hold of the dress and lifted the hem several inches up her leg. That looked better. Grasping the material tighter, she raised the skirt even higher, turned, and twisted her upper body in an effort to glimpse the calf below her knee. "Not bad looking legs, I'd say."

"I agree." A voice from behind startled her, and she whirled around.

A young man wearing a white shirt with Richland Creek embroidered in red letters on the pocket smiled at her. It took her a moment to realize he must be one of the baseball team members. His dark eyes sparkled with laughter.

"Hello. I hope I'm not interrupting you."

Sarah's skin warmed under his cool appraising gaze that drifted over her body and came to a stop at her ankles. A smile pulled at his lips, and he looked up. The intense scrutiny in his dark eyes sent a tremor racing through her body.

A sudden thought struck her, and she glanced down at her dress. She still had the skirt raised. With a gasp she released the dress and jerked her hands away.

She balled her fists and glared at the man. "H-how long have you been standing there?"

"Long enough to admire your. . ." His smile deepened, and he glanced down at her hemline again. "Your, uh. . .dress."

Her faced burned with embarrassment, and she took a hesitant step toward him. "H-how dare you spy on me. You, sir, or no gentleman, or you would have announced your presence."

His smile grew bigger as he walked forward. "I assure you I am a gentleman, but you're right. I should have introduced myself instead of being overcome by the scenery."

Her mouth gaped open. "The scenery? I'll have you know, sir, I am not some floozy who enjoys being spied on."

His grin grew larger. "I know that. You're Sarah Jordan. You've moved to Richland Creek with your mother, and you're living on your grandparents' old farm two miles from here."

She crossed her arms and glared at him. "My, my, news travels fast around here, doesn't it?"

He raked his hand through his dark hair and shook his head. "Look, I'm sorry if I've upset you. I saw you walk to the back of the store, and I wanted to meet you. I'm really not a bad person. I didn't mean to cause you any embarrassment."

"Well, you did. Now if you'll excuse me I have to get to the ballgame."

He took another step toward her. "It's not going to start for a few more minutes. We have time to get acquainted."

She ducked her head and hurried past him. "I don't want to know someone who sneaks up on people."

"Aw, come on. I've apologized, so there's no need for you to run off mad."

"I don't accept your apology." She clenched her fists at her side and stormed past him.

He stepped back to let her pass, but she didn't look up at him. She'd only gone a few feet further when he called out. "I hope we meet again."

She stared straight ahead without giving any acknowledgement that she'd heard him. When she rounded the corner of the store, she looked over her shoulder, but he hadn't followed. She headed to the field where the game would be played but stopped at edge of what was somebody's pasture and studied the people gathering in the field.

Aunt Clara had already arrived and sat in a chair under a shade tree where she chatted with a group of women. To their left, two long benches stretched a few feet back from the baseline that ran from third to home plate. Uncle Charlie and a group of men stood huddled behind them. Several of the men sitting on the benches wore shirts like the one she'd seen on the young man at the pump.

Her heart pounded when she thought how the young man's gaze had swept over her. She pressed her hands to her hot cheeks. What must he think about her after witnessing her shameful behavior? In a community as small as Richland Creek, she was bound to run into him again. What would he say? Worst of all, what would he tell his friends?

She clenched her fists at her side and lifted her chin. He was the one at fault, not her. He shouldn't have sneaked up on her. She would put the whole incident out of her mind and go to the ballgame.

She'd only taken one step when a sudden thought popped into her head. The man at the pump had on a shirt with the local team embroidered on the pocket. That meant he'd be at the game, too. Maybe she should go back to the store and stay with her mother. She dismissed that thought right away. Her mother would insist she come back with her. There was no way around it. She had to stay.

Maybe she could find a place where she could sit alone, a quiet spot where no one would notice her. Her gaze swept the field and came to rest on a woman sitting alone near the first base line in a straight-backed, cane bottomed chair. A parasol shielded her from the rays of the sun, and another chair rested beside her.

Sarah looked at the women chattering under the tree near home plate and back at the person in the chair. Maybe the solitary figure reminded her of the isolation and fear she'd felt since coming to this community. She couldn't be sure what it was, but some unknown power urged her forward.

She eased up to the woman, placed her hand on the back of the empty chair, and cleared her throat. "Excuse me. Would you mind if I sat beside you for the game?"

The woman looked around, and Sarah almost gasped aloud at the kindness that radiated from her dark eyes. Tanned skin stretched across high cheekbones, and her black hair lay twisted into a simple bun at the back of her neck. Tiny lines crinkled the corners of her eyes as her mouth curved into a smile.

"Gracious, have I finally found me a female baseball fan in Richland Creek?" The woman's voice reflected the rural drawl heard throughout the area. She laughed and waved Sarah into the chair. "I brought this other chair just in case I was lucky enough to meet up with somebody who didn't want to spend the afternoon gossipin' under that shade tree over there."

Sarah sank into the offered chair. "Thank you. I'm Sarah Jordan. I wouldn't have anything to gossip about. I've only lived here a few weeks."

The woman turned in her chair, reached over, and patted Sarah's knee. "Land sakes, child, I know who you are. My name's Ellen Taylor. I grew up with your Mama, and I met your pa before he married her and took her off to parts unknown."

"You knew my father, too?"

"Sure did. Why, he was one of the best looking men to ever come visitin' in Richland Creek. Swept your mama right off her feet."

Sarah smiled. "He died two years ago. Ever since I can remember he would take me to baseball games in Memphis. He wanted me to love the game as much as he did, and he taught me the rules and what each player's responsibility was. And I do love the game. It always reminds me of him."

A tiny frown wrinkled Ellen's forehead. "I was real sorry when I heard about your pa dying. Pneumonia, wasn't it?"

Sarah glanced down at her dress and smoothed the wrinkles with her hands. "Yes."

"Well, it's good to have you and your mama living here. And I'm glad you came over here to sit with me this afternoon." Ellen laughed, nodded in the direction of the chattering group under the tree, and winked her eye. "Them women over there think I've taken leave of my senses when I get excited over a silly ballgame. 'Course today I got me a special reason for liking it. My brother is the pitcher."

Sarah pointed toward the home team's bench where Uncle Charlie talked with one of the players. "That's my Uncle Charlie over there. He told me there was a new pitcher today."

Ellen glanced at the huddled men. "I know Charlie." Her gaze lingered for a moment before she turned back to Sarah. "My brother's name is Alex. He's been off in Nashville in school for the past few years. He played on some local teams while he was there. He's home for the summer, and the team asked him to play with them again. I think he's a better pitcher than he was before he left."

A roar from the crowd signaled the team had trotted onto the field. Ellen jumped to her feet, and her chair tipped backwards. Sarah hopped up, ran behind Ellen, and replaced the seat to its upright position before facing the players.

She turned towards the field and froze at the sight of the young man headed to the pitcher's mound—the same one she'd seen earlier at the pump. He looked in Ellen's direction, tipped the brim of his cap, and walked to the center of the diamond.

He paused to dig his toe into the dirt and looked up again. This time straight at Sarah. Their eyes locked for a moment. He smiled at her before he turned his attention to the catcher positioned behind home plate.

Sarah groped for her chair with a shaking hand to steady herself. "Is-is that your brother?"

"Yep, that's him. That's Alex."

15

"His name is Alex?"

"Yep. William Alexander Taylor. Alexander was his mama's maiden name, and we always called him Alex out of respect for her 'cause she died when he was born."

"Didn't you have the same mother?"

Ellen shook her head. "No, his mama was our pa's second wife. I been taking care of that boy since the day he was born, and I'm mighty proud of the way he turned out. He's a good man and smart, just like our pa."

There was no mistaking the pride for her brother that sparkled in Ellen's eyes. Sarah looked from Ellen to Alex. "I can see the family resemblance."

His tall, slender body and straight back looked like his sister's. His unruly black hair, the same dark color as Ellen's, stuck out from underneath the cap he wore. Sarah's heart skipped a beat at the sight of the rippling muscles that stretched the shirt material across his broad shoulders as her gaze drifted down to the mitt on his right hand. "He's a southpaw."

Ellen slapped her leg and laughed. "You're sure right. I'll bet there's not another woman out here today who ever heard of a southpaw. Honey, I know we're gonna be great friends."

A wobbly smile pulled at Sarah's mouth, and she looked from Ellen to her brother getting ready for the first pitch of the game. After Alex Taylor told his sister about the encounter at the pump, she doubted if either one would want to be friends with her. For some reason the thought made her sad.

Alex could hardly believe his eyes when he walked onto the pitcher's mound and saw Sarah Jordan sitting next to his sister. His heart had fluttered when he'd seen her at church last Sunday, her hands folded and a cool expression on her face. It hadn't taken long to find out her name, and after that, he couldn't get her out of his mind. He'd never experienced anything in his life like the need he had to know her better.

When he'd seen her go behind the store, he couldn't stop himself from following. Perhaps he shouldn't have done that. He'd certainly made a mess of his attempt to introduce himself. But he couldn't help it. When he walked around the corner of that store and saw her skirt lifted, he responded before he had time to think.

Alex pounded his fist into his ball glove and groaned. Now she probably would never speak to him again. He frowned and shook his head to rid it of thoughts of Sarah Jordan. Right now he needed to concentrate on the batter waiting at the plate. Three up and three down, he had promised the team before they took the field. His goal for the afternoon was to restore Richland Creek's pride in their community baseball team that hadn't beaten Mt. Pleasant in four years.

Later he could try and make amends to Sarah for his behavior earlier. The memory of how beautiful she'd looked with her skirt raised and her face red with embarrassment flashed into his head, but he frowned and shook it from his mind. Then he raised his arms above his head and inhaled deeply before delivering the first pitch of the game.

Two and a half hours later in the bottom of the ninth inning with two outs and a full count on the batter, Alex took a deep breath and hurled what he hoped was the last pitch of the game. The Richland Creek spectators roared at the umpire's shrill cry. "Stri-i-ike!"

With a grin on his face, Alex walked off the pitcher's mound toward the men who'd cheered for their team throughout the afternoon. Charlie Weston was the first to grab his hand. "I can't believe it, Alex. A no hitter. We've been waitin' for the day when our team could beat Mt. Pleasant, and you do it with a no hitter. Congratulations."

Alex smiled and glanced around at several men who slapped him on the back. "Thanks, fellows. I'm glad we won. Our team worked well together this afternoon."

Three more men ran up and joined the crowd that gathered around him. Charlie turned and headed toward the store. "All you fellows on the team come on back over to the store and have a free soda pop in honor of our win."

Alex watched the men follow Charlie before he turned and stared in his sister's direction. It wasn't Ellen he had his sights on, though. He couldn't take his eyes off the young woman beside her. The sun sparkled on her blonde hair that was pulled to the back of her head. He wondered what it would look like if released and allowed to tumble around her shoulders.

His gaze traveled over her body, and he remembered the pleasure he'd gotten from standing close to her earlier. The fire in her blue eyes had hinted she was a woman not easily intimidated, and he longed to see what else lay below her cool exterior.

Taking a deep breath, Alex forced himself to walk forward. In a few moments he'd know if he had ruined any chance of getting to know the most beautiful woman he'd ever seen.

Chapter 2

Sarah couldn't believe how quickly the afternoon had passed, but she knew it was because of how much she'd enjoyed being with Ellen. They'd talked and cheered for the home team, and Sarah was sad to see the game come to an end. Now as she watched Ellen gather up everything she'd brought with her, Sarah couldn't help but smile.

Ellen propped her hands on her hips and frowned as she looked on the ground around the chair where she'd sat. "Where on earth did I put that parasol?"

"When your brother struck the last batter out, you tossed it into the air. It's behind your chair."

Bending over to pick up the umbrella for Ellen, Sarah stiffened at the sound of a deep voice. "What did you think of the game?"

Sarah turned to look behind her, and her breath caught in her throat. Alex Taylor stood just a few feet away. The hair sticking out from under his sweat-stained cap lay plastered to his skin, and perspiration had left trails in the dirt on his cheeks. Fatigue lined his face, and yet Sarah didn't think she'd ever encountered a more handsome man.

The intense look he directed at her bored into the depths of her soul as if it searched for the spots of hollowed-out loneliness in her heart. Her skin warmed, and she licked her lips that suddenly felt dry. His gaze flicked to her lips and back to her eyes.

Sarah took a step backward to put some distance between them. Ellen stepped forward and hugged her brother. "Boy, I nearly died before you struck that last batter out. Next time, just get it over fast so I don't have to suffer."

Alex pulled his attention back to Ellen, threw back his head, and laughed. "Aren't you a little bit proud of me?"

Ellen smiled and punched his shoulder. "I'm proud of you. I've never seen you pitch better. I guess you heard Sarah and me screamin' for you. I know we gave the ladies something to talk about with all our carryin' on."

Alex returned his gaze to Sarah. "I could hear you, both of you."

Sarah's chest tightened. The memory of their encounter at the pump faded as the new emotions produced by Alex's presence swirled through her. Her heart pounded, and she forced herself to smile.

Ellen's voice cut through her thoughts. "Oh, Alex, I haven't introduced you to my new friend. This is Sarah Jordan. She's a baseball fan. Knew right off you were a southpaw."

Alex's smile directed toward his sister revealed straight, white teeth. "I know Sarah."

Ellen frowned. "You do? How?"

Fear of what he was about to say replaced the warm feeling of a few moments ago. She should have known he wouldn't keep her lapse in judgment a secret. What would Ellen think when he told her about what happened?

His forehead wrinkled as if he was in deep thought. "I saw you. . . I saw you at church last week, but I didn't get to introduce myself. I'm glad to finally meet you."

His eyes twinkled, and she breathed a sigh of relief. "I'm glad to meet you, too, Alex."

He tilted his head and stared into her eyes. "So, you're a baseball fan."

"Yes, but today's game is the best I've seen in a long time." She swallowed hard. "I'm glad I came."

His smile deepened. "I'm glad, too."

Ellen turned back to Sarah. "I hope we see you and your pretty mama at church tomorrow. You know it's dinner on the ground, and I have a feelin' that the men will get up another game in the afternoon."

Sarah reached out and grasped Ellen's hand. "Uncle Charlie and Aunt Clara are coming by to get us tomorrow. I'll make sure I see you, Ellen."

Alex reached for the two chairs. "I hope I'll see you, too."

"Maybe so." Sarah glanced around for her aunt and uncle, but they weren't in sight. "I'd better find Uncle Charlie and Aunt Clara now. They're going to take Mama and me home as soon as the last customer is gone from the store. It's been a wonderful afternoon, and thank you again, Ellen."

Sarah walked away, her heart beating so hard she could almost see it pumping through her dress. What was the matter with her? Earlier she'd been angry with Alex Taylor, and then she'd melted like a silly schoolgirl when he flashed his crooked smile at her.

Against her will, she turned and looked in the direction of the Taylors. A wagon, driven by a young boy, pulled to a stop next to them. Alex set the chairs in the back, and then picked up Ellen as if she was as light as a feather and set her in one of them. He climbed onto the driver's seat beside the boy and slapped him on the back.

She'd heard people speak of hero worship before, but she'd never seen it until the boy looked into Alex's face. It made her feel good to know that Alex was the recipient of such obvious respect. They exchanged a few words before the boy picked up the reins and flicked them across the team of horses.

He guided the pair into the road headed in her direction. Alex looked down at her when they passed, smiled, and tipped his cap.

Sarah watched the wagon lumber down the road and thought back to how different she felt now than she had earlier. Suddenly she didn't feel as alone as she had before. Maybe her mother had been right after all. She had wanted Sarah to meet the people she'd known all her life. She'd insisted there were good people in this community, and they took care of each other.

Sarah smiled at the thought of Ellen and Alex Taylor and the young boy who'd looked at Alex with such admiration. She thought she'd just met two of the ones her mother had meant.

Alex Taylor leaned against the front porch post and stared into the night. Owls hooted in the trees near the barn, and the eerie sound drifted through the still air. Fireflies blinked across the front yard, and a hound bayed in the distance. It felt so good to be surrounded by the familiar night sights and sounds he'd known all his life.

Coming home always filled him with contentment, but tonight there was something else that filled his thoughts. He pictured a lovely young girl with beautiful blue eyes and long blonde hair.

The screen door banged behind him, and Ellen stepped onto the front porch. "Well, I got the pies baked for tomorrow, the bread risin', and the supper dishes washed. I'm about ready to turn in, but I wanted to say good-night first."

"Great supper, Ellen. I can't wait to see what you cook up for tomorrow."

"I'll need you to bring in a ham from the smokehouse first thing in the mornin'. I want to fry up some of it for the dinner."

"Will do."

Ellen stepped closer. "What did you think of my new friend today?"

For a moment he didn't answer as he tried to think of a response that wouldn't convey the fascination he had the first time he saw Sarah. He straightened from leaning against the porch post and smiled at his sister. "She seemed nice."

"Nice, huh? Boy, you can't fool your sister. I saw how your eyes popped outta your head when you talked to her."

Ellen's words brought him back to reality, and he laughed. He wrapped his arm around her shoulders and pulled her close. "Was it that obvious? I don't know what it is about her, but I can't shake the feeling she's different from anyone I've ever known."

"I've known her mama since we were girls, and I knew her father, too. He died two years ago. I never expected Julia to come back here to live. She never visited much after she left." Ellen put her hand over her lips to stifle a yawn. "But I guess it's none of my business. So I think I'll just git myself to bed."

Ellen patted Alex's hand resting on her shoulder and turned to reenter the house, but he reached out and stopped her. The lamp light flickering through the front window cast a soft glow across her face, and he could make out the tiny lines that were beginning to crease the corners of her eyes.

Once again guilt filled his heart. This woman was more than a sister to him. She was the only mother he'd ever known. Only seventeen when he was born, she'd put aside her own plans to take care of him, and she'd never faltered in that commitment. How could he ever repay her for all she'd done for him?

He cleared his throat and blinked back the moisture in his eyes. "Ellen, it's so good to be home for the summer. To be here with you."

"I'm right glad to have you home."

His arm tightened around her shoulder, and he pulled her closer. "But I'm not going to stay, and that's bothering me. I don't feel right about leaving you to take care of the farm when I join Mr. Buckley's law firm in Memphis. On the other hand, I'll be making more money than we've ever made on the farm, and I can take care of you better. But I worry about you here alone. I wish you'd come to Memphis with me."

Ellen reached out and patted his arm. "We've talked about this before, and you know my answer's always gonna be the same. This is my home. I could never leave it. You weren't meant to stay here forever. God gave you a love of the law, and you're going to make a great lawyer. I'm so proud of you."

"I worried about you all the time I was in school, but I kept thinking that it would all be worth it when I graduated. Now that I have a job, we can get a house in Memphis and be together again. You won't be alone here on the farm."

A laugh rumbled in her throat. "Alone? I ain't seen a day yet that I was alone. Ever since you brought Augie home after his pa left him, I've had him under my feet. I have to admit, though, I've loved every minute of it. He ain't going nowhere, and neither am I."

"I do feel better knowing he's here. What if he decides to get married and move out? What then?"

"Married? I don't think that's going to happen any time soon. That boy can't even talk to a girl without swallowing his tongue. But if it does, it'll be fine. The important thing to remember, Alex, is that we have to do what God wants. Right now He's put you on a path to work at a law firm in Memphis and me on one to stay right here. If we trust Him, then things will work out for the best."

He exhaled a slow breath before he leaned over and kissed her cheek. "Thank you, Ellen. You have a way of making me see things clearer. No matter where I go or where I work, I promise I'll always take care of you. I love you."

"I love you, too. Now I'm goin' to bed. You have sweet dreams."

"Good night."

Alex waited until Ellen had disappeared into the house before he turned and stared into the night. The moonlight danced across the young cotton plants that lined the straight rows of the field next to the house. Thank goodness for Augie and the tenant farmers who lived on their land. He could trust them to keep the farm going, but Ellen was his responsibility. She was more than his sister. She was his compass and had steered him in the right direction all his life. With the money he'd be making, he finally had the opportunity to repay her for all she'd done for him.

His heart stilled, and the old resolve flowed into his heart. He intended to work hard and show Mr. Buckley he was a good candidate for partner in the firm. If he achieved that, he would be able to take care of Ellen for the rest of her life.

★ ★ ★ ★ ★

Sarah didn't think she'd ever been so hot. The humid air hung over the group of Sunday morning worshipers gathered in the small church. Every woman in the congregation held a fan stamped with the name of a funeral home in Mt. Pleasant and waved it back and forth with whip-like precision. Whether the members stood to sing, bowed their heads to pray, or sat in the pew, the rhythm of the swishing fans never wavered.

The men held no fans. Every once in a while one would pull a large handkerchief from his pocket and mop the dripping perspiration from his forehead. The choir members were an entirely different matter. They appeared oblivious to the heat as they raised their slightly off-key voices in praise to the glory of God.

Sarah wanted to stick her fingers in her ears, but instead she clutched her hands in her lap. The soprano in the first row hit a high note that pierced her ears, and Sarah winced. She glanced around to see if anyone noticed her reaction. Alex Taylor smiled at her from across the aisle. He raised his eyebrows and shook his head as if to chide her.

Her face warmed, and she grabbed a fan from the hymnal rack on the back of the pew in front of her and whisked it back and forth in front of her face. Determined not to glance in Alex's way again, she turned her attention to Brother Hughes, as everyone called him, who'd walked to the pulpit. He held a Bible in his right hand, his index finger wedged inside the book.

A smile pulled at his lips as his gaze drifted over the congregation. "All of you know Alex Taylor has returned home for the summer from law school. We've all known Alex his entire life, and we're proud of his accomplishments. He'll be leaving again soon to join a law firm in Memphis. Today before I begin my sermon, I want Alex to voice our prayer."

Alex rose from his seat and gripped the back of the pew in front of him. He closed his eyes, and a serene expression covered his face. With his head bowed, he began to pray.

"Oh, sweet Jesus, our Lord and Savior. We come before You to thank You for the gift of life and for the many blessings You give us each day. We praise your name for watching over us and providing for us. These are days we don't understand, Lord. Nations are at war and men are engaged in battles far from here. We ask You to watch over them. I thank you, Lord, for the faithful people of this church and their witness in this community. We pray that your spirit of love will fall upon each member of this church and that we will take it with us wherever we go. Thank You for loving us and caring for us, and we give You the honor and glory. Amen"

Loud amens rang throughout the congregation as Alex took his seat. Out of the corner of her eye Sarah saw him glance in her direction, but she didn't turn her face. She stared straight ahead seemingly intent on what Brother Hughes said as he opened his Bible.

She hoped the look on her face disguised how pleased the announcement of Alex's plans had been to her. So they were both going to be in Memphis. Of course he'd be busy starting a law practice and she'd be teaching, but the thought still excited her.

The sermon seemed to go on forever, and Sarah's aching body reacted to the hard, wooden pew. It was all she could do to sit still. After what seemed an eternity, she realized the droning words of the preacher had halted. She sprang to her feet and joined the congregation to sing a closing hymn.

When the song ended, a deacon stepped forward. "All the tables have been set up outside. But before we have our closing prayer, I've been asked to make an announcement. Mr. and Mrs. Charlie Weston are having a party in Miss Clara's garden behind the store next Friday night to welcome his sister and niece to the community. All of you are invited to come and get to know them better."

Sarah glanced at her mother in surprise. She hadn't heard of this before. Her mother smiled, patted her hand, and leaned closer. "Isn't that nice of Charlie and Clara?"

Outside after the prayer, Sarah rushed to Uncle Charlie's buggy and retrieved the basket of food she and her mother had cooked. She looked around for her mother and saw her already helping place bowls of food on the table. As she watched, her mother grimaced and she clutched at the side of the table as if needing support. Sarah's breath hitched in her throat at the sight. Her first thought was to get to her mother's side right away, but before she could react to what she'd seen, her mother straightened and smiled before continuing her work.

The sight of Aunt Clara, her curls bobbing up and down, hurrying toward her pulled her attention away from her mother. Aunt Clara reached for the basket. "Let's get this on the table so we can serve the men and children. Then we'll fix our plates."

Men first? How many times had she heard that in her life? With a sigh Sarah followed Aunt Clara and took a place next to her beside the table as the men lined up and began to fill their plates. She'd just placed a piece of fried chicken on a little boy's plate when she looked up to see Alex Taylor facing her from the other side. The look in his dark eyes made her stomach clench. "Hello, Sarah. I'm glad you came today."

Sarah gulped and busied herself with the food. "Thank you, Alex. Would you like some fried chicken?"

"Yes, I would. Did you fry it?"

The friendly tone of his voice relaxed her, and Sarah laughed aloud at the thought of her mother sitting at the kitchen table giving her step by step instructions on how to fry chicken. "Let's just say it was a joint effort. My mother has always been the cook in our family, but I'm learning."

Alex smiled and moved along the table. Sarah watched him go, and the warm glow she felt watching him troubled her. She gave her head a shake to clear her thinking.

Aunt Clara's voice interrupted her thoughts. "I think all the men and children have been served. I'll help my plate and eat with your mama. You get yours and go enjoy eating with the young people."

Sarah glanced around to find someone near her age, but they looked like they'd already formed small groups across the area. Maybe she could find a spot where she could be alone. She followed her mother and Aunt Clara to the other end of the table, picked up a plate, and began to fill it with food. Her mother chatted with Clara and didn't notice when Sarah moved to the shade of a tree some distance from the group.

She studied the grass underneath the tree, balanced her plate in one hand, and attempted to sit without staining her dress. A familiar voice sliced through her thoughts. "Do you mind if I join you?" Alex stood over her with a plate of food.

She willed her heart to quit racing. "I suppose it'll be all right."

He eased down on the soft grass beside her. "I saw you were alone, and I thought this might be a good time for us to get better acquainted and for me to apologize again for yesterday. I shouldn't have followed you to the pump, and I shouldn't have spoken to you like I did. I'm really sorry, and I hope you'll forgive me."

His gaze didn't waver from her. She realized he'd offered a sincere apology, and she smiled. "If you'll forgive my unfriendly attitude. I reacted out of surprise because I was caught in such an unflattering position."

Alex grinned. "From what I saw, it wasn't unflattering at all. In fact I thought it was rather attractive." His eyes twinkled, and he arched his eyebrows. "Maybe I shouldn't have said that. I don't want you angry with me again."

A laugh rattled in her throat. "Now you're teasing me." His amused expression disappeared and was replaced with an intense stare. She reached for her fork, but her fingers trembled. "And embarrassing me."

He blinked and shook his head. "I'm sorry." He cleared his throat and sat up straighter. "Now back to my apology. Let me assure you if you'll forgive me, I promise never to mention the incident at the pump to you or anyone else ever again."

The teasing look had returned, and she smiled. "All right. I forgive you."

Alex took a deep breath. "Good. Now that's out of the way, and we can get on with getting to know each other better. Tell me all about yourself."

She shoved a bite of ham into her mouth and chewed to gain some time before answering. His dark eyes watched her intently. "There's really not much to know. I've lived in Memphis all my life. My father died two years ago right before I started school at the West Tennessee Normal School in Memphis. Last month I received my teaching certificate, and I'm going to teach at the private girls' school in Memphis where I attended when I was growing up."

"Ellen told me your father passed away. What did he die from?"

Sarah closed her eyes for a moment and took a deep breath. "Pneumonia. It happened so quickly. One day he was fine, and the next day he was near death. He lived a week after getting sick."

"I'm so sorry, Sarah."

She wiggled her nose and tried to keep the tears from filling her eyes. "Losing him gets better with time, but the grief never goes away."

His eyes mirrored the sadness that filled her every time she thought about her father's death. "Oh, Sarah. . ." Alex reached over and squeezed her hand. "I'm sorry I brought up such a painful subject. I can't imagine how hard this has been for you and your mother."

He released her, but the brief contact they'd shared sent a tingle of pleasure up her arm. "Yes, it has. I don't think my mother will ever recover. She and my father were so close."

"Is that why the two of you came back here?"

Sarah picked up a piece of cornbread but didn't put it in her mouth. "At this point in her life, my mother needs to be near family. I came with her, but I'll go back to Memphis in the fall." She glanced at him. "Now tell me about you."

Alex stretched his legs out in front of him and set his plate on his knees. "There's really not much to tell. Ellen probably told you yesterday that she raised me after my mother died giving birth to me. My roots go deep here. I love the farm, and you won't find better people anywhere. When I first went to Nashville, I was so homesick I almost ran away and came home. I knew Ellen would take a hickory stick to me and tell me to get myself back to school."

Sarah set her plate in her lap and picked up her cup. "And now you're glad you stayed."

A slight frown crossed Alex's face, and he looked down at his plate. "I am, but I worry about leaving Ellen when I start my job in the fall. It was different when I was in school. I still thought of this as home, but I know that's going to change when I start my new life in Memphis."

A troubled look crossed his face, and Sarah wondered what he was thinking that pained him so. Perhaps she should change the subject. "I enjoyed sitting with Ellen yesterday. You have a wonderful sister. Do you have other family members?"

Alex shook his head. "There's just Ellen and me. Our pa died about ten years ago. Ellen's always been there for me. Before Pa died, he made me promise I would always take care of her. I intend to do that."

His dedication to his sister reminded her of how she felt about taking care of her mother. "That's very admirable of you." She paused before saying more. "It seems we have a lot in common. I feel a responsibility to take care of my mother."

"I know your mother must appreciate that."

Sarah swallowed the food she was chewing and glanced back at Alex. "I saw a young boy in your wagon yesterday. Is he related to you?"

Alex shook his head. "No, his name's Augie Hooten. His folks were tenant farmers close to where we live. About ten years ago after Augie's mother died, his pa just took off one day without saying a word. I found Augie by himself a few days later. He was hungry and scared. I brought him home with me, and he's lived with us ever since. He's a big help on the farm."

Sarah smiled at the memory of how the boy had looked at Alex. "I could tell he has a big case of hero worship where you're concerned. Now I know why."

"I wouldn't say that. We just get along fine." They ate in silence for a few minutes before Alex looked back at her. "Sarah, I'd like to get to know you better. Would you mind if I called on you?"

She hesitated before she answered. She liked Alex, but she didn't want to run the risk of getting to like him too much. After all, they would only be here for a few months, and then they'd each start a new life in Memphis. It would probably be better if she said no, but the truth was she didn't want to. "Mama and I would love to have you visit anytime. When will you be leaving for Memphis?"

"The last of August. I'm going to begin work at the law firm the first of September."

"I know you're excited. Memphis is a great place to live. What law firm are you joining?"

"Buckley, Anderson, and Pike. They have offices down on Front Street."

Sarah's eyes grew wide, and the fork she held clattered to her plate. "You're joining James Buckley's law firm?"

Alex smiled. "Yeah. Can you imagine a boy like me who grew up on the farm getting a chance to work in one of the best firms in Memphis?" He glanced at her, and his smile faded. "You look shocked. Is there something wrong?"

Sarah blinked and took a deep breath. "No, it's just that. . ."

He leaned closer. "What?"

"Well," she cleared her throat. "I guess it startled me because I've read so much about Mr. Buckley in the paper. He's one of the biggest opponents of suffrage in the city. I hear he's done a lot to influence legislators to oppose it, too."

Alex shrugged. "I don't know much about that. I'm fortunate to land a position there."

Sarah scooted closer. "But if you work with anti-suffragists, won't they expect you to support whatever they do?"

"I guess so. I never really thought about it because I haven't given suffrage a whole lot of thought."

Sarah's eyes narrowed. "And why not? It's one of the biggest issues of the day, and you've been in law school. Didn't you study about what's going on in the world while you were there?"

His face flushed, and he frowned. "Of course I did, but I didn't see how it affected me. I can already vote."

Sarah jumped to her feet, and the plate sitting in her lap clattered to the ground. She clenched her fists at her sides. "Of course you can. You're a man. But what about Ellen? Did you ever stop to think how she might feel?"

Alex pushed to his feet and held his hands up in surrender. "Whoa, there. You're getting a little emotional, aren't you? I can tell you have strong feelings on the subject, but you won't find any women around her who do. And that includes my sister. So why don't we drop this conversation and call a truce? It's too pretty a day to spend it angry."

His words produced a feeling as if someone had poured ice water over her head. She'd promised Mama not to mention suffrage while she was here. Now she'd just attacked the one person she wanted to get to know better.

She inhaled and swallowed hard. "I'm sorry, Alex. I shouldn't have gotten so upset. You're right. It is a beautiful day, and I don't want to ruin it for you."

Without speaking, he picked up her plate from the ground and stacked it on top of his. They remained silent as they walked back toward the group around the tables. He set their plates with the others and turned to her. "I think we're going to get up a ballgame. They're going to have music inside the church. Do you want to sit with Ellen and watch, or are you going back inside?"

Before she could answer, Ellen's voice cut through her thoughts. "Well, I've been wonderin' where you two young 'uns went. I thought I was gonna have to send out searchers so we could have a pitcher for the ballgame. They're ready to start, Alex. Get yourself on over there. I'll take care of Sarah."

The muscle in Alex's jaw twitched as he looked toward the field where the men prepared for the game. He sighed and turned to Sarah. "I'd better go. Maybe I'll see you later."

Sarah nodded. "Maybe."

Ellen shoved her brother in the direction of the waiting men. "Get yourself out there. They're waitin' for you." Ellen watched Alex hurry across the field before she faced Sarah. "Alex looked upset. Did something happen?"

"Not really. We just had a friendly disagreement." Sarah paused a moment, unsure whether she should pose the question on the tip of her tongue. "Ellen, have you ever given any thought to the fact that you can't vote?"

Ellen cast a quick look around before she grasped Sarah's shoulder. "I reckon I have, Sarah. But if I was you, I wouldn't talk about it in these parts. Some folks don't take kindly to such ideas."

Sarah nodded. "I know, but it's the same wherever you go. Maybe it's time women quit worrying about what people are going to say and get busy doing something about it."

Ellen regarded her with a stern look. "I don't know if your disagreement with Alex is the reason you're talking like this to me. But I want you to know one thing about Alex. God gave him a tender heart for other people, and I have to say it makes me right proud."

Sarah nodded at Ellen's words. "I'm sure he owes it all to you, Ellen. He loves you a lot."

"And I love him, too. I'd give my life for that boy."

Ellen's words pierced Sarah's heart. "I know you would. Please forgive me for bringing up things we don't need to be discussing. I hope you'll hold it in confidence."

"I will."

Sarah forced a smile to her face. "I'm getting a little warm out here in the sun. I think I'll go back in the church with my mother and listen to the singing. It's been nice to see you again, Ellen. Tell Alex I enjoyed spending time with him today."

Sarah turned and walked toward the church. With each step her heart sank lower, and a heavy weight crushed her chest. She brushed hot tears from her eyes and blinked to stop the flow that threatened to flood her face.

In the short time she'd spoken with Alex today, she'd realized their goals in life were very different. Last night she'd even fantasized that something special might happen between them, but she was a foolish woman for having such thoughts. Alex's life and hers were both laid out before them, and there was no changing either one. It would be better if they didn't complicate matters by getting to know each other better.

She and Alex Taylor were set on different courses in life, and nothing could change it.

Chapter 3

On Friday afternoon Sarah sat on the front porch waiting for Uncle Charlie to arrive. She closed her eyes and inhaled deeply in an effort to dispel the thick veil of silence that had hovered over the house all week. Her mother's face seemed to grow more pallid each day, but every time Sarah had asked her about it, she had dismissed her concern.

To add to the gloom, she hadn't been able to quit thinking about her argument with Alex. Right before it happened, he had told her he wanted to call on her, but so far he hadn't showed up. She supposed her outburst had taken care of that.

When she would begin to think such thoughts, she'd shake her head and tell herself it was all for the best. She couldn't afford to be friends with someone who would work for a man like James Buckley. It was better to keep a distance from Alex before it was too late to do so.

The screen door creaked, and Sarah jumped to her feet. Her mother, wearing her best dress, stood just outside the front door. She took a step, and her legs wobbled. Sarah rushed to her. "Are you sure you're up to going to the party."

Her mother took a ragged breath and held out her hand. A heart-shaped locket dangled from her fingers. "I want you to wear this tonight." She dropped the necklace in Sarah's open palm.

Sarah's fingers closed around the cool metal. For a long moment she stood still, unable to speak. "Mama, Poppa gave you this for a wedding present."

Her mother's somber expression revealed nothing of her thoughts. "It's my most cherished possession, but I'm giving it to you."

Sarah rubbed her thumb across the pendant set with small diamonds and gently pried it open. A wave of emotion swept over her at the images of her parents' young faces inside. She turned the locket and traced her finger over the small indentions on the back. "I can't believe my teeth were ever small enough to make these marks."

Her mother laughed. "I suppose I was too interested in the sermon that Sunday to notice you chewing on the locket. Those marks have just made it more special to me, though."

Sarah closed the locket, placed it around her neck, and snapped the catch in place. Tears welled in her eyes as she stood and faced her mother. "Oh, Mama, thank you."

Her mother reached over and centered the heart in the small of Sarah's throat. "Your father would be pleased to see what a beautiful young woman you've become. I'm so proud of you."

Sarah gulped and tried to stem the threatening flow of tears. "Mama, I love you so much."

Their arms encircled each other, and they stood without speaking until the sound of an approaching horse parted them. Uncle Charlie's buggy rumbled over the ruts in the road and rolled into the yard.

They stepped closer to the edge of the porch as he lumbered from the carriage. He looked up at them, took a white handkerchief from his hip pocket, and mopped the edges of his receding hairline. He hooked his fingers around the waistband of his pants and hitched them up over his potbelly before ascending the steps.

Sarah bit her tongue to keep from laughing out loud, for Uncle Charlie's trousers inched down again with every step he climbed. When he reached where they stood, he wrapped his arms around her mother and lifted her off her feet, his usual greeting. "Julia, my dear little sister. I'm so glad you're back home where you belong."

"I am, too, Charlie. We're excited about the party you and Clara have planned for us."

He laughed, and his jowls jiggled. "Good. I think there's going to be a big crowd there. If you're ready, we need to go."

Sarah and her uncle supported her mother on either side as she descended the porch steps. When they had her seated in the front seat of the buggy, Sarah climbed into the back. She smoothed her skirt and leaned forward. "Uncle Charlie, do you know who's coming tonight?"

He grabbed the reins and wrapped them around his hands. "Oh, lots of folks. I reckon about everybody in the community will be there."

Although she told herself not to ask the question in her mind, she couldn't stop. "Do you think Ellen and Alex Taylor are coming?"

Uncle Charlie snapped the reins across the horse's back and guided him into the road. "I don't know. Ellen was in the store earlier this week. She said she was coming, but she didn't know about Alex. Seems like he's been working late in the fields every day and is tired when he gets home."

Sarah leaned back against the leather seat and sighed. "I see."

Uncle Charlie glanced over his shoulder. "But don't worry. There'll be lots of other young people there. You're gonna have a good time."

She nodded. "I'm sure I will."

It would be better if Alex didn't come. She needed to concentrate on getting to know the ones who would be there, not fretting over a man who hadn't bothered to follow through on his request to call on her. But no matter what she knew she should do, she couldn't ignore the fact she wanted to see him again.

If truth be told she was the one who needed to offer an apology this time. Her words to him last Sunday had been harsh, and she regretted that. She had tried not to think about him all week, but he crept back into her thoughts all the time. She remembered the hurt in his dark eyes and wondered if he would ever want to see her again. She closed her eyes and uttered a silent plea.

Please come tonight, Alex.

Alex plodded along the path toward the house from the cotton patch where he and Augie had worked since sunup. He'd attacked the weeds and grass around the young plants like a madman in an attempt to rid his mind of Sarah. The question of what to do about tonight had rung in his head all day. One minute he convinced himself he wouldn't go to Sarah's party, and the next he wanted to see her again.

He wondered about Ellen's whereabouts as he stepped onto the back porch and slipped his work shoes from his feet. He trudged to the dry sink against the wall and dipped some water into the wash pan from the bucket.

As the water trickled down his lathered arms, he wished he could rinse his troubled thoughts from his mind that easily. He'd never been as shocked by anything in his life as he had by Sarah's accusation that he opposed suffrage. As he thought back on the conversation, he realized she hadn't actually said those words, but she had sure implied them.

It wasn't that he was opposed to women voting. He just didn't see a need in it. Most of the married men he knew were the decision makers in their homes, and that's the way he'd always thought it would be when he married. The world was getting along just fine the way it was, and he didn't see any need for a change right now.

He picked up the towel, dried his hands, and threw it into the sink. "Maybe I shouldn't go tonight."

The screen door banged shut. Ellen, carrying a basket of onions and radishes from the garden, stepped onto the back porch. "What're you talking about?"

Alex turned away from her. "I'm trying to convince my-self not to go to the party tonight."

Ellen's eyes grew wide. "Why don't you want to go? Everybody from church is going to be there. It just seems right that we welcome Julia and Sarah to Richland Creek."

He sighed. "Sarah and I had a difference of opinion on Sunday. She said some things that bothered me. I think it might be better if we didn't become any friendlier."

Ellen set her basket down. "Was it about suffrage?"

He gasped. "How did you know?"

"Because she said something to me, too. I warned her she shouldn't be talking like that around here. Lots of folks might take exception to it."

Alex nodded and pursed his lips. "Good for you. She needs to be told."

Ellen tilted her head to one side and sighed. "Now I think I may have done wrong. Just 'cause people are against some-thing don't mean they don't need to hear another side of the issue."

"I don't understand what you mean."

Ellen pulled the sunbonnet from her head and patted her hair into place. "Do you remember the night you told me you wanted to be a lawyer?"

He rubbed the back of his neck and grinned. "Yeah. I think I was about sixteen, and I'd just finished reading a biography of John Adams for school. You were sitting in front of the fireplace reading your Bible, and I sat down on the floor next to you."

"You looked so much like Pa I thought my heart was gonna burst open." Ellen smiled as if she was reliving the memory of that night. "You were all excited 'cause you'd read something you wanted to tell me about."

Alex smiled. "It was the account of how John Adams had defended eight British soldiers who had killed some people in the Boston Massacre."

Ellen nodded. "That's right. John Adams had been outspoken against the occupation of Boston, but in this case he realized nobody knew who fired first or who was responsible for those killed. He took the case because he believed everybody is entitled to be defended in court. He got a lot of criticism over doing that, but he did what he believed was right."

Alex sighed and shook his head. "You've made your point, Ellen. Because of John Adams's defense, six of the soldiers were acquitted, and two were charged with manslaughter. In his later life he called it one of the most gallant actions of his life and said it was the best service he'd ever done for his country."

"And that's what I want you to do. Be gallant in dealing with folks who have differing opinions, and I want you to defend those whose cases may appear hopeless. Give them what John Adams gave those British soldiers, and don't be so set on something just 'cause other folks say it's so. Find out for yourself."

Alex put his arms around his sister and hugged her. "You're a very wise woman, Ellen."

Ellen pulled back and stared into his eyes. "One more thing I hope you'll remember in dealing with folks. We can't make other people do what we want. But we can't change the way we feel about 'em just 'cause we don't like their choices. Sarah may need you as a friend more than you can even imagine. Just pray about it. God will tell you what to do."

Much as he hated to admit it, Ellen sensed the need in people better than he. "You're right. I can't change Sarah. But maybe I can be her friend." He took a deep breath. "Now about that party. Are you going?"

Ellen grinned. "I wouldn't miss it for anything."

He headed toward the kitchen door but stopped and looked back at Ellen. "And I'm going with you. I'll be ready before you know it."

"I'll be waiting."

When he reached his bedroom, he closed the door and sank down on the bed. Second thoughts about attending tonight's party flashed through his head. Maybe he shouldn't go. Sarah might prefer not seeing him again.

He'd never known a woman before who spoke with such passion on a subject. All the girls he'd met while in school had one thing on their mind—finding a man to marry. From what he'd observed with Sarah, that was probably the last thing on her mind. But that was good. He didn't need to get involved with anyone. He had a new life waiting for him in Memphis, and he couldn't afford to do anything to compromise what he'd worked so hard to attain.

Alex pounded the mattress with his fist and pushed to his feet. One party wasn't going to affect his life. There would be lots of his friends there, and he'd enjoy the evening with them. He didn't even have to spend any time with Sarah Jordan.

He strode to the armoire across the room, jerked the door open, and gasped at the sight of his baseball shirt hanging inside. Ellen must have washed it and hung it there. He reached out and ran his index finger over the team's name embroidered on the shirt pocket.

The memory of a young girl standing with her skirt lifted above her ankles returned, and his heart dropped to the pit of his stomach. A sigh drifted up from the depths of his soul. He wasn't fooling himself. All his protests that he didn't care about seeing Sarah again weren't true. In his heart he knew he had to see her.

From the moment he laid eyes on her, all he could do was think about her. He had to find a way to push her from his mind. Maybe tonight he'd find the answer of how to do that.

Chapter 4

Sarah stood to the side of the yard behind Uncle Charlie's store. The sweet smell of blooming roses drifted on the night breeze, and Japanese lanterns blinked a warm glow across Aunt Clara's garden.

One after another Uncle Charlie and Aunt Clara introduced the arriving guests to her, and Sarah wondered how she would ever remember all the names. Beside her, Uncle Charlie's voice boomed out. "Dr. Lancaster, so good of you to come." He turned to her mother. "Julia, this is the new doctor I was telling you about. He just came to Richland Creek a few weeks ago. He's set up his office in one of those houses across the street from the store."

Sarah glanced at the man shaking hands with her uncle. Gray speckled his dark hair, and a pair of wire rimmed spectacles perched on his nose. His blue eyes reminded Sarah of the summer sky. "Mrs. Jordan, I'm so glad to meet you." He moved to Sarah and grasped her hand. "And you, too, Miss Jordan. You're uncle has told me so much about you."

Sarah smiled. "So you're new to this area, too?"

He nodded. "I am. I practiced in Memphis for over twenty-five years. After my wife died, I decided I'd like to find a place where I could have a small practice and enjoy life more. A medical school friend over at Mt. Pleasant suggested Richland Creek. And here I am."

Uncle Charlie laughed. "And we're mighty glad to have you. Go on over and get you something to eat, and I'll talk with you later."

Sarah watched the doctor walk away and stop to talk with some people seated at one of the tables. "He seemed nice."

"Yes." Her mother took a deep breath and patted Sarah's arm. "I think I'm going inside and lie down for a while."

Sarah turned startled eyes to her mother. "Are you all right?"

Her mother patted her hand. "I'm fine. Just a little tired."

"I'll go with you."

"No, you stay here and meet your guests. I won't be gone long."

Sarah watched her mother walk to the back of the store. Sarah glanced at Aunt Clara. "Do you think she's all right?"

"I think so, dear. I'll check on her in a few minutes."

Several people crowded in front of Sarah and blocked her view of the outside staircase that led to the upstairs living area. She pushed up on her tiptoes, but it was no use. She couldn't see where her mother had gone. She turned her attention back to the guests and smiled as she shook one hand after another.

When the line of people grew shorter, Sarah glanced back at the stairway. Her mother was nowhere in sight. Her aunt grabbed her arm and pointed at a man and two women walking toward them. "Oh, here comes the Jenkins family. I've wanted you to meet Mary Lou. She's just about your age."

Mrs. Jenkins stopped in front of her and grasped Sarah's hand. "So you're Julia's daughter Sarah? You look just like your mother did when she married your father. Julia and I grew up together and have been good friends all our lives. I'm so excited to have you both living here."

"Thank you, Mrs. Jenkins. I'm afraid you just missed Mama."

"Oh, no we didn't. We met her as she was going inside and talked to her for a few minutes. She's just as beautiful as ever." She put her arm around her daughter and nudged her closer to Sarah. "This is our daughter Mary Lou. She's looked forward to meeting you."

The young woman smiled as she reached out to shake Sarah's hand. "Hello, Sarah. It's good to meet you at last. I've been at my grandparents' home in Mt. Pleasant for the past few weeks, but I've heard wonderful things about you. The girls have all told me how pretty you are, and they were right."

Sarah felt her face grow warm. "Thank you, Mary Lou. I'm glad you came tonight. I hope we can get better acquainted."

She smiled. "Me, too. Maybe after you've welcomed all your guests we can talk." She glanced at the side of the store where two fiddlers, a guitar player, and a banjo picker huddled together. "It looks like the musicians are getting ready to play. I'll see you later."

"I'll look forward to it."

Sarah watched Mary Lou walk across the yard and join a group of young women. Within seconds they were laughing together, and the sight reminded her of Martha Ann and Rebecca, her friends back in Memphis. She'd never realized how important it was to have friends until she'd found herself in a place without any. If she could make just one friend, things might be different. She didn't think she could stand another minute of feeling like she was on the outside looking in at everybody else's life.

Her mother had often told her the secret to having a friend was to be one first. It was time to try and fit in with the young women her age in Richland Creek. She squared her shoulders and braced herself to join one of the groups. A rustle behind her halted her step.

"Hello, Sarah."

She whirled at the sound of the familiar voice and came face to face with Alex. Her heart lurched, and joy coursed through her body. The loneliness of a moment ago lay forgotten in the thrill of seeing him.

"Alex, I'm so glad you're here. I was afraid you weren't coming."

He moved out of the shadows and closer to her. "I worked late in the field, and I didn't know if you wanted to see me. Our last parting wasn't very cordial."

Sarah stared at this handsome man who created strange reactions in her. His presence lifted her spirits, and suddenly the night came alive for her. She moved closer to him and placed her hand on his arm. "Let's not talk about the last time we met. Let's have a good time and enjoy each other's company. I'm so glad you're here."

Alex looked down at her. "That sounds good to me."

Uncle Charlie approached and extended his hand in welcome. "Well, Alex, I'm glad you got to come. I'm still reliving that game last week. That was mighty good pitching."

Alex clasped Charlie's hand. "Thanks, Charlie. I thought the whole team did a good job."

"Not one to take all the glory, huh? Sounds just like your sister. By the way, is Ellen with you?"

"She is. She's with Sarah's mother right now. We met her going inside the store when we first arrived, and she asked Ellen to go upstairs with her."

Uncle Charlie nodded. "Julia wasn't feeling well. I'm glad Ellen went with her. She's always taking care of somebody."

Aunt Clara's shrill voice cut through the conversation. "What's this about Ellen?"

"I was just telling Alex and Sarah that Ellen's always taking care of someone. That seems to be her mission in life."

Fire blazed in Clara's eyes, and red splotches circled her cheeks. "I'm sure you're right." She turned and stared at Alex. "Well, it's a surprise to see you, Alex. I didn't think you were coming."

Uncle Charlie's face flushed. "Why, Clara…"

Sarah's mouth gaped open. "Why would you think they weren't coming? Alex and Ellen are the only friends I've made since coming here, and I couldn't stand to have this party without them."

"And we're glad to have you, Alex." Uncle Charlie grabbed his wife's arm and steered her towards the food table. "Now you two young people go have a good time. Clara and I have work to do."

Sarah stared after them. "What was that all about?"

Alex shrugged. "It's a long story. I'll tell you sometime."

After a moment, Sarah turned her attention back to Alex. She had wanted him to come tonight, and he had. "I'm glad you came. I've wanted to talk to you all week."

His stony expression gave no hint what he was thinking. "What about?"

"I-I wanted to apologize to you. Mama says I speak before I think sometimes, and that's what I did Sunday. I didn't mean for it to sound like I was judging you. I'm really very happy that you've gotten a position in such a well-known law firm."

A smile pulled at his mouth. "Thank you."

"And I promise I won't say anything else about the head of your firm, no matter what I think of him."

Alex threw back his head and laughed. "So you'll just keep your thoughts to yourself. Right?"

She nodded. "Yes."

His gaze moved over her face. "Somehow I don't think that's possible for you to do, but I don't mind. I'm just glad to be with you again."

For a moment Sarah stood transfixed. It was as if they were the only two people in the world, and they didn't care. Suddenly applause shattered the night air as the musicians made their way to the edge of the yard. Sarah turned away from Alex to join in the ovation.

Uncle Charlie's voice called out from across the garden. "Come on over and put your chair in the circle. We're gonna play musical chairs."

"That sounds like fun. I'll bet I can last longer than you." Sarah reached for Alex's hand and tugged.

Alex wrapped his fingers around hers and laughed "Oh, you think so? How can I refuse a challenge like that?"

The guests grabbed chairs from the tables scattered about and converged on the center of the yard. Alex released Sarah's hand, scooped up two chairs, and handed one to her. "If you're determined to beat me at this game, the least you can do is carry your own chair. But I warn you. I'm a formidable foe, and I intend to win."

She took the chair from him and batted her eyelashes. "When you get to know me better, sir, you will find that I never back down from a challenge. Consider yourself warned."

"I will. In fact. . ." He stopped abruptly and frowned as his gaze swept the yard. "Did you hear somebody calling?"

"No."

"It sounded like. . ." His eyes grew wide. Frowning, he raised his hand and pointed toward the back of the store. "It's Ellen. She's standing at the top of the stairs, but I can't make out what she's saying."

Sarah glanced in the direction he pointed, and gasped. She tried to speak, but she choked on the fear rising in her throat. A wail erupted from her throat. "Alex, my mother. . ."

A sudden hush spread across the yard as the partygoers turned to stare at Ellen. "Charlie," she yelled, "something's wrong with Julia."

Dr. Lancaster jumped up from his chair and raced toward Ellen. Sarah wanted to follow, but her feet felt frozen to the ground. Alex grabbed her hand and pulled her forward. "Come on, Sarah. I'll go with you."

She nodded, and they joined the crowd that surged toward the back of the store. When they reached the steps, Alex wedged their way through those already gathered and pulled her up the stairs until they stood on the landing next to the doctor and Ellen. Sarah tried to push past Ellen to the door, but Dr. Lancaster reached out and touched her arm.

"Miss Taylor tells me your mother has collapsed. Let me examine her first. Then I'll call you. Is that agreeable with you?"

A chill swept through Sarah's body, and her teeth chattered. "Just please help her."

"I'll try." He turned to Alex. "Will you run over to my house and get my bag? It's in the front room. Bring it to me inside."

Alex nodded and turned to Sarah. "I'll be right back."

Dr. Lancaster disappeared into the house and closed the door behind him as Alex bounded down the steps. Sarah closed her eyes and took a deep breath. Minutes ago she'd been laughing with Alex, and now she stood alone waiting for word on her mother's condition. She should pray, but since her father's death she hadn't been on very good terms with God.

A hand touched her shoulder, and she opened her eyes to Uncle Charlie and Aunt Clara standing beside her. Aunt Clara put her arm around Sarah's shoulders. "Come downstairs and sit down, darling. The doctor will let us know something soon."

Tears pooled in her eyes, and she looked from one to the other. "But I want to be near my mother."

Uncle Charlie nodded. "I know you do, but Dr. Lancaster needs to take care of her right now."

He led her down the stairs and to a chair at one of the tables. She'd just taken her seat when Alex reappeared with the doctor's bag and bolted up the steps. When he came back down, he walked over and dropped into the chair next to Sarah. "Did you see my mother?"

He shook his head. "No, she was in the bedroom. Dr. Lancaster was with her, so I gave the bag to Ellen."

Sarah folded her arms on the table and buried her face in them. She tried to ignore the voices speaking in hushed tones around her. All she wanted at the moment was to know what was going on behind that closed door at the top of the stairs.

Then an arm circled her shoulders, and Uncle Charlie whispered in her ear. "Brother Hughes couldn't come tonight, but Alex's offered to step in and lead the folks in a prayer for your mama."

She raised her head and stared up at Alex whose hand in the air signaled for attention. "I think while we're waiting to hear from Dr. Lancaster it would be a good idea to pray for Mrs. Jordan. Let's all bow our heads and pray silently."

Sarah watched as the people bowed their heads and closed their eyes. She saw lips move but no sound came from their lips. The people who'd come to welcome her and her mother to their community now stood offering up a plea for her mother's well-being.

The truth hit her then. Her mother had been right. She had never been alone. Her loneliness had come about because she'd refused to accept people she thought very different from herself. All she'd needed to do was reach out to her mother's friends.

He gaze fell on Alex who stood with his head bowed, and she let her gaze drift over him. A tiny frown wrinkled his forehead, and his lips moved as he prayed. The first time she'd encountered him she'd thought him flirtatious and a ladies' man because of his thinly veiled remarks about her ankles. Neither of those assumptions had dampened the attraction she felt toward him, though.

Then she'd spent time with him and discovered she couldn't have been more wrong about him. The truth was he stirred her in ways no one else ever had. Her father had told her many times how he'd fallen in love with her mother at first sight, and she hadn't really thought it possible. A fairy tale, she'd called it, but now she wasn't so sure. Maybe it was possible after all, but that didn't mean it always led to a happy ending.

Chapter 5

An hour later most of the guests had offered their regrets and left with the promise they would continue to pray for her mother. Sarah sat with Alex, her uncle and aunt, and the Jenkins family. They all jumped to their feet when the door at the top of the stairs opened and Dr. Lancaster came down the steps.

He stopped in front of her and smiled, but it didn't reach to his eyes. He glanced at the people around her before he spoke. "Do you want me to speak openly, or would you rather we talk privately?"

Sarah turned a questioning look toward Uncle Charlie. He bit his lip, dropped his gaze to the ground, and gave a curt nod. She took a deep breath. "I suppose after what's happened tonight everyone in the community will want to know what's wrong with my mother. So it's okay to share that with my family and friends."

"All right. Your mother tells me she suffered complications to her heart from rheumatic fever when she was a child. The heart muscle's pumping action was damaged. Now it's developed into a condition where the heart is unable to pump enough blood to the body."

Sarah swallowed the fear that rose in her throat. "But you can fix that, can't you?"

Dr. Lancaster smiled. "I wish I could, but I'm afraid that's impossible. Your mother is going to need constant care to make sure she doesn't overexert herself."

"I'll do whatever it takes," Sarah said. "Just tell me what to do."

The doctor glanced from her uncle back to Sarah. "Your mother tells me you're supposed to start a new job in Memphis in the fall. She doesn't want you to put your plans on hold for her."

Sarah shook her head. "It doesn't matter what my plans are. She comes first, and I want to take care of her. How is she?"

"I've given her something to help her rest, and she's sleeping right now. I don't want her disturbed tonight. If she's feeling better tomorrow, you can take her home. Miss Taylor is with her and says she'll stay the night if needed."

Uncle Charlie spoke up. "That won't be necessary. My wife and I will take care of her tonight."

Dr. Lancaster nodded. "I'm going back to check on her once more before I leave, and I'll tell Miss Taylor." He turned his attention to Sarah. "I'll come by your house to check on her in the next few days. In the meantime keep her comfortable. Don't let her exert herself, and enjoy your time with her."

Her time with her? The doctor's words sent a chill down Sarah's spine. She reached out and stopped him as he turned back to the stairs. "Dr. Lancaster, thank you for all you've done tonight."

He patted her hand and smiled. "I'm glad I was here to help. Your mother is very fortunate to have such a caring daughter."

Sarah watched as he, Uncle Charlie, and Aunt Clara climbed the stairs and disappeared into the living quarters above the store. Someone touched her arm, and she glanced around to see Mrs. Jenkins next to her.

"Sarah, we're going now, but I'll be by to check on you in a few days, and Mary Lou can stay if you'd like to have someone in the house with you."

Sarah shook her head. "That won't be necessary now. Maybe later."

Mary Lou stepped forward and grasped Sarah's hand. "Let me know if you'd like some company. I don't like to think about you staying alone with your mother so sick."

"I will. Thank you."

Mrs. Jenkins put her arms around Sarah's shoulders and drew her close for a hug. "We're here for you, Sarah. And we'll be praying for Julia. Don't hesitate to call on us if you need help."

Sarah bit her lip and nodded. She couldn't take her eyes off the family as they trudged across the yard that only a short time ago had been filled with well-wishers who'd come to welcome her and her mother to the community. Now she was left standing with Alex in the middle of empty tables and chairs.

She glanced toward the table where the food had sat earlier and for the first time noticed it had been cleared. "Where did the food go?"

"The ladies from the church cleaned it up while we were waiting for word about your mother."

"I didn't notice. I should have helped."

He reached for her hand and closed his fingers around hers. "They were glad to do it. They knew you were too concerned at that point and wanted to help clean up before they left."

She looked up at the Japanese lanterns that still twinkled across the yard and then to the upstairs where her mother lay. Beside her stood a man with a caring heart who'd stayed by her side tonight. His sister and a doctor she'd met earlier had helped her mother, and people she'd considered as being unimportant and having less value than her Memphis friends had demonstrated kindness.

She groaned, and tears spilled from her eyes. "Oh, Alex, I'm so ashamed."

A startled expression covered his face. "For what?"

"The way I've acted since I've been here. I've been angry because I wanted to spend the summer in Memphis instead of coming here. I've looked for all the bad things about this place, and I've never tried to see the good in it. I can't believe what a snob I've been."

Her body shook with sobs as her tears flowed down her face. Alex put his arms around her and drew her close until her head rested on his chest. With one hand he stroked her hair. "Don't cry. I think you're being too hard on yourself."

She shook her head. "No, I'm not. I've tried to keep my feelings from my mother, but I sensed she knew. What if I made her sicker?"

He laid his cheek against the top of her head, and the touch made her want to burrow deeper into his embrace. "You can't take responsibility for that," he said. "I've watched you with your mother, and I know you're a devoted daughter. As for Richland Creek, I understand why you were concerned about coming here. It's a far cry from Memphis, but the people really are good. They'll do anything to help a neighbor."

"I'm beginning to see that. It makes me ashamed I didn't look for it sooner."

He put a finger under her chin and tilted her head up until she stared into his eyes. "Ellen's always told me that our lives are ruled by the choices we make. Sometimes we make good ones. Sometimes we don't. It's not too late for you to make the right choice. I believe you can show the people here that you're not only a beautiful woman but that you also have a beautiful spirit. It's your choice to make."

Sarah stared into his eyes for a moment before she spoke. "Do you really think I'm beautiful?"

His Adam's apple bobbed, and he tightened his arm around her waist. "Yes, I do."

He lowered his head, and her heart pounded at the thought that he was going to kiss her. She closed her eyes, and then her heart plummeted as his lips brushed her forehead. Slowly his hold on her released, and he stepped back.

The sting of rejection pierced her soul, and she searched his stony features for an answer to what had just happened. "Alex. . ."

The muscle in his jaw flexed, and he took a step back from her. "I think it's time for me to leave and for you to check on your mother. Go on upstairs, and tell Ellen I'm waiting for her."

She heard the words, but she couldn't force her feet to move. She swallowed the disappointment of moments ago and nodded. "I'll tell her." She willed herself to take a step but stopped and glanced back at him. "When will I see you again?"

He swallowed hard and exhaled. "I don't know. Maybe soon."

"I hope so." She tilted her head and smiled. "It's your choice."

His eyes lit with surprise, and she struggled to keep from laughing out loud at the way his mouth dropped open. Before he had time to answer, she whirled and headed up the steps. When she reached the landing, she glanced down, and Alex still stood in the same spot watching her.

He liked her. She could tell. And he'd wanted to kiss her but hadn't. Perhaps he thought it was too soon in their friendship for such an intimate moment, or maybe he didn't want to complicate his life just as he was about to begin a new career. Whatever his reasons might be, she hoped he would visit her soon. All she could do was wait and see.

She waved once more before she opened the door and went inside.

The next afternoon Alex pulled his buggy to a stop in front of the house where Sarah and her mother lived. He glanced over at Ellen in the seat next to him. Neither of them had said much since they left home.

His gaze drifted over the small farmhouse and back to Ellen. "Well, here we are."

Ellen frowned at him. "You don't seem too happy about it. I thought you wanted to come."

"I did. It's just that maybe it's too soon for me to be showing up at Sarah's house."

Ellen regarded him with a puzzled look. "Too soon? I told Sarah I'd be by today to check on her mama. If you didn't want to come, you could have stayed home. I've been driving a buggy by myself ever since I was old enough to hold the reins. Don't you go a-thinkin' I can't still do it."

He laughed and climbed down. "I know you can do whatever you want. I just meant that maybe *I* shouldn't have come."

He tied the horse's reins to a tree and stepped back to help Ellen to the ground. "Why didn't you want to come?"

"I like Sarah a lot, but I don't think there's any future in it. I'll be leaving for Memphis soon, and from the way things look now she'll be staying here."

Ellen nodded. "I see. Well, I won't ask you to drive me here again. Next time I'll come alone."

Alex didn't answer. Instead he reached back into the buggy and pulled out the basket of food Ellen had brought. Then he took a deep breath, grabbed her elbow, and held her arm as they climbed the steps to the porch. "Okay, let's go see how Mrs. Jordan is today."

When they reached the front door, he doubled his fist and rapped his knuckles against the screen door. Sarah's voice rang out from the back of the house. "I'm in the kitchen. Come on in and make yourself comfortable."

Alex looked down at Ellen, and she shrugged. Together they walked into the house and entered the parlor to the right of the front door. Ellen sat down in a wing-backed chair to the side of the fireplace, and Alex set the basket beside her. As he straightened, he caught a glimpse of several framed photographs on the mantel. He walked over and picked up the first one, a picture of Sarah's parents. Their unsmiling faces stared at him from behind the frame's glass.

Sarah's hair and complexion resembled her mother, but she had her father's eyes. Another picture sat next to her parents', and he picked it up. His chest tightened so that he could hardly breathe as he gazed at Sarah's profile. Never had he seen anything so beautiful in his life. She reminded him of the illustrations he'd seen of Charles Gibson's ideal of feminine beauty.

Soft footsteps padded on the wood floor of the hallway. "Uncle Charlie, you didn't have to. . ."

Alex turned toward the sound of her voice and almost staggered backwards at the sight of her standing in the doorway. She stood there gaping at them as if she couldn't move. Damp tendrils of hair lay plastered to her forehead, and smudges of dirt covered the apron over her dress. His gaze swept over her and came to a stop at her bare feet. He glanced at her, then back to the photograph in his hand before he set it back on the mantel.

Trying to stifle the laughter that rose in his throat, he turned back to her. "I hope we haven't come at an inconvenient time."

"N-no," she stammered. "I thought you were Uncle Charlie. He was supposed to come back this afternoon."

Ellen rose and picked up the basket. "I brought some food for you and your mama. I'll put it in the kitchen and then go check on her. No need for you to show me the way. I reckon I've been in this house enough times to know where the rooms are."

Sarah nodded but didn't take her eyes off Alex. "Mama's in the bedroom at the top of the stairs. She was sleeping when I was up there earlier."

"Well, I'll just peek in on her." She cast a glance at Alex before she pushed past him and Sarah and left the room.

Sarah reached up and pushed her wet hair off her fore-head. "I didn't expect company. I've been working in the garden."

He struggled to keep from smiling, but it was no use. "Are you going to get mad at me again?"

She frowned. "Why?"

He pointed to her feet. "You nearly took my head off when I saw your ankles. There's no telling what you'll do now that I've seen your feet."

Slowly she bent her head and looked down. Her eyes grew wide, and she let out a loud shriek. "Oh, my goodness. I forgot I don't have my shoes on."

Without another word she turned, ran from the room, and dashed up the stairs. Alex collapsed in the chair Ellen had sat in minutes ago and laughed at what had just happened. One minute he was looking at her picture and comparing her to a Gibson girl and the next she was standing there looking like an urchin from a Charles Dickens novel.

One thing about Sarah—she wasn't predictable. He never knew what the next minute would bring with her. And to his surprise he found that it just increased his attraction to her. He'd never met anybody like her, and any idea he'd had of keeping his distance had just died.

Chapter 6

Sarah raced up the stairs and flew into her bedroom. She yanked her dress and apron off and hurled them into the chair by the window. Mama had cautioned her over and over about going barefoot, but she hadn't listened. Now she'd paid the price. She'd never been as embarrassed in her life as she was when she realized she must look like she'd been working in a cotton patch all day.

She jerked the armoire door open and rifled through the dresses hanging there. She stopped, her hand on the white muslin with its long pink sash, at the thought of her skirt lifted above her ankles. Maybe that had been more embarrassing. She covered her face with both hands and shook her head. Why did Alex Taylor bring out the worst in her?

Now wasn't the time to be debating that question. Quickly she grabbed the dress and pulled it over her head, then dropped to her knees to search underneath her bed for shoes. Once she was dressed and her hair combed, she looked in the mirror, pinched her cheeks, and closed her eyes. Breathe deeply, settle down, and don't let him see how flustered you are, she told herself. Then she hurried from the room.

She paused at the bottom of the stairs and pasted a big smile on her face before she reentered the parlor. Taking a deep breath, she swept into the room with a bravado that belied the nervous twitch of her legs. Alex rose from the chair where

Ellen had sat earlier. He smiled as she walked back in. "That didn't take long."

She arched her eyebrows and responded in a cool tone. "I didn't want to keep you waiting, and I certainly didn't want you to leave with the image of what I looked like when you arrived."

He shook his head. "You shouldn't think like that. It was evident you'd been working, and there's nothing wrong with honest labor. In fact I admire a woman who's willing to dig in the earth and make things grow." He studied her for a moment. "You have many fascinating sides to your personality, Sarah, and I'm enjoying seeing each one."

His words made her heart skip a beat. She tried to pull her eyes away from his piercing stare, but it was useless. "And what have you seen so far?"

He stepped closer. His gaze traveled over her face in a caress that left warm trails across her skin. "I've seen the loving daughter who wants to care for her sick mother, and I've seen the young girl who can still pout over the length of her dress. Then there's the baseball fan who knows about southpaws and no hitters, and the gardener who doesn't mind a little dirt getting on her hands."

"Anything else?" Her heart pounded so hard she wondered if he could hear its beat.

He reached out and clasped her hand in his. "Yes. There's the woman who excites me more than any other ever has and makes me want to know her better." He eased closer until they stood only inches apart. "You have a hold on me, Sarah, but if you don't feel it, too, then tell me now. I'll leave and won't bother you again."

She looked down at their hands and back up at him. "I feel it, too, Alex, but it scares me."

"I know. It does me, too. We don't know each other well yet. We need to give our friendship time to grow and see where it leads us."

She nodded and directed a somber look at him. "I'd like that, but next time let me know when you're coming. I'll have my shoes on."

He stared at her for a moment before he threw back his head and laughed. "Oh, Sarah, you're delightful. You also know how to shatter a mood." His eyes twinkled with happiness. "I wish you could have seen your face when you stepped through that door. It's a sight I won't soon forget."

He took a step back from her, and she sighed in relief at the break in their close contact. His amusement infected her, and a smile crept across her face. "Don't tease me. I've always loved to go barefooted, but Mama says that well brought up young ladies don't do that. I just can't seem to break the habit."

"Don't worry. I've buried this secret with the one about your ankles. My lips are sealed, and we'll mention it no more."

On impulse she pointed toward the door. "If you'd like to see another side to me, walk with me to the pond. This is my favorite time of day, and we might catch sight of a catfish coming up to feed."

"Let's go." He curled his fingers around hers.

Her heart raced at the pressure of his hand holding hers as they walked from the house and down the path that led to the deserted barn. She pointed to the corn crib in the center of the barn. "When I was a little girl and would visit here, my grandfather would let me stay in there and watch him milk."

His brow wrinkled, and he cast a glance at her. "I wonder why I don't remember ever seeing you when we were children."

She shrugged. "We didn't come here often. Maybe once a year. It was difficult for my father to get away."

They walked to the field behind the barn, and she guided him to the drooping willow trees that surrounded the pond. "I called this my secret place when I was a little girl. Now I come here every chance I get."

Sarah ducked underneath the bent branches and led him to her favorite spot in the grass where they were shielded from the sun by the thick foliage. The leaves stirred like a fan in the late afternoon breeze, a welcome respite from the heat of the day.

They sat side by side for a moment without speaking before Alex picked up a pebble from the grass and tossed it into the water. The stone skipped across the surface and disappeared beneath, triggering large ripples that floated toward the bank and washed over the edge of the small pond.

A comfortable silence enveloped them, and Sarah basked in the serenity that surrounded them in their shelter from the outside world. Alex turned to her and gazed at her as if he wanted to tell her something.

"I was serious when I said those things to you earlier." He picked up another stone and tossed it into the water. "The first time I saw you at church I knew you were different from anyone I'd known before."

"I meant what I said, too. But right now I have so many problems in my life I don't know if you need to become involved with me."

He scooted closer. "I'm so sorry about your mother's illness. I know this must be very hard for you, especially after losing your father."

She pulled a blade of grass out of the ground and rolled it between her fingers as she thought about the man with the laughing eyes who had been the center of the universe for her and her mother. "At least this time I know what's coming. My father's death was such a shock."

"I can imagine."

Alex didn't say anything for a moment. Then he took a deep breath and shook his head. "You really have had a rough time. Now that you're here, I want you to know Ellen and I will do everything we can to help you get through what you're facing with your mother's illness. All you have to do is tell us what you need."

She reached over and squeezed his hand. "Thank you for that. You'll never know how much that means to me. It seems for the past few years our problems have come non-stop." She sighed. "Now I have another one I have to address."

He frowned. "Can I help you with it?"

She shook her head. "Thank you, but. . ." She paused and her eyes grew wide. "Why didn't I think of this before? You're a lawyer—just what I need."

A look of surprise crossed his face. "A lawyer? Well, I won't officially be one until I'm admitted to the Tennessee Bar, but I'll help you if I can."

"Oh, Alex, I've been out of my mind with worry, and I've been afraid my mother would find out. If I'd told her before, it might have triggered an attack that she wouldn't overcome."

He reached over and grabbed Sarah by the shoulders. "This sounds serious. Tell me what's wrong."

She took a deep breath. "About ten years ago my father decided he needed to make a will. He wanted to make sure my mother and I would be cared for if he died. When the will was drawn up, he asked his cousin to be executor. My father had grown up with this cousin, and he trusted him. After my father died, this relative came to see my mother and me and told us not to worry he would take care of everything, that he would send us a check each month from my father's estate. Several months ago the checks stopped coming."

"Did you ask what happened?"

"At first I thought it was an oversight. Then I went to see him and asked him what had happened. He told me we had used up everything my father left us and that we needed to sell the house. By that time Mama had decided she wanted to come back here, so I told him to sell it. Several weeks before we moved he told me he had found a buyer for the house and that I would begin receiving money monthly as soon as all the papers were signed. But nothing has come. I've written him letters, but I've gotten no response. The bank won't help me, either. We're about to run out of money, and I don't know what to do."

"You haven't told your mother anything about this?"

She shook her head. "No, I didn't want her to worry. I thought I could work it out, but I haven't been able to."

A sad look flickered in his eyes. "Oh, Sarah, I'm so sorry you've had to bear this alone. Of course I'll help you. I'm going to Memphis next week to take the bar exam and spend some time at the firm. While I'm there, I'll see what I can find out. In the meantime, if you need money, I'll be glad to help you out."

She pushed to her feet and shook her head. "No, I didn't tell you this so you'd give me money. Uncle Charlie will help us if we need anything. I just want to find out what's happened. We weren't wealthy, but I know my father had saved some money."

Alex stood up and faced her. "I'll see what I can find out. What's your cousin's name?"

"Raymond Jordan. He works in a bank down on Union Avenue."

He put his hands on her shoulders and stared into her eyes. "Don't worry about this, Sarah. I promise I'll look into it."

Relief coursed through her body, and she smiled. "Thank you, Alex. You have no idea what this means to me."

"I should be home toward the end of the week. I'll come to see you and let you know if I found out anything. Please try not to worry."

She smiled. "I'll try. But don't let my problems distract you. I want you to pass the bar exam."

He pursed his lips. "It's a tough test, but I've studied hard for it."

"I'm sure you'll do well."

They stared at each other for a moment before Sarah turned and led the way back to the house. For the first time in months she felt some relief. With her mother's present condition, they needed the money. If she couldn't teach this fall, she didn't know how she'd be able to support them.

She could only hope that Alex would bring good news on his return from Memphis.

Chapter 7

By the end of the next week Sarah was about to go out of her mind. Alex hadn't returned, and she hadn't heard from him. All she could think about was whether or not he would be able to find out what had happened to her father's estate. Added to that worry was the fact her mother was beginning to suspect something was bothering her. So far she'd been able to dismiss her mother's questions, but she doubted if she could much longer.

She discarded the needlepoint piece she'd been working on and dropped it on the table next to her chair. With her mother in bed for her afternoon nap it was a perfect time to get outside for a while. She headed to the front porch and had just stepped onto it when she spied a buggy coming down the road.

Her lips curled into a smile as she recognized Dr. Lancaster with Ellen sitting beside him. Since the night of the party, the two had become close friends, and now Ellen accompanied him on his patient calls. She waved as the buggy rolled into the yard.

"Good afternoon. Get out and come in."

Dr. Lancaster hopped down from the buggy and tied his horse to the small tree in their yard before walking around and assisting Ellen to the ground. Sarah couldn't help but notice how they smiled at each other before they turned toward the house.

Dr. Lancaster reached back in the buggy for his bag and took Ellen's arm. Together they climbed the steps. "We were making rounds this afternoon, and I thought I'd better check on your mother."

"She's asleep right now, but you can wake her if you need to."

He shook his head. "I won't do that now. We can visit some first."

Sarah reached out and hugged Ellen. "I'm so glad you came today." When she straightened, she opened the door and motioned for them to come inside. "Can I get you some tea? And I have some cookies I made this morning."

Dr. Lancaster nodded. "That sounds good. How about you, Ellen?"

"I'm always up to a cup of tea."

Just as they stepped into the house, her mother's voice called out from upstairs. "Sarah, do we have company?"

"It's Dr. Lancaster and Ellen, Mama. I thought you were asleep."

"I've been awake for a few minutes. Tell Dr. Lancaster to come on up."

"I'm on my way."

Ellen reached out and put her hand on his arm. "Do you need me to help, Edmund?"

He shook his head. "No, you go on and have your tea. I'll come to the kitchen when I'm through."

Sarah watched him climb the stairs and enter her mother's room before she turned back to Ellen. She propped her hands on her hips and arched her eyebrows. "Edmund? I sense there's more to this relationship than just a doctor and his helper."

Ellen's face turned red, and she waved her hand in dismissal. "Quit your teasin', Sarah. There ain't nothing but friendship between us."

Sarah glanced up the stairs once more before she looped her arm through Ellen's and pulled her into the kitchen. "I don't know about that. I think the good doctor is smitten with you, Miss Taylor."

"And I think the sun's done gone to your brain, Miss Jordan. Now how about that cup of tea?"

Laughing, they entered the kitchen, and Ellen sat down at the table. It had been a lonely week for Sarah, and she was glad to have company. She glanced over her shoulder at Ellen as she pulled the kettle from the stove. "I thought Alex would be back by now. Have you heard from him?"

Ellen shook her head. "I know the bar exam was earlier this week, but I don't know when to expect him. I reckon he'll be over here the minute he gets home, though."

Now it was Sarah's turn to blush. She felt her cheeks grow warm, and she smiled at Ellen. "I hope so. I like Alex a lot."

"And he likes you, too, darlin'."

"I'm glad." Sarah grinned and bit down on her lip as she finished making the tea.

Fifteen minutes later Dr. Lancaster joined them. Sarah smiled and pushed to her feet to get him a cup of tea, but the expression on his face made her sink back into her seat. She tried to speak, but her throat felt paralyzed.

He sat down across from her and exhaled. "I had hoped your mother's condition would be better today, but it's not. I can see a marked difference in her since the night of the party. I'm very concerned."

Ellen reached over and grasped Sarah's hand. "Are you all right?"

Sarah nodded and clutched Ellen's hand tighter. "I-I don't know." She turned back to Dr. Lancaster. "Is there anything I can do to make her more comfortable?"

He smiled and shook his head. "I've never seen anybody do more than you've done for your mother. See that she eats and don't let her over exert herself. She doesn't need to climb those stairs. It might be a good idea to move her bed downstairs, maybe in the parlor, so she can look outside."

Ellen leaned forward. "I'll get Alex and the boy who lives with us to come do that as soon as Alex gets home."

"Thank you, Ellen." She hesitated before asking the question she didn't want to ask. "Do you know how much time she has?"

Dr. Lancaster shook his head. "I leave those matters in God's hands. I try to treat my patients as long as He sees fit to leave them here."

A tear rolled down Sarah's cheek, and she wiped at it. "It doesn't matter. I'll be with her until the end."

"And we'll be here helpin' you," Ellen said.

Dr. Lancaster cleared his throat. "She said she's been having trouble sleeping. I've given her a light sedative. Maybe she'll sleep for a while. I hate to leave you on such a sad note, but I have some other stops to make this afternoon. So Ellen and I need to be going, but we'll be back in a few days. If you find yourself facing an emergency you can't handle, call for help right away."

Sarah turned a questioning look toward him. "And how would I do that? There are no telephones in Richland Creek."

Ellen laughed and patted her on the back. "I guess nobody's told you about our distress call. Have you noticed that post with the big bell hanging from it out back of the house?"

"Yes."

"Well, that's what we call a dinner bell. The farm wives use it to call their family from the fields when it's time to eat. But if somebody starts ringing their bell over and over without stopping, ev'rybody knows it's an emergency, and folks come

71

runnin' to help out. So if you need anything, you just pull the cord on that bell, and you'll have neighbors here before you can bat an eye."

Sarah breathed a sigh of relief. "That's good to know."

She led them back through the house to the front porch. They stepped outside and stopped just as another buggy rattled to a stop. Ellen's face lit up when she spied her brother holding the reins.

"Alex, when did you get back?"

He grinned and jumped from the buggy. "Just a little while ago."

She turned to Sarah and smiled as he tied the horse to another limb of the tree where Dr. Lancaster's buggy sat. "Didn't I tell you he'd be over here as soon as he got back?"

Sarah couldn't take her eyes off Alex as he ambled toward them. His dark eyes sought hers, and he smiled before he glanced at his sister. "What are you doing here?"

Dr. Lancaster laughed, met Alex at the bottom of the steps, and stuck out his hand. "I'm afraid I'm the cause of it. Your sister has been going with me on my rounds so she can show me where everyone lives in the community. She has really been a tremendous help."

Alex shook the doctor's hand and smiled at Ellen. "I'm sure she was happy to do it."

"I was." Ellen joined them at the bottom of the steps and smiled at her brother. "And I'm glad to have you back home. How did you make out on the exam?"

He rolled his eyes and shook his head. "I have no idea. It was two days of question after question, and I won't know if I passed or not until October. I don't know how I'm going to make it until then."

Ellen gave him a playful punch on the shoulder. "You'll be fine, and I'm sure you passed. You studied hard enough for it." She inclined her head toward Dr. Lancaster. "I'm going with Edmund on the rest of his rounds, then I'll be home to fix supper. Edmund's gonna eat with us."

Alex smiled. "That's nice. You'll get to see what a good cook Ellen is."

"Oh, I already know. I've eaten supper with Ellen and Augie every night this week. I've never had such wonderful meals."

Ellen blushed and shook her head. "You gonna make me have the big head if you don't watch out. Let's go. You got patients waitin'."

Sarah struggled to keep from smiling at Alex's bewildered look as Ellen and Dr. Lancaster climbed into the buggy and pulled out of the yard. When they'd driven down the road, he turned to Sarah. "Did I miss something?"

She laughed. "I think while you were away Dr. Lancaster and Ellen became interested in each other."

His eyes grew wide, and his mouth dropped open. "What? She can't be interested in anybody."

"And why not?"

He climbed the steps to the porch and shook his head. "Because. . .Because she's too old to be thinking about stuff like that."

Sarah burst out laughing. "Oh, Alex, don't be ridiculous. You should be happy for her. She's probably lonely, and she'll be even lonelier after you leave for Memphis."

"I asked her to come live with me." He glared at her which only made her laugh harder. He turned and stared in the direction of the buggy. "I can't believe it. I've been gone all week, and she barely has time to say hello before she runs off with another man."

Sarah grabbed his hand and pulled him toward one of the chairs that sat on the front porch. "Quit acting like a spoiled child and come tell me about your week in Memphis."

He started to say something else, but then he grinned at her and allowed her to lead him to the chair. He dropped down in it, and she sat next to him. "Well, like I said, the bar exam was tougher than I thought it would be. I don't know. . ."

She held up her hand. "I want to hear all about the exam, but I'm dying to know if you found out anything for me."

He threw back his head and laughed. "Now who's acting like a child?" He reached over and chucked her under the chin. "Only interested in what concerns you, Miss Jordan?"

"Oh, Alex, quit teasing and tell me."

He swiveled in his chair so that he faced her. "All right. I won't keep you in suspense. I found your father's cousin at the bank where he worked. Since he'd set up the account with your money at the same bank, I confronted him about why you hadn't received any checks lately. At first he denied any wrong doing and ordered me out of his office. I went back to the law firm, and Mr. Buckley called the bank president who happened to be a friend of his. He checked into the matter, and it soon became evident your cousin had been taking money from the account."

Sarah's mouth dropped open. "But why? I thought he had money of his own."

Alex shook his head. "He did, but he'd about spent it all. He'd started frequenting the illegal gambling back rooms down on Beale Street and had lost nearly all of his. Not only was he taking your money, but he was embezzling from the bank as well. Fortunately for you and your mother he had just started dipping into your funds, so most of it's still there. But if we had waited much longer, it would all be gone. He's been arrested on the embezzlement charge and will probably go to jail for a long time."

Her breath caught in her throat. "So we have our money back?"

He grinned. "Well, most of it. It should be enough to take care of you and your mother for a long time."

She gave a squeal of happiness, threw her arms around him, and hugged him. "Thank you, Alex, for helping us."

His arms tightened around her. "I took the liberty of telling the bank to put your name on the account. I didn't see any need for another executor. You can manage your money as well as anybody else can."

His vote of confidence in her brought tears to her eyes, and she pulled back and stared up into his eyes. "I don't know what I would have done without your help. I feel like you've saved us. I'm very grateful to you."

His eyes narrowed, and he pulled her closer. "I don't want your gratitude, Sarah. I just want to be with you and know that you want to be with me, too."

"I do," she whispered. "I thought about you the whole time you were gone."

He was so close she could feel his warm breath on her face. She closed her eyes and tilted her face up as his lips descended on hers. In his kiss she could sense he'd missed her as much as she had him. She curled her fingers into the hair at the back of his neck. After a moment he broke the contact and pulled her against him.

She pressed her cheek to his chest and felt the steady throb of his heart beating. It felt so right to be in his arms like this, and she wished the moment would never end. He bent down and whispered one word in her ear.

"Sarah."

And with that one whispered word she knew without a doubt her relationship with Alex had entered a new phase today. No matter what happened in the future or where she went, she would never be able to break the invisible bonds that tied her heart to his for the rest of her life.

Chapter 8

Sarah tiptoed into the room, stopped beside the bed, and stared down at her sleeping mother. Just as she'd promised, Ellen had sent Alex and the young boy who lived with them the next day after Alex returned from Memphis to move her mother's bed downstairs. After two weeks, though, it didn't seem to have mattered. Her mother grew less spirited each day, and when she was awake she did little more than lie on her side and stare out the window next to her bed. Whereas she hadn't been able to sleep before, now she spent long hours unable to stay wake.

Today Sarah barely recognized the pale face and frail body of the sleeping woman. Just a few weeks ago her mother had accompanied her to a party, and now she struggled for every breath she took. Her mother shivered, and Sarah tucked the cover around her before she sat down on the parlor sofa.

Dr. Lancaster and Ellen had continued to come, and Sarah could tell her mother's condition troubled him. Sarah realized his cheerful attitude was his attempt to keep her from being frightened. It hadn't worked. She'd never been as scared in her life. When they'd first come to Richland Creek, Sarah thought she was prepared for what lay ahead. As the time grew nearer, she realized there were some things in life one could never be ready to experience. She hadn't wanted to lose her father, and she didn't want to see her mother die.

She wiped at her eyes and picked up the needlework that lay on the table beside the sofa. Before she could take a stitch, she heard the whinny of a horse from the front yard. She rose and walked to the front door. When she opened it, she smiled at the sight of Alex tying his horse to the tree in the yard.

She stepped on the front porch and watched him as he strode toward her and bounded up the steps. When he stopped beside her, he gave her a swift kiss on the cheek and looked past her to the door. "How's your mother today?"

"Not good. She's been sleeping most of the day." She pointed to the chairs on the porch. "Let's sit out here where we can talk and not disturb her." She sank down in one and closed her eyes as a cool breeze swept over her. "That feels good. Mama stays so cold I have to keep the house closed up. Sometimes I think I'm about to roast."

He reached over and covered her hand with his. "I'm sorry you're going through such a hard time. Do you need anything?"

"No. I'm fine. I'm just taking it day by day." She settled back in her chair and ran her hands down the front of her dress to smooth out the wrinkles. "How's Ellen?"

A grunt of disgust rumbled in his throat. "She's acting like a schoolgirl. Every day she's off with our good doctor, and I don't see her until nearly supper time. Then he's there to eat with us. You'd think the man didn't have a home of his own."

Sarah giggled and shook her head. "Alex, you should be ashamed of yourself."

"What are you talking about?" His wide-eyed expression only made her laugh harder.

"You should be happy for Ellen. She has a nice man showing some attention in her, and she looks happy. You'll be leaving soon, and she'll be alone. I'm glad she has Dr. Lancaster to keep her company."

"Well, that's what bothers me," he grumbled, "Dr. Lancaster keeping her company."

"You like him, don't you?"

Alex shrugged. "He's okay, I guess. But I don't think he's Ellen's type."

Sarah leaned forward and grinned. "And what type does she need?"

"Somebody like, uh. . ." His forehead wrinkled as if he was trying to think. "Somebody like. . .your Uncle Charlie, for instance."

Sarah's mouth dropped open, and she stared in disbelief at him. "Uncle Charlie? Whatever made you think of him?"

"Because they were engaged once."

Stunned, Sarah fell back in her chair and gaped at him. "Engaged? I never knew that. When?"

"She was awfully young at the time, just seventeen."

Sarah frowned and tried to digest what Alex had just told her. "You told me that's how old she was when you were born."

He exhaled a long breath. "Yeah. When my mother died, Ellen promised her she would always take care of me. Ellen wanted her and your uncle to raise me together, but he didn't want to start married life with a ready-made family. So Ellen broke the engagement."

Sarah shook her head slowly from side to side. "I can't believe I've never heard this story." A thought popped into her head, and she sat up straight. "Is that the reason Aunt Clara was so rude to you the night of the party?"

"Yes. I think she has a fear that deep down Charlie still loves Ellen, and she takes it out on both of them. Of course it's ridiculous, but that's what Clara thinks."

Sarah thought about all Alex had said for a moment before she crossed her arms and directed a smug smile at him. "Now I understand why you're upset about Ellen and Dr.

Lancaster. Ellen gave up the man she loved for you, and it's always just been the two of you together. You're jealous Dr. Lancaster may take your place with her."

He frowned and jumped to his feet. "I'm not jealous. I just don't want her to be hurt."

She rose to face him, grinned, and wagged her finger in a mocking manner. "Protest all you want, counselor, but you won't change my mind."

He raked his hand through his hair and grimaced. "Sarah, you are the most exasperating woman. . ."

Her gaze strayed to the road, and she held up her hand to stop him. "Hold that thought, Mr. Taylor, I see the mailman coming. I'm hoping to get a letter."

She whirled and ran to the side of the road just as the buggy pulled to a stop. Mr. Wardlow, the mailman, leaned out and smiled at her. "Afternoon, Miss Jordan. How's your mama today?"

Sarah looked past him to the stack of mail lying beside him on the seat. "She's not doing too well."

Mr. Wardlow pushed his hat back on his head and stroked his white beard that hung to his chest. "I'm sorry to hear that. She able to be up much?"

"No, not much." She cleared her throat. "Do you have any mail for us?"

His eyes grew wide, and he chuckled. "Oh, I guess you're right anxious to see if that there letter came from Memphis you've been asking me about."

Sarah glanced once more at the stack of mail. "I am."

He laughed, reached down, and picked up a white envelope. He studied the front of it as if memorizing every word. "Yep, this one right here's for you. It's from a Miz Edna Simpson in Memphis. Is this the one you've been a-lookin' for?"

She held out her hand. "Yes, it is."

He nodded. "Well, it came all right." He looked at the envelope again. "Who is this Miz Simpson?"

"A friend. Now may I have my mail?"

A startled look flashed on his face. "Of course you can. That's my job, to deliver the mail."

He handed the letter to her, and she clutched it in her hand. "Thank you for bringing it, Mr. Wardlow."

He tightened his grip on the horse's reins. "You got anything to send?"

"Not today, but I may have tomorrow."

He touched the brim of his hat. "I'll stop by then. Good day, Miss Jordan."

"Good day, Mr. Wardlow."

Sarah waved the letter above her head as she raced back to the porch where Alex waited. He met her at the top of the steps. "What's the matter?"

She hopped onto the porch and held up the letter. "This is from the lady who owns the school where I was supposed to teach this year. Her name is Edna Simpson. She owns a private girls' school in Memphis. I went there until I graduated. She has always liked me, and she kept in touch with me during the two years I was studying for my teaching certificate. When I graduated, she had a job waiting for me." Sarah glanced back toward the house. "After Mama got sick, I wrote her and told her I had to give it up."

"So why is she writing you now?"

Sarah took him by the arm and led him to the far end of the porch away from her mother's window. She leaned close to him and spoke in a soft voice. "We've written back and forth since I've been here. Her letters have cheered me so much when I felt down. She's been my one link with the outside world, and I get so excited when one arrives. Do you mind if I glance over it quickly?"

"Of course not. Go ahead and read it."

She ran her finger underneath the seal and pulled the letter out. As she read, her heart began to pound, and tears filled her eyes. When she finished, she looked up at Alex. "I can't believe it."

He frowned. "What does she say?"

She sniffed and cleared her throat before she began to read.

"My dearest Sarah, I can't tell you how saddened Roger and I are by your last letter. I know this is a difficult time for you, and we think of you all the time. In fact, it has been all I could do to keep Roger from descending on Richland Creek with an entourage of nurses to lighten your load. I explained to him this is a private time between you and your mother and he should respect your wishes. However, this has not dampened his desire to be of service to you since you have always held a special place in his heart."

"Who's Roger?" Alex interrupted.

"Roger Thorne, Mrs. Simpson's nephew. He's quite wealthy and owns the school. Mrs. Simpson runs it for him." She directed her attention back to the letter.

"Although we don't want to think about it, it seems we must face the inevitable. Whenever the time comes, I want you to know your job is waiting for you. Roger and I decided to staff the position with a substitute until your circumstances allow you to return. The room you will occupy in my house awaits you as do Roger and I. Whenever you are able to come, send us word when you will arrive, and we'll meet you at the train station.

On another note our suffrage group is becoming more active, and we have many meetings and demonstrations planned for the coming year. Your place in that group also awaits you. Roger has also planned several fund raisers for the spring so some of our volunteers can join Alice Paul's organization in Washington as she continues to petition the government for our cause.

I will keep you informed of our progress. Please continue to write and update us on your mother's illness. Roger and I both send you our love.

Edna Simpson

When she finished reading, she looked up at Alex. "Can you believe that?"

He frowned. "I certainly can't. Who does that woman think she is writing you a letter like that?"

Sarah blinked and shook her head. "I don't understand what you mean."

"That letter sounds like she can hardly wait for your mother to be out of the way so you can come back to her."

"No, no, you misunderstood her. She only wants to help me. I know I can't live on the money my father left me for the rest of my life. I will have to have a job to support myself. She's making that possible."

Anger lined his red face, and he clenched his fists at his side. "And she's keeping a room for you in her house? Do all the teachers live there?"

She didn't understand why Alex was so upset, and she hesitated before answering. "N-no, but she knows we sold our house. I'm sure she's trying to help me."

Alex's eyebrows arched, and he glared at her. "And what about this Roger? It sounds like he's more than a possible boss. He wants to bring nurses here, and you have a special place in his heart? He must really be in love with you."

She didn't know whether to be angry or to laugh. She chose the laughter. "That's the funniest thing I've ever heard. He's fifteen years older than me. He always treated me like a daughter."

Alex pointed to the letter. "The feelings she describes in that letter are far from fatherly. But what about you, Sarah? Is there a part of you that's in love with this obviously wealthy man who has special feelings for you?"

Now the anger won out. "No!" As soon as she screamed the word, she regretted her outburst. She didn't want to upset her mother. "No," she whispered. "I'm not in love with him. I've never had feelings for any man until. . ."

He stepped closer and put his hands on her shoulders. "Until when?" She swallowed hard and tried to pull away, but he gripped her shoulders tighter. "Until when?" he repeated.

"Until I met you." She closed her eyes.

He wrapped his arms around her and pulled her close. His lips brushed her hair on the top of her head. "And I've never had feelings for another woman until you. I'm sorry I overreacted to your letter. I didn't mean to upset you. Hearing how another man feels about you drove me crazy for a moment." His husky voice sent a warm rush through her veins.

"You're so wrong about that. But none of it matters anyway. The only way I will ever go to Memphis is if Mama passes away, and I can't stand to think about that. I love her so much, Alex. "

"I know you do. Please forgive me." He nuzzled her ear with his lips. "I have to leave for Memphis in a few weeks, but I want you to know I'll take the train to Mt. Pleasant every Friday afternoon so I can be here on the weekends with you. We'll face this together."

She cuddled closer to him. "Thank you."

They were silent for a moment. "Although there is one more thing about that letter that upsets me."

She sighed. "What is it?"

"The part about the suffrage movement."

She stiffened. "What about the suffrage movement?"

"You'll have to give up your involvement with them."

She pulled back and stared up at him. "And why would I do that?"

He loosened his grip, and she stepped out of his arms. "Don't get upset, Sarah. I know you have strong feelings about it, but sometimes it's more expedient to keep your thoughts to yourself."

She frowned and shook her head. "I don't understand what you're talking about."

He sighed and directed a look toward her that made her feel like a child being reprimanded by her father. "We've only known each other for a few months, but in that time we've grown close. It's plain to see we care deeply for each other. But I'm about to start my career, and I have to be careful that I have the right kind of friends if I want to make partner in the law firm."

"By right kind of friends, are you saying you can't associate yourself with the radicals who support suffrage?"

He winced. "Well, I wouldn't call them radicals, but that's the kind of people I'm talking about."

Sarah clenched her fists at her side and gritted her teeth. "The kind of people? What do you know about any of the people who are working to give women the right they should have had years ago? Are you so narrow-minded that you think women aren't intelligent to make the right choice in electing our leaders?"

"No, I'm not. I'm just saying that you should respect my wish to succeed in my job and help me do it."

She crossed her arms and stared at him a moment. "Where did you get the idea you couldn't make partner if you had friends in the suffrage movement? Was it from James Buckley?"

His face turned crimson, and he held out his hand. "Sarah, please try to understand. . ."

She could see the truth in his eyes, and it broke her heart. "It was Mr. Buckley, wasn't it? When did he tell you this? Was it when he helped you with my executor problem?"

He hung his head and nodded. "Yes. He recognized your mother's name as one of the leaders in the Memphis suffrage movement, and he asked me if I had a relationship with you. He told me he couldn't have associates in his office who support such radical ideas. Then he said he was sure you were a sensible girl who wouldn't want to hurt my career."

Tears stung her eyes, and her chin trembled. "Why didn't you tell me this when you got back?"

"Because I thought it was something we could face in the future. You have enough to worry about now with your mother's illness. Please understand my position on this, Sarah. I want to rise to the top of my profession so I can afford to take care of Ellen and repay her for all she's done for me. Don't you want that for me?"

She nodded. "I want you to have whatever will make you happy, Alex. Just remember that Ellen may need more than money, though. She might like to have a voice in who represents her in the government."

"I know. She kind of hinted at that after you and I had our first argument about suffrage. So do you understand why I'm asking you to do this?"

For a moment Sarah couldn't respond. Her mother had been right when she told her to keep her thoughts to herself while she was in Richland Creek. Alex had let her know that day at the picnic what he thought of the suffrage movement, and she'd dismissed it. She'd thought he'd change his mind when he saw how passionate she was about the cause, but now she realized that was a silly idea. From the look on his face she knew there was no changing his mind. She should have known better than to let herself fall in love with Alex, but it was too late. She fought back tears at the thought that her fairy tale would not have a happy ending.

She took a deep breath and stared into Alex's eyes. "Yes, I understand," she said. "I want you to tell Mr. Buckley when you see him that I appreciate his help in getting my money back, and that he's right about me not doing anything to hurt your career. I would never do anything to harm you, Alex."

Alex sighed with relief. "I knew you would see it my way."

Her lips quivered, and she shook her head. "But I don't. I can't turn my back on a cause that I believe in so whole-heartedly. I will continue to support enfranchisement for women until my last breath." She hesitated and took a deep breath before she spoke the words that she knew would break her heart. "Our relationship is never going to work, Alex. We have to end it now while we still can. You go to Memphis and play Mr. Buckley's game to get you to the top, and make a lot of money on the way. But I won't be there with you."

He took a step toward her. "You can't mean that. I know I haven't said it, but I love you, Sarah."

She shook her head. "It's no use, Alex. There's no future for us. I don't want to see you again."

He reached for her, but she flinched. A hurt expression darkened his eyes, and he swallowed. "You're sure about this?" His agonized whisper broke her heart.

"Positive. Now please leave and don't come back here again."

He let out a ragged breath before he pushed past her and bounded down the steps. She didn't turn around, but she heard his horse gallop out of the yard. Then she walked back in the house and leaned over the bed to check her mother.

She wanted to rush upstairs to her bedroom, throw herself on the bed, and cry until she couldn't feel the pain anymore, but she couldn't. Not now. Her mother needed her, and she had to put her own problems aside. There would be time later to grieve for the loss of Alex.

She bent over her mother's still form. "Mama, can you hear me?"

There was no response except labored breathing. So far she'd been unable to get any food down her mother today, and that concerned her. Maybe she could get her to take some of the soup she'd made earlier. She went into the kitchen and returned with a warm bowl of broth, sat down, and attempted to feed it to her mother. Nothing she did could coax her to open her lips and swallow. Most of it trickled down the side of her face and onto the bed.

After a few minutes Sarah gave up and set the bowl aside. She sat down, scooted her chair closer to the bed, and clasped her mother's hand in both of hers. She sat quietly for a few minutes lost in thought before she began to speak.

"Mama, do you remember the time when I was a little girl, and you and Poppa took me to downtown Memphis shopping. We rode a streetcar and got off at the corner of Main and Beale. The first thing I saw was a store on the corner with dolls in the window, and I ran toward it. I was pointing out which doll I wanted for Christmas when I heard voices shouting in the distance. I was so scared, but you took me by the hand and led me to the edge of the sidewalk. I saw a large group of women in the middle of the street walking toward us. Some of them carried flags. Some held signs, and all chanted at the top of their voices."

"For a minute I was scared, and I looked up at Poppa. 'What is it, Poppa? I asked.'"

"He grasped my other hand and pointed to the women. 'It's all right, he said. It's a group of suffragists marching.'"

"That word sounded so strange to me, and I struggled to say it. 'What's a suf-suf-suffragist?'"

"He just smiled at me in his patient way like he always did and said, 'They're women who want our lawmakers to give them the right to vote like men.'"

Sarah sighed and settled back in her chair. "Of course at that age I'd never given a thought to the fact that women couldn't vote, but it dawned on me that one day I would be a woman. So I asked him. 'Why can't women vote, Poppa?'"

"He reached up and ran his finger over his mustache like he did every time he was going to tell me something really important. 'Well,' he said, 'I suppose because men who have the power have never passed a law which allows them to vote.'"

"I remember I propped my hands on my hips, cocked my head to one side, and looked up at him. 'Do you think women should vote, Poppa?' I asked."

"He never avoided any of my questions, and he didn't that day either. 'I certainly do. Women have been trying for about forty years to get the lawmakers to change the law,' he answered."

"As far as I was concerned, that settled the matter. I crossed my arms over my chest and gave a curt nod. 'When I'm grown, I'll make them change the law, Poppa,' I said."

"I can still hear how his laugh echoed across Beale Street. He dropped down on one knee and chucked me under the chin. 'I think you could. I feel sorry for the lawmakers if you get after them. You'll be a formidable adversary.'"

"I'd never heard that big word before and asked him what it meant."

"It's someone who opposes something and works to change things,' he told me."

"I knew I could do that so I smiled. 'Then I'm going to be an adversary and get Mama and me the right to vote like you, Poppa.'"

Sarah tightened her hold on her mother's hand. "I haven't forgotten that promise, Mama. As long as I live, I won't give up working to give women the right to vote. I want you to know that."

There was a slight pressure from her mother's fingers, and then her hand relaxed. Sarah sat by her bed without moving as the afternoon gave way to night, and dark shadows covered the room. When the clock struck six o'clock, Sarah rose and lit the oil lamp on the table beside the bed, then took up her post again. Just after the clock struck nine o'clock, Sarah heard a peaceful sigh, and she leaned closer as her mother took her last breath. She sat on the edge of her chair for a few minutes and studied how peaceful her mother's face appeared in death.

The reality of what had occurred struck her, and she eased back into her chair and closed her eyes. Her father was gone, and now so was her mother. But they weren't the only ones. Today within the span of a few hours, she'd lost her mother and the man she loved. She felt as if her heart had been gouged out and thrown away.

She leaned her head on the back of her chair and let the tears roll down her face. Now she truly was alone in the world. All she had left was a promise she'd made years ago. She cried until she felt exhausted, but she didn't move from her chair.

She sat there until the clock struck six o'clock the next morning. Then she rose from her chair, walked to the back yard, and began to toll the bell that would alert her neighbors to her distress. She stood there, her hands wrapped around the bell's rope, and pulled without stopping. A horse galloped down the road and came to a stop in the front yard, but she didn't quit pulling the rope. She heard running footsteps coming around the side of the house, and she wished Alex would appear. But it was Mr. Jenkins instead. When she saw him, she finally let go of the rope and collapsed against him.

Chapter 9

The gloom of the approaching storm hung over the mourners at the gravesite like a heavy veil. Sarah sniffed the fresh scent of approaching rain and glanced at the smoky haze hovering in the air. Dark clouds rolled across the sky, and a hot wind stirred the leaves on the trees at the edge of the cemetery. Horses snorted and shook their harnesses in warning of the impending storm.

Uncle Charlie and Aunt Clara sat on either side of her under the canopy covering the grave. The mourners had followed them from the church after the funeral and now stood outside the tent. She glanced at the familiar faces and was suddenly struck by the thought that she would miss the people she'd come to know here.

There had been a steady stream of visitors bearing food and well wishes after her mother's condition became evident the night of the party, and she had found the friendships her mother had told her awaited her in the small community. Now they gathered to offer her comfort.

She heard Brother Hughes reading a scripture verse and then say a prayer, but she didn't listen to his words. All she could do was stare at the simple coffin sitting atop the grave. Her gaze drifted to her grandparents' graves next to it, and a tear ran down her cheek. Mama's wish had been fulfilled that she would rest in the cemetery where members of her family were buried.

She jumped at the touch of someone's hand on hers and looked up into the Brother Hughes's kind eyes. "We'll be praying for you, Sarah. Remember that God's with you."

Sarah stared at him and didn't respond. Those same words had been said to her at her father's funeral, but so far God hadn't bothered to show up in her life. She closed her eyes, bit her bottom lip, and wished she could wake up and this would all be a dream, but it wasn't.

She felt the pressure of Uncle Charlie's hand on her elbow. "We have to go now, Sarah. The workers are going to fill the grave. We can come back later."

He led her into the open air, and they stopped as one by one the people filed by to offer their condolences. Her heart skipped a beat when she caught sight of Ellen and Alex at the back of the line.

When Ellen reached her, she put her arms around Sarah and hugged her. "I'm so sorry, Sarah. I wish I could take away some of your hurt, but I know I can't. I remember how I felt when I lost my mama. I'll be praying for you."

Sarah straightened and stared into Ellen's eyes. "Thank you, Ellen. You've been so kind to me since I came to Richland Creek. I'll never forget you."

Ellen patted her cheek and smiled. "That sounds like you're leaving."

"I am. I'm staying with Uncle Charlie and Aunt Clara tonight. Then tomorrow he's taking me to Mt. Pleasant to catch the train to Memphis."

A flicker of sorrow crossed Ellen's face. "You take care of yourself."

"I will."

Ellen stepped aside, and Alex moved in front of her. He swallowed as his gaze drifted over her face as if trying to memorize every feature. "You're really leaving?"

Her chin trembled, but she didn't flinch from his gaze. "Yes."

"Where will you be?"

"I'll be at The Simpson School for Girls. It's in Mrs. Simpson's large Victorian house on Adams Street."

He nodded. "I know the area."

"And you'll be at Mr. Buckley's offices on Front Street. Do you know where you'll live?"

"I've rented an apartment on Madison Avenue."

They stared at each other for a moment, but there didn't seem to be anything else to say. Sarah stuck out her hand. "Goodbye, Alex. Thank you for everything you've done for me. If I need a lawyer again, I'll contact you."

He took her hand in his and squeezed it. "Goodbye, Sarah. I wish you the best."

She pulled her hand away and turned to Uncle Charlie. "Please. I want to go now."

He nodded and took her by the arm. As she turned away from Alex, she felt as if the life had drained from her, and she clung to her uncle's arm for support. She wanted to look back, but she didn't.

She felt the stares of the silent crowd boring into her all the way to the buggy. Uncle Charlie helped her and Aunt Clara in. Then he climbed into the driver's seat, gathered the reins in his hands, and clicked them on the horse's back. As they slowly moved out of the churchyard, Sarah could feel Alex's penetrating gaze burning into her back, but she forced herself to face forward.

Thunder rumbled through the air and lightning flashed across the sky by the time the buggy pulled up to her uncle's store. Uncle Charlie jumped out, helped Aunt Clara and her step down, and hurried them toward the porch. "Clara has the key to the front door," he said to Sarah. "I'll get the horse in the barn before the storm hits."

He hurried back to the buggy and drove around the back of the store. When Aunt Clara had the door unlocked, she turned around. "Come on in, Sarah."

She shook her head. "I think I'll sit out here a few minutes. I'll lock the door behind me and then come on upstairs."

"All right. But don't stay out here and get wet."

Sarah waited for Aunt Clara to go inside before she walked to the edge of the porch and clutched the railing. Only two months ago she'd stood here with her mother and grumbled that she had no friends in Richland Creek. A few minutes later she'd met a man who had opened her heart to what it meant to love. Now that she'd lost both him and her mother, loneliness was eating away at her like a dreadful disease.

The heavens opened, and the rain began to pound on the tin roof of the store. Large drops of rain pelted the yard leaving depressed dusty circles in the dry earth. She watched as the rain grew heavier and formed big puddles in front of the store.

After a few minutes she sighed and turned to go inside but stopped when she caught sight of a horse and rider approaching. The man sat hunched in the saddle, and rain poured from the brim of his hat. Sarah's breath caught in her throat. She would recognize Alex anywhere.

He pulled his horse to a stop in front of the store, dismounted, and looped the reins over the hitching post. He looked up at her, doubled his fists, and strode up the steps until he stood in front of her. His clothes clung to him, and he wiped his wet sleeve across his rain-streaked face.

He took a hesitant step toward her. "I couldn't let you go like this."

She struggled to keep from bursting into tears. "Please, Alex, there's nothing left to say. We have different dreams, and they've set us on different paths. There's no way for us to overcome that."

He took another step toward her. "But I love you, Sarah. I love you. I love you. That's all I can think about." His agonized words made her want to rush into his arms. Instead she backed away and pressed her hands to her ears.

"Don't say that."

He grabbed her hands in his and pulled them away from her ears. "I can't let you leave without telling you I think I fell in love with you the first time I saw you. I knew it would be hard for us, but I wanted to try."

"I did, too."

He grasped her shoulders and pulled her closer. "Is it really too late for us, Sarah? Can we not work this out?"

"Alex, please. . ."

He tightened his hold on her. "Answer me one thing. Do you love me?"

"I. . ."

He gritted his teeth. "Do you love me?"

She closed her eyes and nodded. "Yes, I love you, but I can't be the person you want. I'm going back to Memphis, and I'm going to throw myself into the suffrage movement. In time you'll forget about me."

His dark eyes flickered with pain, and Sarah knew hers must mirror his. "So this is it. We throw away what we could have because we can't find a way to work out our problems."

"Please," she groaned. "How can we find common ground? I've grown up in a household where suffrage was talked about every day. From the time I was a child I've wanted to fight the injustice of women not having the right to vote. You're going to work for a man who forbids you to have contact with people in the suffrage movement. How can we overcome that?"

He shook his head. "I don't know. I just know I'm dying inside."

"I am, too."

He leaned forward and touched his forehead to hers. They stood with their eyes closed for a moment until he spoke. "It can't end like this."

She struggled to blink back her tears, but it was no use. "It has to, Alex. There's no answer for us. Please go while I still have the strength to send you away." Her last words were lost in a sob.

He drew back and looked into her eyes for a moment before he leaned forward and kissed her on the cheek. "I'll never forget you."

Her skin burned where his lips touched her. "You'll always be in my heart, Alex."

He tightened his hold on her and then released her. He took a step back, reached up, and brushed a lock of hair behind her ear. "I'll worry about you on your own."

"I'll be all right. I'm very resilient."

His Adams apple bobbed as he swallowed. "If you ever need me, let me know. I'll come for you wherever you are. That's my promise to you."

Before she could say anything, he turned and rushed down the steps. He grabbed the horse's reins, jumped into the saddle, and galloped down the road. The rain beat down on him so that he soon disappeared from sight.

Sarah watched for several minutes before she turned and entered the store. She locked the door behind her and leaned against it. The locket her mother had given her hung around her neck, and she opened it. The smiling faces of her parents peered up at her. She stared at them for a moment before she snapped it shut.

A sudden burst of thunder shook the store, and she flinched. Outside the fury of the story unleashed itself. The house shook, and lightning flashed across the sky. Rain pounded the tin roof like the sound of a beating drum, and thunder rattled the windows.

She thought of Alex riding through the storm and her knees grew weak. He'd be nearly drowned before he reached home, but Ellen would take care of him. But who would do the same for her?

Now she was alone and would be responsible for herself from now on. But she could do it. As she had once promised her father, she could be a formidable adversary, and she could face whatever the future threw at her.

★ ★ ★ ★ ★

A week later Ellen stood in the middle of Alex's bedroom, her hands on her hips. "Do you want to take all this furniture when you move to Memphis?"

He scratched his head and looked around at the room's furnishings he had used all his life. "If you don't need it, I think I'll take all in this room. I can buy me some things after I get settled."

"I couldn't believe the size of that apartment when I saw it," Ellen said. "You'll have more room than you'll know what to do with."

Alex walked over to the cedar chest and opened it. "Do you mind if I take these quilts and sheets with me? I don't think I could sleep if I didn't have one of your quilts covering me."

Ellen laughed and looked over his shoulder at the contents he rifled through. "Oh, I imagine when you get married your wife will want something other than old homemade quilts from your sister."

Her words caught him off guard, and the cedar chest's top slipped from his hand. He caught it before it banged shut and eased it down. For days he'd tried to put his last meeting with Sarah out of his mind, and yet it returned at the most unexpected moments. He pinched the bridge of his nose and shook his head. "I don't think I'll ever marry, Ellen."

"Why not?"

"I gave my heart away, and I have nothing left to give anyone else."

Ellen took his hand and pulled him toward the bed. They sat down facing each other, and Ellen looked into his eyes. "Alex, you can't go on the rest of your life thinkin' about Sarah. You've got to look for happiness somewhere else."

Alex shook his head. "I won't ever love anyone else like I love her." He faced his sister. "She said she loved me, Ellen, but she couldn't give up her dream. If she really loved me, why was her dream more important to her than me?"

"I don't know. Have you ever turned that question around on yourself?"

He frowned. "I don't understand."

Ellen took a deep breath. "Well, if you really love her, why couldn't you find a position in some other law firm that didn't oppose her cause?"

Alex leaned forward and clutched his hands between his knees. "I've asked myself that. Then I tell myself what an honor it is to get a chance in James Buckley's law firm. It's the best in Memphis, if not in the whole state. This could open up all kinds of doors for me. And for you, too."

Ellen's eyes grew wide. "How's it gonna help me?"

"Because I'll have more money to take care of you. That's what I've always wanted."

Ellen chuckled and patted his arm. "You don't have to take care of me. I've been in charge of this farm and all the tenant workers that help us for years. I think I've done a mighty good job of keeping a roof over my head and food on the table."

He straightened and put his arm around her. "You have, but I don't want you to keep working so hard. I want to make life easier for you."

"I hope I didn't do anything to make you think you had to repay me for taking care of you. I did it because I loved you. The only repayment I want is for you to be the best lawyer you can be. It don't matter a bit to me how much money you make as long as you remember to let God lead you."

He nodded. "I'll remember, Ellen. You taught me that."

Ellen sighed and pushed to her feet. "Then I guess we better get you packed to leave for Memphis. When do you think you'll go?"

"Mr. Buckley wants me there in two weeks. I thought I might go the middle of next week. That would give me some time to get settled before I report to the office."

Ellen lifted her hands and stared upward. "My baby brother a lawyer and working in a big law firm. Thank you, Jesus, for blessing us."

Alex smiled at Ellen's display of gratitude toward God. She'd offered him the only support he'd ever had in life, and he intended to make her proud of him. Right now she might not understand how money would make a difference in her life, but she would later. He intended to give her a life of ease. He'd build her a new house on that rise in the field next to their house, and he'd fill it with the best furniture.

She'd have dresses that would come from the finest stores in Memphis, and there would be a maid to clean her house and a cook to prepare her meals. And they'd travel. First off, he'd take her to South Carolina where their ancestors had lived before traveling to Tennessee in a covered wagon, and maybe later they'd take an ocean liner to Europe.

Although he'd never spoken of this to her, he'd had these dreams for years. When he realized he was falling in love with

Sarah, he had included her in his plans. She would be his wife and together they'd give Ellen the life she deserved.

That dream had died when Sarah left to pursue her life with Edna Simpson and Roger Thorne. Just the thought of the man's name made Alex's skin crawl. Although he'd never seen him or even heard of him until Sarah read him the letter, Alex didn't trust him. At first he'd thought it was only jealousy that spurred these feelings, but in the days since Sarah's departure he'd recognized his concerns went a lot deeper.

One of the first things Alex intended to do when he got to Memphis was find out everything he could about the man who supposedly had "fatherly" feelings for the woman he loved. If he harmed Sarah in any way, Roger Thorne would have to answer to him.

Chapter 10

As a student at Mrs. Simpson's school, Sarah had never appreciated the small class sizes and the well-equipped classrooms. Now as a teacher, she realized how privileged she'd been to attend school here. Her father must have sacrificed to pay the tuition she never thought about. Now after two weeks in the classroom she was overcome again with how fortunate she was to work with such an elite group of teachers who were dedicated to their students. As a first year teacher, she felt lost at times, but the staff had been quick to come to her aid, especially her former teachers who accepted her as an equal. She'd made the right decision in coming here.

Lost in thought, she walked from the building that housed the classrooms into the garden that separated it from the main house and sat down on a bench. She'd just finished reading the first page of the book she'd brought from her classroom when Christine Donovan, another first year teacher, exited the school.

Sarah scooted over to give her room to sit. "Are you just now leaving for the day?"

Christine dropped down on the bench. "Yes. I had some papers to grade, so I'm later than usual. You don't know how lucky you are to live here at Mrs. Simpson's house. I have a long streetcar ride to my apartment over on Union."

Sarah only nodded. This wasn't the first time one of the teachers had said something about her living arrangements.

It seemed she was the first teacher to be allowed to live with Mrs. Simpson. "I'm very thankful Mrs. Simpson asked me to live here this year. I'm sure it was because I had just lost my mother and had nowhere else to go. I'll probably have my own apartment next year."

"You'd better enjoy living here while you can. It's a lot better than being on your own like I am. I grew up in an orphanage and worked my way through Normal School to get my teaching certificate. I don't mind telling you it's been a struggle."

Sarah's heart pricked at Christine's words. "I had no idea. But look how it's worked out. You have a teaching job now, and you're able to support yourself."

A smile pulled at Christine's mouth. "Yes, and there's a man in my life, too. Maybe it won't be too long before I won't have to teach. Instead I can be a wife."

Sarah squeezed her hand. "I hope it works out for you."

Christine straightened. "Well, enough of that talk. How was your day?"

Sarah slipped her bookmark between the pages and closed the book. "It was fine. I really enjoy working with the younger children. I'm so glad Mrs. Simpson assigned me that classroom."

Christine smoothed her blonde hair into place and straightened the wide-brimmed black hat she wore. "Be thankful you don't have the eighth grade girls. I don't know if I will survive them or not."

Sarah laughed and nodded. "I remember what I was like at that age. I must have driven my parents out of their minds." She patted Christine's hand. "But don't worry. You'll survive."

She sighed. "Mr. Thorne said the same thing. I hope the two of you are right."

"Right about what?" Mr. Thorne's voice startled Sarah, and she glanced up to see him standing in front of them.

Christine rose to her feet. "We were just talking about our classes."

His eyes twinkled. "And you're still worried? I thought you'd gotten over that."

"I'm trying, but some of those girls are a handful."

His reassuring smile lit up his blue eyes. "My aunt and I have assured you we have faith in you. I hope you won't worry about it anymore."

"Thank you, Mr. Thorne. I appreciate the confidence you and Mrs. Simpson have in me." She glanced back at Sarah. "I need to go. I don't want to miss the streetcar. I'll see you tomorrow."

Sarah nodded. "Have a good evening, Christine." She waited for Christine to get out of earshot before she turned her attention back to Mr. Thorne. "Did you need to see me?"

His eyes twinkled, and a mischievous smile pulled at his mouth. He glanced over his shoulder at Christine's retreating figure before he leaned forward and whispered in conspiratorial manner. "I saw you sitting out here with your shoes off, and I thought I should come warn you before Aunt Edna spots you. She might not approve."

Sarah laughed and reached for her shoes that sat underneath the bench. "Then I'd better put them back on. I don't want to be reprimanded after only two weeks on the job."

His smile deepened, and he pointed to the bench. "Do you mind if I sit with you?"

"No, please do." He eased onto the bench in a graceful move that reminded her of the ballet dancers she'd seen at the Orpheum Theater last year. He crossed his legs and pressed the crease in his trousers with his fingers.

"You should know you have nothing to fear as far as reprimands go. Aunt Edna and I are so happy to have you back we wouldn't dream of upsetting you."

"Thank you, Mr. Thorne. I'm glad to be back, too."

A small frown flashed across his forehead, and he tilted his head to one side. "There is one thing I would like for you to do, Sarah."

"Of course. What is it?"

"I know you had to call me Mr. Thorne when you were a student here, but you don't have to now. I would like for you to call me Roger."

She gave a small gasp. "I don't know if I can do that. It doesn't seem respectful enough. After all, you are my employer."

"I know, but we're also members of the suffrage group. I have a feeling you're going to be one of our brightest stars, Sarah, and I want us to work together as equals." He reached over and covered her hand with his. "Won't you do this for me, please?"

He bent forward, and the afternoon sun sparkled on his blond hair. A pleading look lit his eyes, and she nodded. "If that's what you want, I'll try."

He smiled and stood. "That's all I can ask. Now I almost forgot why I really came out here. Aunt Edna wanted you inside for an early dinner. She's having something to eat in her room while she gets ready for the meeting here tonight to plan the reception we're having for Mrs. Catt when she comes to Memphis in October."

Sarah jumped to her feet and clasped her book to her chest. "I haven't forgotten. I can't believe Carrie Chapman Catt is coming to Memphis. It's like a dream come true that I'm going to meet her."

"I know. We're all excited. She's taking her second term as president of the National American Woman Suffrage Association very seriously and is traveling all across the country. We were fortunate to get one of her stops scheduled in

Memphis." He held out his arm. "Now if you'll allow me, I will escort you inside for dinner."

Sarah stared as his arm several seconds before she hesitantly looped her arm through his. He reached over with his other hand and covered hers as he led her inside to the dining room.

When they entered the dining room, she was greeted with a chorus of welcomes from the student boarders who sat at a long, linen-draped, mahogany table. One reproachful glance from Roger quieted the girls, and they sat silent with their hands folded in their laps.

Roger held Sarah's chair for her to be seated and moved to sit at the other end. Dora, the cook's helper and serving girl, pushed the swinging door from the kitchen open and backed into the room. Steam rose from the large platter of chops she held, and her face sparkled with sweat. She set the meat in front of Roger and cast a quick smile in Sarah's direction before she disappeared into the kitchen.

Within minutes she returned to the dining room with bowls of peas and potatoes. Roger served the food onto plates stacked in front of him and passed them to either side. As Sarah reached for her plate, she noticed Roger studied her from the other end of the table. As his gaze traveled over her face, she remembered how Alex had looked at her, and her hand trembled.

The choice she had made closed a door when she came here, and nothing could change it now. Her thoughts might return to Alex and Richland Creek from time to time, but that life lay in the past. Her heart might cry out for the young man with piercing dark eyes, but he was as dead to her as her parents.

She lifted her fork to her mouth but halted in midair as she caught sight of Roger again. He sat hunched in his chair with his elbows resting on its arms. The water goblet in his hand rotated in small circles, and the candlelight reflected off the large diamond ring on his finger. He studied her with an arched eyebrow and a half-smile on his face.

Alex's warning about Roger returned, and she realized he'd been right. She might think of the older Roger Thorne as a father figure, but from the look on his face she realized that his feelings for her were anything but fatherly. She had no idea how she was going to deal with this situation.

Two weeks later Sarah glanced around from where she sat in Mary Windsor's living room and stared at the people gathered there. At times an impulse to pinch herself popped into her mind. She could hardly believe that she was really in the presence of a woman she'd admired for years—Carrie Chapman Catt. Like others before her she had dedicated her life to seeking enfranchisement for women and worked tirelessly for the cause.

As Mrs. Catt brought her speech to an end, Sarah and the other guests rose to their feet and applauded. Sarah had never felt so stirred in her life. As those in attendance pushed forward to speak with their guest, Mrs. Windsor grabbed Sarah's hand. Her face flushed with excitement, she steered Sarah in Mrs. Catt's direction.

"Sarah, I want you to meet our guest of honor," she said.

Sarah's mouth dropped open, and she turned to Mrs. Windsor who now had positioned them behind the women talking with Mrs. Catt. "Me? Why would you want me to meet her?"

"Because, my dear, I have been very impressed with you since you've been attending our meetings with Edna and Roger. I feel like you have much to contribute to our cause, and I want Mrs. Catt to meet you."

Before Sarah could protest more, the women in front of her stepped aside, and Sarah looked into the smiling face of a woman she'd read and heard about since she was a little girl. She swallowed her nervousness as Mrs. Windsor pushed her forward.

"Mrs. Catt, this is Sarah Jordan. She's new to our group, but I sense in her a true dedication to our cause. I wanted you to meet her."

Mrs. Catt extended her hand, and Sarah grasped it with her trembling fingers. "Oh, Mrs. Catt, it's such an honor to meet you. My parents were both avid supporters of suffrage, and I've heard them talk about you all my life."

The smile on Mrs. Catt's face grew larger. "I'm happy to meet you, too, Sarah. I assume from what you've said your parents are no longer alive."

"No, ma'am. They both passed away, but I've taken up their cause. I intend to see it through until women are granted the right to vote."

Mrs. Catt motioned to a sofa across the room. "There's a young reporter who wants to take some pictures of me. While he's setting up his lights, why don't we sit down? I like to talk to young women who join our movement about their commitment and what they feel they can contribute to our cause."

Sarah's heart pounded with excitement as Mrs. Catt led her across the room. As they settled on the sofa, Sarah glanced toward the door that led into the dining room and spotted Roger and Mrs. Simpson watching her. Roger's eyes sparkled, and he stroked his mustache. He gave her a slight nod before he took his aunt's arm and escorted her into the room where refreshments were being served.

"Now," Mrs. Catt said, "tell me about yourself, Sarah."

She'd had other people ask her that in the past, but somehow it had always seemed like only a polite request. With

Mrs. Catt it was different. The tone of her voice made Sarah know this woman was really interested in what she had to say. Maybe that was the quality that had made her a great leader in the suffrage movement.

Sarah cleared her throat and sat up straighter. "There really isn't much to tell." For the next few minutes Sarah spoke of her upbringing in Memphis, the loss of her parents, and her return to Memphis to teach. "All I want is to help achieve what you've worked so hard for."

Mrs. Catt studied her carefully. "You haven't mentioned a young man. Is there one in your life?"

"There was one, but not anymore." Sarah tried to keep her voice from cracking. "His boss didn't like the idea of my being involved in the suffrage movement."

Mrs. Catt sighed and shook her head. "I'm sorry, Sarah. That's not uncommon. My husband is very supportive of my work. If he wasn't, I wouldn't be able to travel about the country so much. Maybe you and your young man will be able to reach some kind of compromise."

She shook her head. "I don't think so." Sarah sniffed and straightened in her seat. "But I want to know more about your work. It must be exciting traveling around the country and meeting like-minded people who want to see you succeed."

Mrs. Catt laughed. "Yes, it's nice to meet the supporters of our cause, but there are a lot who don't. That's not always pleasant. But I've set myself on this course, and I can't walk away from it."

"You've been doing this for years. Do you think your efforts are paying off?"

"I hope so. As I said in my speech, I believe the way to win is through reaching our elected leaders. A lot of my time is spent working in local elections so we can get candidates elected to office who are sympathetic to our cause. And I spend a lot of time with those already elected to Congress. We also need to gain their support. So the role of our organization is a more peaceful one fought in the political arena. Of course there are other suffragists who disagree. They have a more militant attitude."

Sarah knew immediately who she spoke of. "Like Alice Paul?"

"Yes, Alice is a wonderful woman, and she's spent years working for suffrage just as I have. But she's become disenchanted with the slow progress our National American Woman Suffrage Association is making. As I'm sure you know, she left our party and founded the National Woman's Party. Her group is the one working in Washington right now. I worry about her and the women affiliated with her. With the uncertain times in the world and America trying to stay out of the war in Europe, President Wilson may grow tired of her demands."

Sarah thought about what Mrs. Catt had said for a moment before she responded. "But don't you think perhaps both groups may serve a purpose in this fight. It's important to reach the elected people, but there's also a need for the common man to be stirred to the point of addressing his beliefs to the elected leaders from his state."

Mrs. Catt smiled. "Ah, spoken like a true Alice Paul supporter."

Sarah's face grew warm. "I do admit I admire her. In fact, I would love the opportunity to go to Washington and work with her."

Mrs. Catt reached over and patted Sarah's hand. "Maybe you'll get your chance. But if you do, be careful. I'd hate to see anything happen to a sweet, young girl like you."

She was about to respond when a man's voice startled her. "Ladies, look this way, please."

Mrs. Catt laughed and pointed to a young man standing behind a camera on a tripod. "That's the reporter, dear. Smile. You might make the newspaper tomorrow."

Sarah smiled for the camera and then looked around at the people waiting to speak with Mrs. Catt. "I don't want to keep you from the other guests. I've enjoyed our chat."

Mrs. Catt took a deep breath. "Yes, I suppose I should talk with some of the other people here tonight, but I've really enjoyed our conversation."

"This has been a wonderful experience. You are a great inspiration to me."

Sarah pushed to her feet and stepped away from the sofa. She smothered a smile when a woman dropped down next to Mrs. Catt and settled herself for a picture. Sarah ambled toward the dining room and stopped next to the table laden with an assortment of sandwiches, cakes, and candies.

Her conversation with Mrs. Catt replayed in her mind. It was true she believed in everything Mrs. Catt had said, but nothing excited her like the thought of what Alice Paul and her supporters were involved in at the capitol. If only she could be there and experience what it was like to confront those opposed to suffrage.

Movement next to her caught her attention, and she turned to see a young man she'd noticed in the group earlier. He cleared his throat before he spoke. "Miss Jordan, I'm Timothy Windsor from St. Louis. I'm visiting my aunt and uncle, and she told me who you are. I've been watching you since you arrived, and I knew I had to meet you."

He held out his hand, and she placed hers in it. The breath almost left her body. His dark eyes and his hair that tumbled across his forehead transported her back to a baseball field and another young man. Her limp hand could not respond to his fingers gripping hers. "Th-thank you, Mr. Windsor."

"I understand you're a teacher." He picked up a cup of tea and handed it to her. She gripped the saucer with her trembling fingers.

"Yes, I teach at Mrs. Simpson's school." She took a sip of tea and walked to the far side of the room. He followed behind.

"Would you like something to eat?"

The cup rattled against the saucer. "No, thank you. I-I'm waiting for my friends to join me."

He glanced toward the table and back at her before he smiled. "When I saw you come in tonight, I thought the man with you was probably your father. But when my aunt introduced us, I knew he wasn't."

"No, he's not. I teach at his aunt's school."

His dark eyes smiled down at her. "Aunt Mary insisted that I come tonight to meet her friends. I didn't want to, but now I'm certainly glad I did. I never expected to meet such an attractive young woman in the group."

She steadied her trembling hand and clutched the saucer firmly. "Thank you, Mr. Windsor. I hope you enjoyed Mrs. Catt's speech. I certainly found it stirring."

His dark eyes twinkled. "That wasn't the most stirring thing for me." He cleared his throat. "Miss Jordan, I'm going to be in town for several days. Would you mind if I called on you at Mrs. Simpson's?"

Call on her? Those words had been spoken to her before. Tears threatened to fill her eyes. This man might remind her of Alex, but he wasn't. And no one would ever take his place in her heart.

She glanced at Roger who was talking with a woman at the table and hoped her expression alerted him to the panic building inside her. He halted his conversation, looked from her to Timothy, and headed toward her. When he stopped beside her, she inched closer to him and smiled at Timothy with trembling lips.

"Roger, this is Timothy Windsor."

"Yes, we met earlier." The two men shook hands, but Roger turned a quizzical look to her. "Is everything all right, Sarah?"

She handed him her cup and saucer. "Yes, I'm just tired and ready to go home. Would you help me find my coat?"

"Miss Jordan, I….," Timothy began.

Sarah linked her hand through the crook of Roger's arm and took a step back. "It was very nice to meet you, Mr. Windsor. I hope you enjoy visiting with your aunt. Have a safe trip home."

She turned and hurried away, pulling Roger after her. He handed the cup he held to a servant by the door as they pushed through the crowd. Mrs. Simpson followed them into the room where they'd left the lightweight shawls they'd worn.

Roger pulled Sarah to a stop. "What's the matter? Why are you in such a hurry to leave?"

"Timothy Windsor asked if he could call on me, and I wanted to get away from him."

Roger fixed her with a stony glare. "Did he now? What did you say?"

"I tried to get your attention so I could get away from him. I didn't want to hurt his feelings, but I have no desire to know him better."

Roger's body relaxed, and he smiled at her. "Good girl. Let's get out of here before he comes after us."

Sarah draped her wrap over her arm and headed toward the front door. Just as Roger put his hand on the knob she heard his voice. "Miss Jordan, wait." She glanced over her shoulder and saw Timothy Windsor approaching.

Roger opened the door, and she rushed onto the front porch and gulped a big breath of the chilly October air. He turned his back to block the door and faced Timothy. "Miss Jordan is very tired, and we're leaving now. She has a long day ahead of her in class tomorrow. I'm afraid she's going to be very busy for the next few weeks. It was nice to meet you, Mr. Windsor."

Roger turned and hurried his aunt and Sarah to their parked car. As they pulled away from the curb, Sarah watched Timothy Windsor standing on the porch with his hand on the column at the top of the steps. She settled back in the seat and wiped away a tear that trickled from her eye.

No one said a word as they drove through the dark streets of Memphis. When they pulled up in front of Mrs. Simpson's house, Roger got out, helped them up the steps, and followed them into the entry hall. His aunt stopped at the foot of the stairs and turned to him. "Did you want to speak to me before you go home?"

He glanced at Sarah. "No, I'd like to talk with Sarah for a few minutes."

"Very well. Then I suppose we'll see you for dinner tomorrow night."

He smiled. "Since tomorrow is Saturday, I may be here in the early afternoon. It will depend on whether or not I decide to finish up some work at the office."

Sarah watched Mrs. Simpson climb the stairs and enter her room at the top of the landing before she turned back to Roger. "You wanted to talk to me?"

"Yes." He grasped her arm and steered her into the parlor. They stopped in front of the fireplace, and he gripped her arm tighter. "I want you to tell me what happened with that boy tonight. Did he do anything inappropriate? If he did, I'll see that he regrets it."

113

She pulled away from him and shook her head. "No, no. It wasn't anything like that. It was my fault. He reminded me of someone, and I got upset."

Roger's eyes narrowed. "Reminded you of someone? Who?"

She sighed and shook her head. "It doesn't matter. It was someone I met in Richland Creek."

"A man?"

She frowned. Why was he asking these questions? "Yes, but. . ."

He took a step toward her. "What's his name?"

"Roger, please. . ."

"Sarah, I want to know the name of the man. You obviously still care for him or you wouldn't have gotten so upset tonight. Now tell me who he is."

She threw up her hands in defeat. "His name is Alex Taylor. He's a lawyer and works in James Buckley's firm. But there is nothing between the two of us anymore."

"James Buckley's firm?" He chuckled and shook his head. "Then that's why he hasn't been around here to call on you. Buckley's not about to let any of his lawyers associate with members of the suffrage movement."

"No, he's not. I don't know why I got so upset when Timothy approached me. All I could think about was getting out of there."

A smile pulled at his lips. "And I helped you. Don't forget that."

A chill went down her spine. "I promise I'll never forget anything you and your aunt have done for me, Roger."

He gave a sigh of relief. "Good. And I have a promise for you, too, Sarah."

"What is it?"

114

He reached out and took her hand in his. He stared into her eyes a moment before he brought her hand to his mouth and kissed it. "I promise I'm going to make you forget you ever knew a man named Alex Taylor."

His words stunned her so she couldn't speak. Wide-eyed, she watched as he released her hand and strode from the room. The front door slammed, and then she heard the sound of his car pulling away from the house.

After a few minutes she sank into one of the chairs that faced the fireplace and buried her face in her hands. As the tears rolled from her eyes, she shook her head in denial. Roger was wrong. She would never forget Alex Taylor. Never.

Chapter 11

Alex heaved another box off the floor of his office and set it on his desk. He propped his hands on his hips and let his gaze drift over the small room he'd been assigned as his first office at Buckley, Anderson, and Pike. It would be all right for a start, but he didn't intend to stay in here long. He would work hard, and before long he would have one of the larger offices with big windows that looked out onto Front Street and the river beyond.

He opened the box and was about to pull out a book when a tap at the door interrupted him. "Come in." The door opened, and Lydia Stevens his secretary stuck her head in the door. "Lydia, what are you doing here on a Saturday afternoon?"

"I heard you say yesterday you planned to come in and get your office in order today. I thought I might be able to help."

He shook his head. "But I don't want to interfere with your personal time. I'm sure you have other things you need to do on your day off."

She shrugged, and he recognized her no nonsense attitude in the gesture. "Days off don't mean a lot to me. My life has revolved around this firm for the past twenty years, and I expect it will continue to in the future." She straightened her shoulders. "But I really came in to help Mr. Buckley with some work. He sent me down here. He wants to see you in his office."

The senior partner wanted to see him in his office? And on a Saturday afternoon? This couldn't be good. In the weeks since he'd been here Mr. Buckley hadn't called for him. In fact he'd been under the tutelage of John Deadmon, one of the junior partners. Alex gulped before he spoke. "He wants to see me? What for?"

Lydia smiled, and the reproachful gaze she directed at him reminded him of Ellen. "I'm not in the habit of asking the senior partner of the firm why he does anything, Mr. Taylor. I learned a long time ago it's much easier to follow instructions than to determine the reason behind them."

He grimaced and nodded his agreement. "I understand, Lydia. Just keep reminding me of that. I don't want to say or do the wrong thing." He picked up his suit coat that he'd hung on the back of a chair and shrugged into it. "If I'm being called to the boss's office, I'd better try to look my best."

Lydia crossed her arms and narrowed her eyes as she studied him. "I think you'll pass inspection. Mr. Buckley is not a tyrant like some people think. He's been very kind to me since I've worked here. He has a love for the law, and he wants all his associates to share that love."

Alex studied the woman for a moment. In the short time he'd been at the firm, he'd never heard Lydia mention a husband or a family. In fact, she seemed to spend all her time at the firm, and she'd done everything she could to make him feel at home here.

"I admire your dedication to the firm."

She smiled. "Like I said, it's my life. I've seen a lot of young lawyers come through here. But I must say, I've never been as impressed with anyone as I am with you. I've seen your academic record and read your letters of recommendation. I know you can make partner here if you work hard."

Alex took a deep breath and pulled his coat sleeves over his shirt. "That's what I intend to do. I'm glad to have you on my side. Keep me steered on the right path."

"I will, Mr. Taylor." She glanced at the box on his desk. "Now you go on to Mr. Buckley's office, and I'll finish unpacking these books for you."

"Thanks."

He headed down the hallway toward the suite of offices on the other side of the reception room. When he reached Mr. Buckley's office, he stopped outside the door and took a deep breath before he knocked.

Mr. Buckley's voice growled out a command to enter, and Alex stepped inside. He was struck at once by the difference in this room and the one where he worked. Polished mahogany appeared to be everywhere. Alex had never seen such beautiful office furniture in his life. From behind his desk Mr. Buckley glared at him from the padded chair where he sat.

"Well, close the door and come in, Taylor. No need to stand there like you're scared to enter."

Alex forced a smile to his face and closed the door behind him. He walked to the chair facing Mr. Buckley's desk and waited for an invitation to sit. Mr. Buckley gestured toward the chair, and Alex eased into it.

"Lydia said you wanted to see me, sir."

Mr. Buckley leaned back, propped his elbows on the chair arms, and tented his fingers. "I've been busy since you arrived and haven't had much time to talk to you. I wanted to make sure Deadmon had helped you settle in."

"Yes, sir. He has, and Lydia has been very helpful. Thank you for assigning her to me."

He nodded. "Lydia has worked for me for many years, and she knows how to spot an up and coming lawyer. She tells me you've impressed her more than any other in a long time."

"That's good to know, sir, but I don't know what I've done for her to judge. I've spent most of my time working on appellate briefs for some of the other lawyers."

"I know. I've been keeping up with your work, and I've been impressed."

Alex's eyebrows arched in surprise. "Really?"

"Yes. I've found that more and more cases are being lost on appeal because of an ineffectively written brief. Some lawyers forget they learned about legal writing in the first year of law school. Instead they write what they think the judge wants to hear. Your briefs are tidy and to the point, just what I like to see. I wanted to compliment you on that."

Alex smiled and let his shoulders relax. "Thank you, sir. I hope I can continue to impress you. I'll certainly try."

Mr. Buckley picked up an unopened envelope and tapped it against his desk top several times. "Why don't we see if you continue to impress me?"

A ripple of concern swept through Alex, and he eyed the envelope with a wary expression. "How?"

"A letter came for you today. I wanted to be with you when you opened it."

Alex frowned. "I didn't think the mail was delivered here on Saturdays."

"It's not. I arranged for this one to arrive by special delivery."

Alex's bewilderment increased. "I don't understand, sir. What is it?"

"It's the results of your bar exam."

Alex sat in stunned silence and tried to absorb the fact that Mr. Buckley had arranged with the bar examiners to send his results by special delivery. Did the man's power have no limits?

Mr. Buckley handed the envelope to him, and Alex's heart fluttered when he saw the return address. He swallowed and looked up. "I knew this was supposed to arrive in October. Now that it's come, I'm afraid to open the letter."

Mr. Buckley shrugged and handed him a silver letter opener. "Well, we have to find out the results. You might as well get it over with."

Alex slipped the blade under the seal and pulled out the piece of paper inside. He took a deep breath before he unfolded it and read the results. A wave of relief washed over him, and he breathed a sigh of relief. "I passed."

He glanced up, and Mr. Buckley was beaming. "Good news, young man. I knew you could do it." He extended his hand, and Alex rose to shake it. "Welcome to the firm. I know you're going to be a valuable member."

Alex smiled and sank back in his chair. He stared down at the letter and thought of Ellen. He could hardly wait to let her know his hard work had paid off, but she'd never doubted him. "Thank you for your confidence in me, sir. I'll work as hard as I can for the clients of this firm."

Mr. Buckley's bushy eyebrows drew down over his nose, and he glanced at a folded newspaper lying on his desk. He picked it up. "I'm sure you will. But there's still one area we need to discuss. I wondered if you had read the afternoon newspaper."

Alex shook his head. "I haven't had time. Is there something in it I should see?"

He pushed the newspaper toward Alex. "I thought you might be interested in a story on the front page. I believe the young lady in this picture is a friend of yours."

"A friend of mine?" Alex frowned and reached for the paper. His eyes grew wide, and his hands shook. Sarah, seated next to a woman he'd never seen before, stared at him from the front page of the newspaper. He looked up at Mr. Buckley. "I-I don't understand."

"You haven't read the article yet. The older woman in the picture is Carrie Chapman Catt, president of the National American Woman Suffrage Association. She's in Memphis stirring up trouble for a few days, and she spoke to a large gathering at Mary Windsor's house last night."

Alex looked back at the picture. "And Sarah was there?"

"Evidently so." Mr. Buckley folded his hands on top of his desk and leaned forward. He directed a piercing glare at Alex. "Isn't Miss Jordan the young woman you asked me to help with an inheritance problem a few months ago?"

"Yes, sir.

"And at the time there was some kind of relationship between the two of you."

"Yes, sir."

"And now?"

"That's all over. It has been for weeks."

Mr. Buckley relaxed and smiled. "Good. I can't have my associates mixed up in all this suffrage nonsense. I just needed to make sure you understood what's required of the people in my law firm."

Alex rolled the paper into a cylinder and wrapped his hands around it. "I understand, sir."

"Then I'm glad we had this little talk. Get everything out in the open I always say. Now I'll let you get you back to your office."

Alex pushed to his feet, but before he could move the door to Mr. Buckley's office burst open. A young woman with long brown hair swept into the office and hurried to Mr. Buckley's side. She stared down at him with big, brown eyes. "Daddy, I've been shopping, and I ran out of money."

Mr. Buckley scowled and stood. "Larraine, how many times do I have to tell you to knock before you come bursting in my office? I might have an important client in here."

She laughed and kissed him on the cheek. "But this is Saturday, and you never have clients on days when you're catching up on work. Besides you have that new associate you've told me so much about, and I wanted to meet him." She looped her arm through her father's and batted her eyelashes at Alex. "Are you going to introduce us, Daddy?"

Mr. Buckley smiled at his daughter. "Larraine, this is Alex Taylor. Alex, I'm sure you've already figured out this is my daughter."

Alex flashed a wobbly smile in the young woman's direction. "I'm pleased to meet you, Miss Buckley." He backed toward the door, the newspaper still clutched in his hand. "I'll talk with you later, Mr. Buckley."

Mr. Buckley nodded. "And Alex, congratulations on passing the bar."

"Thank you, sir."

Larraine's eyes widened, and she held up a hand to stop him. "You passed the bar? When did you find out?"

Alex held up the letter. "Just a few minutes ago."

"That's wonderful." She looked up at her father. "Daddy, we should invite Alex to dinner tonight to celebrate his success."

Alex's face grew warm, and he shook his head. "No, I couldn't intrude."

Larraine laughed. "You wouldn't be intruding. You would be our guest of honor. Not all of the new associates here pass on the first try." She looked up at her father. "Tell him what time to be there, Daddy."

Mr. Buckley only hesitated a few seconds before he nodded. "Larraine's right. We should celebrate your success. Dinner is served at seven o'clock. Do you know where we live?"

"No, sir."

"Oh, don't worry about getting there, Alex," Larraine said. "I'll come for you in my car. I saw your address on the office roster, so I know where you live. I'll pick you up about 6:30."

Alex realized her statement didn't require an answer so he simply nodded and walked out of the office. His legs shook so that he wasn't sure if he would make it all the way back to his office. He lurched through the door and came to a halt at the sight of Lydia still unpacking a box.

"How did it go?" she asked.

He shrugged. "Fine. I found out I passed the bar."

"Congratulations. I'm very happy for you." Lydia's nonchalant tone gave no indication whether she was happy for him or not.

"And I've been invited to dinner at Mr. Buckley's house."

That statement got her attention, and she looked up, a frown on her face. "Larraine?"

"Yes. How did you know?"

Lydia closed the box she'd been unpacking and directed an impassive stare at him. "Like I said earlier, I've been around here for a long time and have seen a lot of new lawyers come through here."

Alex frowned. "And what's that supposed to mean?"

Lydia sighed. "I think you're smart enough to figure things out for yourself. Just be careful while you're doing it."

She walked out of his office and left him standing in the middle of the floor trying to figure out what had happened since he'd stepped into Mr. Buckley's office. At first he'd been thrilled over the bar exam and with the compliment he'd received. Then he'd been frightened of the implied threat Mr. Buckley delivered about any friendship he might have with Sarah. And Larraine Buckley? He couldn't even start to understand her.

Nothing had surprised him, though, like seeing Sarah's face on the front page of the newspaper. He laid the paper on his desk, opened it, and smoothed out the picture. He closed his eyes for a moment and remembered how beautiful she'd looked standing with her skirt lifted above her ankles. He'd tried to forget her, but he couldn't.

He dropped down in the chair behind his desk and stared at the envelope containing his exam results. He didn't know how long he sat there, but he finally straightened. Suddenly he had an urgent need to talk with Sarah, to tell her he'd passed the bar, and. . .just to hear her voice. Since it was Saturday, she wouldn't have classes today. Maybe he could reach her. He picked up the telephone receiver. Lydia answered right away.

"Yes, sir."

"Lydia, can you get me Mrs. Edna Simpson's School for Girls? It's located on Adams Street."

"I'll get it right away, Mr. Taylor."

Within a few seconds the call connected, and the voice of a young woman answered. "Mrs. Simpson's School."

Alex cleared his throat. "I'd like to speak with Miss Sarah Jordan, please."

"I'm sorry, sir. Miss Jordan isn't here right now."

"Do you know when she'll be back?"

"I'm not sure, sir. She's gone to a dinner meeting with Mrs. Simpson and Mr. Thorne. Would you like to leave a message?"

If she was out with those two, it could only mean one thing—a suffrage dinner. He slumped in his chair and closed his eyes. "No thank you. I'll call back later."

Alex hung up the phone, but he knew he wouldn't call back later. Sarah had been right. Their paths lay in different directions, and there was nothing he could do to change that.

Chapter 12

October in Memphis had always been Sarah's favorite time of year. Leaves were turning the bright colors of fall, and the nights were getting cooler. It also meant Christmas wasn't too far off, and she could hardly wait. This year she had special plans for Christmas, but she dreaded telling Mrs. Simpson and Roger. They wouldn't understand why she wanted to spend Christmas with Uncle Charlie and Aunt Clara.

In an effort to put the troubling thought from her mind, Sarah looked up at the chimney on top of Mrs. Simpson's house as Roger's car rolled to a stop in front. Smoke curled up the brick chimney and drifted across the night sky. Dora had a knack for knowing how to comfort the people she served, and she'd made a fire to welcome them home from the suffrage dinner.

When the three of them entered the house, Sarah rushed right to the fireplace, turned her back to it, and held out her cold hands to the flames. Roger smiled as he entered the room and came to stand next to her.

Mrs. Simpson sat down in a chair facing them, leaned back, and frowned at Roger. "That was quite a boring dinner. We need some new speakers in our group. I'm tired of hearing the same thing over and over."

Sarah shook her head. "Oh, I thought it was a wonderful evening. I enjoyed every minute of it."

Roger laughed. "That's because this is all so new to you, but you'll come to feel the way we do before long. That's why I think it's time we started preparing you to speak at some of our gatherings."

Sarah turned to him in surprise. "Me? Who wants to hear me?"

"Evidently a lot of people. There were many at the dinner tonight who asked when they were going to hear from you, especially after your picture made the newspaper today."

She waved her hand in dismissal. "That was just luck the reporter chose me. It could have been anybody at the meeting."

Roger cocked an eyebrow and smiled. "You think so?"

"Of course I do. Who. . ." She stopped, and suddenly the truth hit her. "Roger, did you have anything to do with my picture being in the paper?"

He threw back his head and laughed. "It's amazing what you can get in the paper when you slip the reporter a few dollars. Besides, the man is a friend of mine. He was glad to do it for me."

Sarah crossed her arms and directed a stern look in his direction. Her first impulse was to berate him for doing such, but the childish pleasure she detected in his eyes silenced her. Ever since she'd returned to Memphis, Roger had tried to make her happy, and she couldn't be angry. After all, he wanted to promote her within the Memphis suffrage group, and this was his way of doing it.

"I suppose it's all right this time. But don't do it again. I imagine some of the older ladies in the group are wondering why they weren't chosen."

Roger threw back his head and laughed. "Nobody wants to see those women in the paper. They want a beautiful, young girl like you."

The newspaper lay on a table next to Mrs. Simpson, and Sarah walked over and picked it up. She studied the picture for a moment. It really was a good picture, and her pulse raced at the thought that a picture of her sitting next to one of the staunchest suffrage promoters in the country had made the Memphis paper.

She glanced up at Mrs. Simpson. "Would you mind if I cut this out and keep it?"

Mrs. Simpson reached out and patted her arm. "Of course not, my dear. You need to keep it to remember such an important night in your life."

Sarah clutched the paper close to her chest and smiled. "It was one of the best nights of my life. Thank you for taking me."

"It was our pleasure," Roger said. "But it was only the first of more to come." He pulled his pocket watch from his vest and stared at it. "It's getting late. So if you ladies will excuse me, I think I'll go home." He leaned over and kissed his aunt on the cheek. "I'll come by tomorrow afternoon and take you and Sarah for an afternoon ride. Then we can come back here for dinner. Tell the cook I'd like to have her chocolate cake for dessert."

"I'll tell her," his aunt said.

Roger walked over, took her hand in his, and kissed her knuckles. "Good-night, Sarah. I'll see you tomorrow."

The touch of his lips on her hand sent a cold chill up her spine, and she could only nod as he turned and left the room. The memory of another man's lips flashed into her mind, and her heart lurched at the thought. She looked back down at the paper she still held. Had Alex seen her picture? If he had, he was probably telling himself right now how lucky he was not to have her in his life any more. She should be thinking the same way, but every day it grew harder to forget him.

She glanced at Mrs. Simpson who sat huddled in her chair and stared into the fire. A faraway look hooded her eyes, and Sarah wondered what she was thinking. Perhaps both of them had memories tonight that troubled them. Sarah sighed and headed to the staircase.

"Good night, Mrs. Simpson."

"Good night, Sarah. I hope you sleep well."

Sarah nodded, but somehow she didn't think she would. Suddenly her head was too filled with memories of what she'd lost and would never regain.

Larraine pulled her car to a stop outside Alex's apartment building, rested her arm on the steering wheel, and turned to him, a coy smile pulling at her lips. "I hope you had a good time tonight, Alex."

Alex scooted closer to the door and fumbled for the handle. "I enjoyed dinner very much. Please tell your mother again how much I appreciated the invitation."

Larraine leaned closer to him, and the perfume she was wearing enveloped him. "Mother had nothing to do with it. I was the one who invited you." She put her hand on his arm and ran her fingers down to his hand. "You can thank me by taking me out to dinner this weekend."

Alex looked down at her fingers that rubbed against his knuckles, and loneliness washed over him. But it wasn't for the beautiful young woman with dark hair and flashing brown eyes. He closed his eyes and pictured a blonde beauty with brilliant blue eyes that made him think of the summer sun and baseball games.

He opened his eyes, covered Larraine's fingers with his, and moved her hand back to the steering wheel. A voice in his head screamed for him not to ruin his chance of working in Mr. Buckley's firm, but he needed to establish an understanding with Larraine.

She glanced at her hand and back to him. "What's the matter?"

Alex took a deep breath. "Larraine, you're a very beautiful young woman, and I'm flattered that you seem to like me. But the truth is I'm an old-fashioned kind of fellow. I like to be the one who asks a woman out. And I sure don't want to ruin my chances at the firm by upsetting the boss's daughter. So let's just agree we had a good time tonight and leave it at that."

She blinked and leaned back in the seat. "Aren't you afraid I'll tell my father you were rude to me?"

Perspiration popped out on Alex's head, and he nodded. "Frankly, yes. But I don't understand why you would care one bit what I thought or did. I grew up on a dirt farm. We didn't have much money, and we worked hard. My sister sacrificed a lot to get me to law school in Nashville, and I owe her a big debt. I don't want to do anything to endanger the chance I have at your father's firm. I'm sure you have more in common with your other friends than you do with a farm boy who's just out of law school."

She swiveled in her seat, crossed her arms, and settled against the car door. "I saw you, you know."

He frowned. "When?"

"The day you came for your interview. I was in Lydia's office when you walked down the hall. She told me who you were. Later I got the file my father had on you, and I read every word. I know all about you, Alex. And what I read intrigued me. You're going to be a great lawyer."

His face grew warm. "Thank you, Larraine. I'm honored you have confidence in me."

She tilted her head to one side. "But it wasn't your academic record that impressed me. It was the letters of recommendation from your teachers and friends who've known you all your life. I saw something in their words that told me you were a man I wanted to know better. I'd like for you to give me that chance."

"Larraine, I don't know. . ."

She held up a hand. "Maybe I came on too strong today. That's been the way I've gotten what I want all my life, but I see that's not going to work with you. I'd like for you to know the real person I am. I keep that person hidden from most people. Won't you give me the chance to introduce her to you?"

Alex stared at her for a moment. "I'd like to get to know you better. Maybe we need to start over."

She smiled. "Maybe we do."

Larraine repositioned her body behind the steering wheel. "I'd better be getting home now. My parents will be wondering where I am."

Alex reached to open the door but stopped. The picture from today's newspaper flashed in his mind, and he gritted his teeth. If Sarah had been at a suffrage meeting, Roger Thorne was probably close by somewhere. She seemed to be making it fine without him in her life. If she could do it, he could, too.

He turned back to Larraine. "Since we're going to start over, how would you like to have dinner with me Saturday night?"

Her eyes grew wide. "Really?" When he nodded, she smiled. "I'd love it. What time shall I pick you up?"

He shook his head. "I don't feel comfortable with you picking me up. I'll come to your house to get you."

"Will you have a car?"

"No, but we can walk to the streetcar stop and ride it down to Main. That is, if you're okay with a little walking."

She smiled. "I've never ridden a streetcar. It sounds like fun."

He arched his eyebrows. "Never ridden a streetcar? Well, ma'am, you're in for a treat. I'll see you about six."

"That sounds wonderful. And thank you, Alex, for giving me another chance."

The sincerity of her words convinced him she was being truthful. He hoped so, because he'd never been lonelier than he had since he'd arrived in Memphis. It would be good to have a friend. He just needed to remember she was his boss's daughter and not let anything happen that would put his job in jeopardy.

He smiled and climbed from the car. "I'll see you Saturday."

He'd barely slammed the door before she waved and roared off down the street. He watched the car disappear in the distance and shook his head. He'd never met a woman like Larraine Buckley in his life, and he wasn't sure if that was good or bad.

Chapter 13

Sarah could hardly believe the changes that had taken place in her life in the two months since her picture had appeared in the Memphis newspaper. In addition to nearing the end of her teaching semester she had discovered her concern that some of the Memphis suffragists would resent her picture being in the paper had proved unfounded. In the weeks after the meeting at Mrs. Windsor's house, the group had embraced Sarah as the new face of suffrage in Memphis—a symbol of modern young women who would not rest until they achieved enfranchisement for generations to come. She found herself a celebrity in the growing circle of supporters in the local group.

Now talk had turned to sending some volunteers to Washington to work with Alice Paul, the head of the National Woman's Party. This group had begun to apply pressure to the Democratic controlled House and Senate in the past few months, and women were flocking to Washington to take part in this historic confrontation. Sarah hoped she would be one of those to go.

"Sarah, where are your thoughts tonight?"

Mrs. Simpson's voice penetrated her mind, and she sat up straighter on the sofa. The fire Dora had laid earlier blazed in the fireplace and warmed the parlor on this cold December night. She yawned and stretched her arms over her head. "Lost in my thoughts, I guess. It's so good to spend a night at home."

"It is." Mrs. Simpson frowned and glanced at her watch. "I wonder where Roger is. It's not like him to miss dinner."

"Don't worry, Mrs. Simpson. He's been putting in a lot of hours at work lately trying to make up for the time he misses when he's working on our group's projects during the day. I don't know how he does it all."

Mrs. Simpson smiled. "I know. He's really thrown himself into the suffrage activities since you've come back to Memphis. I think you inspire him, Sarah."

Sarah chose to ignore the remark and picked up the evening paper that lay on the table at the end of the sofa. Her eyes widened as she skimmed the articles on the front page. "Oh, I didn't know my name was in the paper."

Mrs. Simpson laughed. "It seems to be nearly every day now. What is it this time?"

"It's a write-up about the meeting at Mrs. Harrison's home last night. It quotes some of the things I had to say."

"Well, read them to me, my dear."

Sarah grew excited as she glanced over the article. "This is what the article says. *Miss Jordan, poised and confident, appealed to the group with well researched material. She related that at present time women comprise one-fifth of the Tennessee workforce. Many work ten to twelve hours a day for wages one-half to one-third that of men. Employers justify this by claiming that women only provide a secondary income. In addition to jobs they also must care for their families at the end of a long work day.*"

"That reporter gave an accurate of account of your speech." Mrs. Simpson leaned forward. "What else did he say?"

Sarah cleared her throat and directed her attention back to the page. *"Miss Jordan ended her remarks by stating that women stand at the threshold of victory. She urged all pres-*

ent to band together to oppose those who would deny women the liberty for which our ancestors struggled. With defiance in her voice, she raised her fist as she delivered her parting statement. 'I say to you, let us go forth with the same resolve the valiant patriots of the American Revolution declared. No Taxation Without Representation!'"

"Excellent! Excellent!" Mrs. Simpson clapped her hands in glee.

Sarah continued to stare at the paper in disbelief. "I'm overwhelmed. I had no idea this would be in the paper."

"What's in the paper?" Roger's voice asked from the doorway.

Mrs. Simpson motioned him into the room and pointed at the paper Sarah held. "Sarah is quoted in tonight's paper. She made quite an impression last night."

Roger took the sheet Sarah offered him and read through it. When he had finished, he smiled at her. "This is wonderful, my dear. Evidently you gained some new followers. I'm pleased with this report, and you should be also."

"Oh, I am."

Roger walked to the fireplace and turned his back to it. "I think you've just become a leader in the Memphis movement."

Sarah shook her head. "Oh, I don't think so."

He nodded and cocked an eyebrow. "But I know you have. I've just come from a meeting with the Executive Board of our group, and they want to send you to Washington to work with Alice Paul."

Sarah's mouth dropped open, and she stared in stunned silence at Roger. Finally she managed to speak. "Me? They want me to go?"

Roger threw back his head and laughed. "They do."

"But, but Roger, why would they want to send the youngest person in the group?"

"Because the face of opposition is changing. We need to get the young women out there, and you are perfect."

"Was there any opposition to my going?"

Roger sighed and nodded. "I'm afraid there was some. A few people were reluctant to send a young girl who is alone in the world into the political arena of Washington, but that's all taken care of now."

"How do you mean?"

"I assured them Aunt Edna and I wouldn't dream of letting you go alone. So we'll accompany you to Washington."

Sarah shook her head. "No, you've both done too much for me already. I can't let you put the responsibilities of your job and this school aside for me."

Roger stepped over to her and took her hand in his. "It's not just for you, Sarah. Now is the time for us to push our cause in Congress, and I want to be a part of it, too. I have influence on Capitol Hill, and I will do everything in my power to help by using it. Aunt Edna has been very generous with her money, and she will continue to be. The three of us will be welcomed by the suffrage leaders in Washington."

Tears pooled in Sarah's eyes, and she looked from Roger to his aunt. "I don't know how to thank you for all you've done to help me. You took me in and gave me a job and a home, and you've helped me work for a cause I'm very passionate about. And now you tell me I may get to go to Washington. It's more than I can imagine."

Roger smiled. "Well, imagine it, my dear. We'll start making our plans now to leave when the second semester ends in May."

Sarah bit down on her lip. "That reminds me of something I've been meaning to tell you. The first semester will be over in a few weeks, and the students and other teachers will be gone. I'm planning to go to Richland Creek to visit my aunt and uncle for Christmas."

Roger's hands curled into fists, and his body went rigid. "You're not going to be here for Christmas?"

"No, my uncle and aunt were very good to my mother and me while we were there, and I would like to see them again."

He took a step toward her. "Are you sure it's them you want to see and not someone else?"

Sarah's eyes grew wide. "What are you talking about Roger?"

Anger flashed in his eyes. "Are you sure you're not planning to meet some man there?"

Baffled by Roger's reaction, she frowned and shook her head. "Don't be ridiculous."

He took a step closer to her, and his eyes narrowed. "Since you're not denying it, there has to be a man. Is it that fellow you told me about? Alex Taylor who works for James Buckley?"

Sarah stared in disbelief at him. What gave him the right to level such an accusation at her? She took a deep breath and raised her chin. "Let me remind you, Roger," she said through gritted teeth, "you are not my father. I don't have to tell you anything."

He reeled as if she'd slapped him. "Your father? Is that how you think of me?"

She was immediately sorry she'd said those words. The hurt look in his eyes made her heart lurch. She closed her eyes for a moment and swallowed. "I'm sorry, Roger. I didn't mean to hurt you. But I really want to see my aunt and uncle. I have no idea if Alex is going to be home for Christmas or not. He's been in Memphis the whole time I've been here, and we haven't spoken. So I don't see any reason we should in Richland Creek."

Mrs. Simpson jumped to her feet and took his hand in hers. "Roger, we can't control Sarah's personal life. We just have to show her how much we care for her." She squeezed his hand. "Do you understand?"

After a moment he glanced down at the floor and nodded. "Yes, Aunt Edna."

"Good. Then I'll leave you two to straighten out this misunderstanding." She kissed him on the cheek. "Good night, Roger."

"Good night," he mumbled.

She turned to Sarah. "Good night. I'll see you at breakfast."

Sarah nodded and waited until Mrs. Simpson had left the room before she turned back to Roger. "Is everything all right now?"

He swallowed and stepped closer to her. "Sarah, I'm so sorry for the way I acted. You're right. It's none of my business. You've been a part of our lives ever since you came to this school when you were six years old. I suppose I thought that gave me the right to question you. Please forgive me."

"Of course I'll forgive you. We've known each other too long to let anything come between us. I'm sorry I spoke so sharply to you. Now I think it would be good if we dropped this subject. I'm going up to bed, and I'll see you at dinner tomorrow night."

His gaze drifted over her, and he sighed. "Good night, Sarah."

Before she could respond, he turned and walked from the room. Then the front door slammed, and she realized he'd left. She sank down on the sofa and buried her face in her hands. The moment she'd been dreading had arrived, but she thought it had ended well. Maybe by tomorrow he would regret the things he'd said. If not, there would only be one solution to the problem. She'd have to quit her job and move out. But the bad thing was that without Roger and Mrs. Simpson's support she would no longer have her contact with the suffrage group.

She had to find a way to preserve her position in the group so that she could get to Washington. Right now all she wanted was to stand with Alice Paul against those who would deny them their rights.

Alex sat at the kitchen table where he'd eaten most of his meals in his life and stared down at his hands wrapped around the cup in front of him. His head ached from lack of sleep, and his body felt drained of energy. He hadn't thought coming back to Richland Creek for Christmas would be so hard, but after nearly a week here he knew he'd been wrong.

Everywhere he looked, he saw something that reminded him of Sarah. It had started almost as soon as he walked in the door. He'd gone to his old room to hang up his clothes and had spotted his baseball shirt first thing. It had only gotten worse since then.

His horse reminded him of the ride through the rain to try and persuade her to change her mind. The buggy even made him think of how embarrassed she'd been to be caught barefooted when he'd driven Ellen to her house. Even Ellen's cooking brought to mind the picnic and the time he'd share with her.

All he'd wanted was to get away from his increasing work load at the firm and Larraine's constant attention and come home to the peace that Ellen always provided. That had turned out to be a joke, too. He'd hardly seen Ellen since he'd been home. She spent most of her time with Edmund, and Ellen acted differently when he was around.

Another surprise had awaited Alex at the farm. Augie, the boy he'd depended on to take care of Ellen while he was in Memphis, had recently celebrated his eighteenth birthday and could hardly wait to go out into the world. Joining the army was all he talked about. Aside from the fact that he needed Augie on the farm, Alex feared America might soon join the conflict in Europe. He couldn't stand to think of Augie in danger.

Alex set the cup down and rubbed the back of his neck to relieve the ache that spread across his shoulders. Maybe it would have been better if he had stayed in Memphis for Christmas. Larraine had certainly begged him to, but he wanted to be with Ellen as he had every Christmas of his life.

A sound at the back door caught his attention, and he glanced up as Ellen, carrying a basket of eggs, walked into the kitchen. She set the basket on the table and hung her bonnet on the wall hook. "I thought I was gonna have to drag you out of bed this morning. What's the matter? Rough night?"

Alex concentrated on the hot coffee in his cup before answering. "I didn't sleep well. I guess I needed a few extra hours this morning to get me started."

Ellen shook her head and moved to the stove. "Do you want me to fix you somethin' to eat?"

"No, the coffee will be enough."

Ellen came back and sat facing him. "Alex, what's wrong? You ain't seemed happy since you got home. It's Christmas, and I don't see none of that spirit in you like you usually have."

He shrugged. "I guess it's because I've been working so hard."

She propped her hands on her hips and directed a stern glare at him. "Are you sure it ain't Sarah you're thinkin' about? Maybe coming back here has reminded you of what happened last summer." Ellen dropped down in a chair beside him. "Alex, you gotta get over her. She's been gone four months now. She's got a new life, and it don't include nobody from Richland Creek."

"I know. But I can't let go. Everywhere I look I see something that reminds me of her."

Ellen reached over and took his hand. "Darling, she made her decision. There's nothing more to do but pray for her."

He shook his head. "I don't think that's going to help."

Ellen cast a surprised expression in his direction. "I never heard you say anything like that before." She paused a moment before she spoke again. "She's home for Christmas."

"Who is?"

"Sarah. She's at Charlie and Clara's."

He sat up straighter, his eyes wide. "How do you know?"

"I saw her yesterday when I was at the store."

Sarah was here? In Richland Creek and no one had told him? "Why didn't you tell me?"

Ellen shrugged. "I didn't really think you wanted to see her. You been talking a lot about that Larraine Buckley, and I figured you were interested in her."

Alex didn't respond for a moment. "I like Larraine." He raked his hand through his hair. "And I don't need to see Sarah. It'll just cause more problems for me."

"Suit yourself." She stood, walked to the cabinet, and took out her mixing bowl. Alex watched her assemble ingredients next to it for several minutes before he spoke.

"What are you doing?"

"I'm gonna make a cake for Christmas dinner tomorrow. Charlie got in some fresh coconuts down at the store, and I want Edmund to taste my coconut cake."

Resentment flashed through Alex. "He's going to spend Christmas with us? Doesn't that man have anywhere else to go?"

Ellen turned around slowly and faced Alex. "I thought you liked Edmund."

Alex raked his hand through his hair. "I do like him, but he's been here every night since I got home. I think he needs to spend time with other families in the community."

Ellen's eyes registered hurt as she stared at her brother. "Alex, are you jealous of the attention I give Edmund?"

He huffed out an angry breath. "Of course not. Why would I be jealous? He's just a friend, isn't he?"

Ellen picked up her apron, tied it around her waist, and wiped her hands down the front. "No, Alex. He's more than a friend. He's come to mean a lot to me, and he tells me he feels the same about me."

Alex's resentment turned to shock as he leaned back in his chair. "Well, I'm glad you finally decided to tell me about it. I suppose I'm the last to know. Are you planning to marry him?"

"He's asked me, but I ain't told him I would yet. I'm planning to tell him yes tomorrow on Christmas Day."

Alex pushed his chair back and stood up. His body trembled, and his hands clenched at his side. "I would have expected better of Edmund. He knows I'm the head of this family. He should have talked to me before he ever said anything to you. I guess my opinion doesn't count for anything."

A tear trickled down Ellen's cheek. "Please don't be this way, Alex. I love Edmund, and I want this chance. Don't ruin my happiness because you're sick over Sarah."

Alex kicked the chair into place at the table and stormed toward the back door. "Sarah has nothing to do with this. It looks like between the two of you I'm doomed. She doesn't love me enough to give up her ridiculous cause, and my own sister plans a wedding without even asking my permission. All I've got to say is congratulations to you both!"

Alex stomped across the back porch but stopped as he opened the screen door. He rested his hand on the doorjamb and bowed his head. A feeling of remorse consumed him. Ellen had told him to pray about Sarah, but he couldn't tell her the truth. He didn't pray as much as he used to. What had happened to him?

He used to turn everything over to God, but somewhere along the way he'd begun to think he could take care of himself. Right now he didn't feel like he was doing a very good job of it. He bowed his head, but no words came to mind.

He opened his eyes and looked over his shoulder into the kitchen. Ellen stood with her apron covering her eyes, her body shaking with sobs. He wanted to go to her and wrap her in his arms, but he opened the door and walked away from the house.

Chapter 14

Sarah straightened from putting a dress in her valise and glanced around the tiny bedroom she'd slept in while visiting Uncle Charlie and Aunt Clara. Satisfied she hadn't forgotten anything, she closed the bag just as Aunt Clara walked through the open door.

"Are you sure you have to go back to Memphis on Christmas Day? School won't be in session until after New Year's. Surely you could stay for a few more days."

Sarah shook her head. "I wish I could, but I have some important meetings this week in Memphis."

Aunt Clara's mouth pursed. "With that suffrage group your mama got you so involved in?"

Sarah sighed in resignation. "We've been through this several times since I've been here. Mama and Poppa both supported suffrage. It was an important cause for them. Now it is for me. I'm sorry you don't approve."

Aunt Clara's eyes widened, and she glanced over her shoulder before she leaned closer. "I may not have said much when Charlie was giving you what-for about your thinking, but I have my own opinions on the subject." She smiled and squeezed Sarah's arm. "I'm real proud of you, darlin'. I don't agree with women being denied the rights our men have."

Sarah's eyes grew wide. "Why, Aunt Clara, you've never said anything before."

She gave a snort of disgust. "I reckon I can't speak too freely around here without somebody getting upset. Charlie doesn't want to lose anybody's business in the store, but I don't care. After all, I put in as many hours working in that store as he does. When it's election time, the men all congregate around that big old wood burning stove in the back of the store, and they talk about who's the best candidate for the job. But I've got no say in that conversation. No more than their wives do. It's right hard to take, Sarah."

"I know, Aunt Clara. That's what keeps me working. It's time women were given the rights they've been denied."

She stepped closer to Sarah. "Think about me, Sarah, when you're talking to folks about suffrage. And you keep working for all us women who have to remain silent or suffer the consequences from our husbands."

Sarah grasped her aunt's hand. "Uncle Charlie would never hurt you."

"Not physically. But he could sure make life hard for me." Tears glistened in her eyes. "And I don't have anywhere else to go, Sarah. I don't have choices like you do. So don't forget all of us who pray for your success."

Sarah stood stunned for a moment as she stared at her aunt. She would never have expected to hear the words she'd spoken today. She swallowed before she grabbed her aunt in a fierce hug. "I'll never give up, Aunt Clara. I'll keep you in my heart while I continue my fight."

They hugged for a moment, then Aunt Clara stepped back, wiped at her eyes, and stared at Sarah's valise. "Are you through packing?"

Sarah sniffed and nodded. "I am. What time does Uncle Charlie want to leave for Mt. Pleasant?"

"He's gone to the barn to hitch the horse to the buggy. It shouldn't be long."

Suddenly she didn't want to leave. She'd enjoyed the quiet time she'd spent with her only family. Although Mrs. Simpson and Roger had been kind to her and included her in everything they did, it still didn't take the place of people who shared your roots. She reached out once more and clasped her aunt's hands in hers. "Thank you so much for having me for Christmas. I know Mama would be happy I spent it with family this year."

Tears filled Aunt Clara's eyes, and her chin trembled. "It's been our pleasure. We miss you and your mama so much. Anytime you want to visit, let us know. Now that we have a telephone in the store you can call. Of course you can call if you just want to talk. We don't want to lose contact with you."

Sarah shook her head. "I don't want that either." She took a deep breath. "Christmas dinner was delicious. I don't know when I've eaten so much." She reached up and touched the cameo pin she'd attached to her dress. "And thank you for the beautiful pin. I'll always treasure it."

"It was our pleasure. I hope you enjoy. . ." She stopped at the sound of a knock on the door and sighed. "That's somebody at the outside stairway entrance. I hope it's not somebody wanting something from the store on Christmas Day."

She turned and hurried out of the room. Sarah glanced around once more before she picked up her valise and followed to the parlor. She'd just set her bag down beside the fireplace when her aunt opened the door and uttered a soft gasp of surprise.

Sarah could tell it was a man's voice that answered her aunt, but she couldn't tell what he was saying. She turned to face the door and felt the breath leave her body when Alex stepped into the room. Her aunt glanced from one to the other as if she didn't know what to say. The veins in her neck stood out, and Sarah realized Aunt Clara was having trouble speaking.

Alex moved closer, and Sarah reached up and grabbed the edge of the mantel to steady her shaking legs. His eyes burned into her. It was all she could do not to run to him. She tightened her hold on the mantel.

"Hello, Sarah." Her name rolled off his tongue like a sweet caress, and she shivered with pleasure.

She swallowed hard. "Alex, what are you doing here?"

"Ellen told me yesterday you came home for Christmas. I tried to stay away, but I couldn't."

Sarah glanced at Aunt Clara with pleading eyes. Help me, she begged silently. With a shake of her head Aunt Clara reached for a shawl hanging on a hook near the door and wrapped it around her shoulders. "I'll go see what's keeping Charlie. It's nice to see you, Alex."

He nodded without turning to face her. "It's good to see you, too, Clara."

She opened the door and stepped outside. When the door had closed behind her, Sarah let go of the mantel and clasped her hands in front of her. "Why did you come, Alex?"

"I wanted to see you." His gaze drifted over her face. "You look wonderful. Teaching must agree with you."

"It does. I've had a good first semester. And how about you? Is the law firm everything you thought it would be?"

"It's all right. I'm working hard." He hesitated a moment. "I saw your picture in the paper, and I've read several articles about you. It seems you're busy in the Memphis suffrage group."

"I am. In fact I may be going to Washington soon to help with the cause there."

Surprise flashed across his face. "Washington? Are you going alone?"

"No. Mrs. Simpson and Roger are going with me."

"Roger?" He spit the word out like it was distasteful. "I might have known he'd be involved."

Her hands balled into fists. "He's been very good to me."

"I'm sure he has. And what does he want in return for it?"

"Maybe the same thing Larraine Buckley wants from you."

His mouth dropped open, and he stared at her in shock. "H-how did you know about Larraine?"

She tried to smile, but she couldn't. "You're not the only one who reads the newspaper. I've seen your picture in the society news several times."

"She's just a friend, Sarah. My boss's daughter."

"And Roger is my friend, as well as one of my bosses."

Alex groaned and raked his hand through his hair. "I didn't come here to talk about anybody else but us. I wanted to see you and make sure you're all right." He wrapped his fingers around her arms above her elbows and stared into her eyes. "And I wanted to tell you I still love you."

She knew she should pull away, tell him she didn't love him, shout at him to leave, but she couldn't. Instead she gazed up at him. "And I still love you."

"Then why can't we fix this problem between us. I thought all women wanted the man she loves to be successful in his profession. Why can't you do that for me?"

"Oh, but I do. I just don't want your success to cost you so much of who you are."

He frowned. "What does that mean?"

"You have a law degree. You can work in any law firm in Tennessee. Why does it have to be in James Buckley's firm? When I met you, I knew you could be a lawyer who sees the needs people have and help them with their problems no matter who they were. A person has to have a lot of money to hire one of the lawyers at Mr. Buckley's firm. You've let your obsession with making money get in the way of how you could help people less fortunate."

"And you're not thinking of yourself?" he scoffed. "You want to be able to walk into a voting booth and cast your ballot. I think you're willing to put that first no matter what it costs you and everybody else who loves you."

She struggled to blink back tears. How she wanted to make him understand what she'd wanted ever since she was old enough to understand about the injustices women suffered in this country. "Alex, I'm not in the suffrage movement for myself alone. I'm representing hundreds of thousands of women all across this country. They need to be recognized as citizens and given the rights that men have. If I gave up their fight, I'd be disloyal to them. There are very few of us who are willing to stand up and be heard. I have to be one of their voices."

A smirk pulled at his mouth, and he shook his head. "So nothing has changed. You're not going to give up this silly fight."

Her tears disappeared, and her skin grew warm at the snide remark. "Why would you call it silly?"

"Since time began, the woman's place has been in the home. It's the husband's place to take care of the family in every way. Men haven't been doing a bad job electing our leaders in the past, and I don't think they will in the future." He took a step closer. "And they will keep doing it because nothing's going to change. You're not going to win this fight, Sarah."

She almost doubled over in pain from what felt like a kick in the stomach. Instead she straightened her shoulders and glared at him. "Well, it's certainly good that I've finally seen your true colors, Mr. Taylor. I thought you were supposed to be a Christian man who cared about other people. I now see your pompous prayers really hid what was in your heart. I lost my faith in God long ago, and now it seems yours wasn't real after all."

Pain flickered in his eyes, and he flinched from her steady gaze. "Sarah, please don't say that. I don't want you to think about me that way."

She brushed at the tears running down her face. "I'm afraid I already do."

He backed away from her. "Then there's nothing left to say."

She shook her head. "No, nothing else."

He turned toward the door, and the slump of his shoulders made her want to run to him and throw her arms around him. She willed herself to stand still. When he reached the door, he put his hand on the knob and stood there with his head bent. Then he turned and faced her.

"Sarah, I meant it when I said I love you, but I'm through trying to put our relationship back together. I want to be happy, so I won't bother you again. I'm going to get on with my life."

She clasped her hands in front of her and nodded. "And I'll do the same."

His gaze drifted over her face once more. "I may be walking out of your life, but I will stand by my promise. If you ever need me, let me know. No matter where you are, I will come for you."

She clamped her trembling lips together and nodded. She didn't move until he had stepped outside and closed the door behind him. Then she fell on the sofa and released the tears she'd held in while he was here. She'd told herself she was slowly getting over Alex, but today that had been proven wrong. It didn't matter where she went or what she did, she knew she would never quit loving the man she'd first met at the pump behind the store.

The only problem was the man she'd met that day didn't exist anymore, and she didn't know how to live without him.

Alex tied his horse to the hitching post beside the church and stared at the building where he'd attended services all his life. To someone just passing by the white clapboard building might appear to be only another small church on a dirt road in a rural community, but to him it was something much more.

Inside the walls of this small church he'd given his heart to God when he was a boy, and he'd promised Ellen and everyone in attendance that day he would always serve the Lord with gladness. He'd done that all his life until last summer when his life had changed. What had happened to him?

He hadn't been inside a church in the months he'd been in Memphis. Instead he'd spent Sundays at his office or with Larraine Buckley. Sarah had accused him of pretending to have faith and that he prayed pompous prayers. Was that really the impression he gave other people?

He glanced at the front door and wondered if the church was unlocked today. He felt an urgent need to go inside and find some answers to all the questions pouring through his head. He climbed the steps, opened the door, and stepped inside.

The dark interior of the church calmed him and sent a peaceful feeling rippling through his soul. He eased down the aisle, slid onto the bench where he'd sat all his life for services, and rested his crossed arms on the pew in front of him. He lowered his head until it lay atop his arms. He wanted to pray, but the words eluded him. Even if he could pray, he doubted God would want to hear from somebody like him who hadn't been in touch in four months.

He buried his face deeper in his crossed arms and thought of all the things Sarah had said to him. Then he thought of Ellen and how her face had looked yesterday when he'd ranted at her because she hadn't told him about her feelings for Edmund. He wondered if he would ever recover from the guilt gnawing at his heart for hurting the two women he loved.

The tap of footsteps on the wooden floor alerted him that someone had entered the church and now walked down the aisle toward where he sat. He looked up in surprise at the figure of Edmund Lancaster looming above him. "Hello, Edmund. What are you doing here?"

"Ellen was worried because you've been gone so long. She sent me to look for you. I saw your horse outside and thought I would see why you're here."

Alex scooted over and motioned Edmund to sit beside him. "I took a ride on my horse for a while. I rode and did a lot of thinking. Then I went to see Sarah. Ellen had told me she was home for Christmas."

Edmund's eyebrows arched. "And how did that go?"

"Not too well, I'm afraid. We both said some things that hurt. After I left Charlie's, I felt the need to come here and pray. For some reason, I can't find the words I want to say."

They sat in silence for several minutes before Edmund spoke. "Alex, Ellen's worried about you. You've taken this break up with Sarah a lot harder than she thought you would. She's afraid your health is going to be affected if you don't get your emotions under control."

Alex rubbed his hand across his tired eyes. "It's not just Sarah and her silly cause. It's the pressures of my new job and all the hours I'm putting in trying to become a valuable member of the firm. Then I come home and find out the boy I intended to run the farm for me wants to enlist in the army. And then I get the biggest shock of all when Ellen tells me she wants to marry you. It's too much at one time."

"I know what it's like when you're first starting out in a new job. I remember when I got out of medical school and joined a practice in Memphis I worked long hours just like you've done to prove myself. I found out I was neglecting important things in my life, things I could never get back."

Alex swiveled in his seat and stared at Edmund. "Like what?"

"Oh, like spending time with my family. Enjoying the blessings of each day. I even got to the point I didn't read my Bible and pray like I should. I strayed from my faith for a while, I'm afraid."

Alex nodded. "Yeah, I know what you mean. Sarah accused me of pretending to be a Christian and said the prayers she'd heard me pray were pompous. But I believe in God, and I love Him with all my heart. Over the past few months, though, I've felt like He's deserted me. He's left me to deal with my problems all alone. "

Edmund looked at the cross on the communion table at the front of the church and back at Alex. "No matter how committed we are to God, we can let circumstances in our lives lead us away from Him if we're not careful. It happened to me, and I had to realize it wasn't God that had deserted me. I had deserted Him."

"How did you get back to the place where you'd been in your relationship with God before?"

Edmund took a deep breath. "I had to take each of my problems and lay them at His feet. I had to come to the point that I realized I couldn't control what was happening to me, and I had to place it all in His hands. When I did that, my whole life changed. You've suffered a lot of changes in your life in the last year, and you're not coping very well. Why don't you turn it all over to God?"

Alex bent over and leaned on the pew in front of him. "I want to do that, but right now I don't even know where to start."

Edmund sat silent for a minute. "Well, why don't we deal with one thing at a time? Let's talk about Augie first. Ellen told me you found him alone in a sharecropper's house after his father had deserted him. His mother was dead, and he had no relatives so you brought him home. You and Ellen gave him a place to live, fed him, and accepted him as one of the family. Did you remind him every day of what you'd done for him and want him to sign a lifetime commitment to you for your kindness?"

Alex sat up, his back straight. "Of course not. I wanted to help him."

"And you have, Alex. You've helped him develop into a fine young man—one who wants to test his wings and fly out into the world. You don't want him to live his life just to help you."

"But what will I do about the farm if he leaves? I need someone to run it for me, and I was depending on him to do that."

Edmund turned his body in the pew to face Alex. "God has given you a brilliant mind, Alex. You have a job in a prestigious law firm, and I know you're going to do well. If God has gone to all the trouble to provide you with these things, don't you believe He's a big enough God to provide a plan for your farm?"

Alex hung his head. "I know that in my heart. But I worry about the tenant farmers and who will oversee them." He stared up at Edmund. "And I feel guilty for leaving Ellen alone with it while I was away in school. Now I'm in Memphis, and I worry about crops that need to be planted and harvested. And the more I worry, the more alone I feel. What's happened to me?"

Edmund reached out and touched Alex's shoulder. "You're human, Alex. When we take our eyes off the example Jesus gave, we all tend to feel alone and desperate."

He knew Edmund was right, but at the moment he felt as if the man he'd once been had disappeared, and he didn't know how to get him back. "Sometimes I question why God doesn't change things the way I want, and I begin to lose my faith."

Edmund arched an eyebrow and directed a somber stare at him. "What do you want God to change?"

Alex pondered his response before he spoke. "One thing I'd have Him change is Sarah's determination about this suffrage thing, and I'd take care of her and Ellen. I wanted to do well and make money so I could give Ellen the things I've always wanted her to have—a big house, clothes, a chance to travel." He frowned at Edmund. "But she doesn't want anything from me anymore. She wants to marry you."

"Ellen's faith brought the two of you through a lot of hard years. She gave up a lot for you, Alex, but she never meant for you to repay her with money and possessions. All she wants is some happiness of her own. You hurt her with your attitude about our wedding."

Anger flared in Alex. "That's your fault, Edmund. I'm the head of our family, and you should have spoken to me before you said anything to Ellen."

Edmund's face showed no emotion. "Maybe the reason you're angry with Sarah and Ellen is because you've never really come to terms with your feelings about women."

Alex's face grew warm, and his pulse pounded. "What do you mean by that remark? Sarah's off working for some hair brained idea that doesn't amount to a hill of beans when she could've been my wife. I would've made her happy. Ellen forgot her place by not asking my permission to marry."

Edmund waited for Alex to finish his tirade before he continued. "Forgot her place? Sarah working for a hair brained idea? Alex, the world is changing. The promise of individual rights built this nation. Right now only men have the privilege to vote, yet women must adhere to the same laws as they do."

"Yeah, I've certainly heard that from Sarah." There was no disguising the disgust in his voice.

Edmund's quiet voice continued. "Ellen raised you to study the Bible and believe the word of God. Think back, Alex, to how it was before Jesus came. Women were nothing more than chattel. They held no rights. They couldn't testify in court because of their lowly estate. Jesus changed all that."

"What are you getting at, Edmund?"

Edmund looked toward the cross on the communion table, and his eyes glistened. "On the morning of the resurrection Jesus revealed himself to two women and charged them with the duty of telling everyone He had risen. Think about it. He entrusted His glorious message to mankind to those the government prohibited from even speaking in a court of law."

Alex pondered Edmund's words. "I never thought of it like that."

"If Jesus loved women that much and raised them to such a place of honor, how can we do any differently? I don't know what will happen with Sarah and her fight. But she believes it's important, and for that reason we should support her."

Edmund placed his hand on Alex's shoulder. "As for Ellen, your sister has devoted her life to you, but you don't own her. She can make her own decisions without your approval. We hope you'll be happy for us. If you choose otherwise, it will make no difference in our commitment to each other. We plan to be married next month and hope you'll attend the ceremony. Let us know."

With that Edmund stood up and walked out of the church. Alex sat in the pew thinking of all Edmund said. A feeling of guilt and shame surged through him.

He moved to the front of the church and fell to the floor in front of the altar. Edmund's words drifted through his mind, and he groaned as his heart and mind wrestled with what he'd said. Was Edmund right?

Sarah had been honest with him since the day of the picnic about her commitment to suffrage, but he had never tried to understand the depth of her allegiance. Instead he had judged her feelings in light of his own desires, the same as he did with Ellen. He had never given a thought to understanding why Sarah felt driven to work for suffrage. His unhappiness over his failure to keep Sarah with him had driven him to lash out at Ellen in his fear of being left alone.

Minutes ticked by, and a battle waged inside him. Finally spent from his ordeal he cried out in prayer. "Father, forgive my selfishness. Show me what to do."

A peace flowed into his heart at the memory of a night he had told Ellen he wanted to become a lawyer. They had talked about John Adams, and Ellen had challenged him to be gallant in his actions with people who had opinions that differed from his.

Instead of trying to understand Sarah and what drove her to follow the cause she believed in, he had willingly accepted the beliefs of his employer. Now he saw that he had done it for selfish reasons—money and prestige. His own desires had taken him down a path that had broken his sister's heart and cost him the woman he loved.

The question he had to answer now was how he could repair the damage he'd caused. He thought again of John Adams and his defense of scared soldiers who were far from home and confronted with a mob. He'd memorized what John Adams had said about the incident and had repeated it to himself all the time he was in law school. Now it returned to send guilt flooding through him. Adams had called it *one of the most gallant, generous, manly, and disinterested actions of my whole life, and one of the best pieces of service I ever rendered my country.*

He'd told Ellen that's what God wanted him to do—stand up and defend those who had no one else to help them. He would never forget how she smiled as she opened her Bible and read words from Isaiah. "Thou art my servant: I have chosen thee, and not cast thee away. Fear thou not: for I am with thee: be not dismayed: for I am thy God: I will strengthen thee: yea, I will help thee: yea, I will uphold thee with the right hand of my righteousness."

She told him there would be many times when he would feel alone and defeated. He would suffer hostility because of those he chose to defend just as Adams had, but he should never waver from the path God had set him on. He had promised her he would let God lead him, but he hadn't. As a result he had not been gallant or manly in his actions, but he had the choice to do something about it.

He raised his head and looked toward the cross at the front of the church. He had no answers how the problems in his life would be solved, but he knew God had promised to be with him. He lifted his eyes toward heaven. "Thank you, Lord, for reminding me of how far I've strayed from the path You set me on. Guide me to where You want me to be."

After a few minutes, he rose and walked up the aisle. He had much to atone for, and perhaps some things would never be changed. Right now his first action required asking Ellen's forgiveness.

Chapter 15

Alex raised his head after the benediction and glanced around the church he'd attended since he'd returned to Memphis after the holidays. He had to admit he liked his choice. After two months of attending services he'd gotten to know quite a few of the members, and he already felt at home.

As he walked up the aisle toward the vestibule, he stopped at the sound of his name being called. He turned and smiled at the sight of Will Page, a friend from law school, waving to him from the front of the church. He stepped into an empty pew and waited for Will to make his way up the aisle to him.

With a big grin on his face, Will pushed into the pew and grabbed Alex's hand. "Alex Taylor, imagine seeing you here."

Alex shook his hand and laughed. "I've been attending here for about two months now."

"I've been out of town since the first of February. I just got back yesterday. It's great to see you."

They dropped down on the bench and turned to face each other. Alex smiled at the man who along with Ben Cooper had been his study partner through law school. "I haven't seen you since graduation. Have you heard from Ben?"

Will laughed and turned to rest his arm on the back of the pew. "Ben headed to Washington after we graduated, you know. He landed a job with Dudley Malone and Matthew

O'Brien, those lawyers in Washington who have been so vocal in supporting suffrage."

Alex gaped at Will and frowned. "Ben's working in the suffrage movement?"

"Yeah, you know he always supported gender equality. I guess he's found some lawyers who think like he does. From all accounts he's happy as can be."

Alex thought of his friend from law school and remembered how passionate he had been when he talked about the injustices women had endured. His stomach roiled, and Alex knew it was from his guilt over dismissing Ben's opinions. If he had listened then, things might have turned out so differently for Sarah and him. Alex sat up straighter and turned his attention back to Will. "But what are you doing in Memphis? I thought you were going to stay in Nashville and practice."

Will laughed. "You know me, always looking for something better. I got an offer from a firm here and decided to take it instead. I meant to look you up, but I've been busy."

"You don't sound too busy, not if your boss let you off for two months. Maybe I need to check him out."

The tips of Will's big ears turned red. Alex had seen that reaction many times in class when he had been embarrassed by one of their professors. "No need to do that. You wouldn't like it there. That firm doesn't practice our kind of law."

"And what kind is that?"

Will frowned. "You know what I mean. Do you remember all those conversations you and Ben and I had about serving the people and helping those who had no one else to stand up for them?"

Alex nodded. "Yes, I remember. We talked about being gallant and our belief that everyone is entitled to a defense." The words reminded Alex of how far he'd strayed from that ideal.

"I found out that the firm I'd joined didn't care about what I believed. I was told who I could represent and who I couldn't. I finally got tired of it, and I quit right before Christmas."

Alex stared at Will in surprise. "You quit? What are you going to do now?"

A big smile creased Will's face. "I'm starting a new job next week. The city of Memphis has decided to fund a new office called the Public Defender's Office. This is the first such office in the state. It will be staffed with lawyers who offer legal services to those who can't afford to hire a lawyer, and I'm going to be one of them. Just think, Alex, I'll be one of the first lawyers in the state to provide legal help to those in need. It's just what we always talked about."

Talking about being noble and providing help for people unable to defend themselves might have sounded good in a college dorm room, but in the real world it took money to survive. "But what about the salary? Surely it doesn't compare with what you were making."

Will chuckled. "The salary's not that great, but it's enough to live on. I found out in a hurry that money can't make up for what you sacrifice in selling out your beliefs. I feel like this is what God is telling me to do, Alex. For the first time since leaving law school I'm happy."

Alex stared at him for a moment before he nodded. "I'm happy for you, Will. It sounds just like what we always talked about."

Excitement lit Will's eyes. "They've still got some openings. Want to come join us?"

Alex shook his head. He'd worked too hard at Mr. Buckley's firm to give up that opportunity. "I'm making it all right at the moment, happy where I am. But since we're now attending the same church, I expect I'll be hearing all about this new job."

A wistful expression covered Will's face. "Just think, Alex, after all those midnight talks about the future, I'm going to get the chance to make a difference." Will pushed to his feet. "It's been great seeing you today. I hate to run off, but I'm expected at my future in-laws' house for Sunday dinner."

Alex rose. "So you're getting married? Do I know her?"

"No, I met her when I started attending church here. How about you? Any woman in your life?"

Alex shook his head. "I'm afraid not, but I'm happy for you."

Will stepped into the aisle. "I'll see you later."

Alex nodded and watched his friend rush up the aisle and out of the church before he sank back down in the pew. He'd tried to get up his nerve ever since returning to Memphis to go see Sarah, but he hadn't been able to yet. There were things he needed to say to her, to apologize for, but he still hadn't come to grips with her need to pursue her cause. Maybe in time he would.

He bowed his head and prayed for God to give him guidance in how to approach Sarah.

★ ★ ★ ★ ★

Sarah knew she would always remember this moment—7:00PM on the first day of spring in 1917. She wanted to stand up and shout, but she doubted if her legs would support her. Her hands clenched the edge of the sofa cushion, and she stared up at Mrs. Simpson and Roger who faced her with their backs to the fireplace.

A smile pulled at Roger's lips. "You look stunned, my dear."

"Are you serious?"

Roger laughed out loud, and Mrs. Simpson dropped down on the sofa next to her. "We are."

Sarah slowly looked from one to the other. "We're going to Washington next week?"

Roger nodded. "If that's okay with you."

"B-but how. . .I mean, school won't be out for two more months. How can we just leave?"

Roger sat down on the other side of Sarah and turned to face her. "I know this is sooner than we'd planned, but there's a reason. As you know, Alice Paul and some of her workers have been meeting with President Wilson every week to press our case for enfranchisement. Those talks came to an end in January, and Miss Paul is now planning her next course of action. The executive board of our group met this afternoon, and we decided we couldn't wait any longer to send her aid. Everybody on the committee had other commitments until the summer, so I told them we would work out something so we could go."

Sarah thought of the girls in her class. Just now they were beginning to accomplish some of the goals she had set for the school year. How could she walk away and leave them? "But you haven't said what we'll do about school. What about my classes?"

Mrs. Simpson reached over and clasped Sarah's hand. "You know how much this school means to me. I've worked hard to build it into one of the best schools in the city. But I look at the young girls here, and I have another obligation to them. I don't want them to leave here with a good education and still be second class citizens because they can't vote. I can get a teacher to cover your classes for the rest of the year. I don't think I can find anyone else better than you to work for their right to enter the voting booth."

Mrs. Simpson's words humbled Sarah, and she reached over and hugged the woman who had played such an important role in her life. "Thank you, Mrs. Simpson. My parents wanted me to attend school here because they knew you shared their dream. They would be so happy to know you're giving me this opportunity."

Roger leaned closer and smiled. "But there's more, my dear. As you know, we're having a big rally at the Orpheum Theater on Saturday night. The committee wants you to be one of the speakers."

"Me?" Sarah's voice rose to a high pitch. "Why?"

"They want to introduce the young girl who is taking our fight to Washington. You do know you'll probably be one of the youngest women working with Alice Paul, don't you?"

The breath almost left Sarah's body as she thought of Alice Paul, the Hicksite Quaker who had been raised to believe in gender equality. To catch a glimpse of her would have been more than Sarah could have hoped for, but to work alongside her was like a dream come true. "I'll do whatever I can to support Miss Paul in her quest for recognition of women across this country."

Mrs. Simpson smiled and patted Sarah's arm. "We know you will. Now since your dear mother is no longer with us, I feel it is my duty to go as your chaperone to Washington." She arched an eyebrow in Roger's direction. "And Roger feels that he must go and watch over the two women in his life. I've already spoken to Miss Abercrombie, the assistant head mistress, about taking over my duties until the end of the year. So we can leave next week."

Sarah turned to Roger. "Can you leave work?"

He laughed. "You forget I own the company. It almost runs without me anyway. Besides I want to spend some time with members of Congress and see if can't influence some of them to our way of thinking."

"Do you know where we'll be staying?"

Roger stood up and walked back to the fireplace. "I called a friend of mine in Washington, and he gave me the number of a realtor. I'll get in touch with him tomorrow. I want you two to have a house, but I'll probably stay at a nearby hotel and take my meals with you. I thought we could take Dora to cook and clean for you."

Mrs. Simpson stood up, walked to her nephew, and gave him a kiss on the cheek. "You think of everything, darling."

"I try, Aunt Edna. I only want to make life easier for you and Sarah."

She smiled up at him. "You do every day." She glanced back at Sarah. "Now I think I'll go up to my room. You two can continue to plan our great adventure, but I think I'll get ready for bed."

"Good night, Mrs. Simpson." Sarah stood and watched her leave the room before she turned back to Roger. "I can't thank you enough for this opportunity, Roger. How will I ever repay all your kindness?"

He took a step toward her. "I don't want any repayment, Sarah. Surely you know I'd do anything for you. I love you, and I want to marry you."

She recoiled from the words she'd hoped he would never say to her. She swallowed hard and tried to regain her composure. "Roger, please don't say that. You are my dear friend, and we share a commitment to a common goal. But I don't think of you like a woman should think about the man she'll marry. In fact I doubt if I ever marry."

His eyes darkened, and he doubled his fists at his sides. "Is it that farmer you met last summer? Is he the reason you don't want to marry me?"

She lifted her chin and stared into his eyes. "First of all, Alex is a lawyer, and I don't like the tone of your voice when you speak of farmers. I met some wonderful people last summer who were farmers, and they were very good to my mother and me."

"You haven't answered my question. Why won't you marry me?"

"Marriage should be based on love, and I don't love you."

He studied her for a moment. Then he walked toward her, put his finger under her chin, and tilted her face up to look at him. "I love you enough to make up for how you feel. I know I can change your mind, and I will. I'm used to getting what I want, and you're going to marry me."

"Roger, please. . ."

"Hush." He put his index finger on her lips. "You will change your mind, and you will be my wife."

He leaned over and kissed her on the forehead. Then he turned and walked out the door. Sarah stood frozen in place until the front door closed. She dropped down on the couch and clasped her hands around her waist.

What was she going to do? Roger seemed certain he could persuade her, and she was just as determined he wouldn't. Maybe this trip to Washington was coming at a good time. Her volunteer work at Alice Paul's headquarters would give her the perfect excuse for staying away from him. In time he would come to see there was no hope for changing her mind.

At least that's what she hoped would happen.

From the minute he'd seen the article in the newspaper that Sarah would be addressing Memphis suffrage supporters at the Orpheum Theater on Saturday night Alex had known he would be in attendance. He pulled his watch from his pocket and glanced at it then back to the stage where chairs were arranged for the speakers to sit. He hoped when Sarah took her seat she wouldn't be able to see him huddled on the back row.

He glanced around the theater as the people entered and took a seat. It surprised him to see some of Memphis's leading citizens at the rally. Obviously not everyone held the same views as did Mr. Buckley. So far he hadn't revealed the changes taking place in his life to Mr. Buckley or to Larraine who he now had dinner with two or three nights a week. He wondered what they would think about his presence here tonight. He might not have to wait long to find out if someone attending tonight told his boss about seeing him here.

Alex sighed and rubbed his hand across his eyes. It didn't matter. The truth was going to come out sometime, and he had a feeling it wasn't too far off. The change in him had been happening ever since Christmas when he and Edmund had talked.

Every time he thought of that day, Alex's face burned with shame. He'd had an entirely different picture of himself than what Edmund had painted, and it sickened him now to think how right Edmund had been.

All his life Alex had taken pride in the fact that he would never discriminate against a person because of social standing, race, or culture. He'd brought Augie, the son of the community's drunkard, home and treated him like family. He had taken food to the tenant farmers when they had no money and never made any difference whether they were black or white. Somehow, though, he'd never thought about his indifference to the plight of women. Not until Edmund had pointed out how much Jesus loved women.

Since the day they'd talked, Alex had read his Bible and prayed about the things Edmund had said. He realized how wrong he'd been in his uncaring attitude, and he understood how that must have hurt Sarah. If only he could go back and do it all over again, but he couldn't, and she had moved on.

A flurry of activity on the stage caught his attention, and he sat up straight as the speakers for the evening entered the stage. When Sarah stepped from behind the long curtains pulled back at the stage entrances, he thought his heart would burst. She wore a blue dress the color of the eyes that haunted his dreams and had her hair piled on top of her head. She smiled and took her seat.

Her gaze drifted over the crowd and came to a stop on someone a few rows from the front in the middle section. Alex craned his neck to see who she smiled at, and his heart dropped to his stomach. A man waved at her and then blew her a kiss. Alex had seen his picture in the paper enough to recognize business owner and socialite Roger Thorne. Alex gritted his teeth and directed his attention back to Sarah.

The moderator for the evening, a middle-aged woman with white hair, stepped to the podium. "Good evening, ladies and gentlemen. My name is Mary Windsor, and on behalf of the Memphis Suffrage Association I am pleased to welcome you to this rally."

She began to introduce each of the individuals seated on the stage, but Alex tuned her voice out. He only had eyes for Sarah. The speaker turned to Sarah last. "And speaking for the first time for our organization, Miss Sarah Jordan, a teacher at Mrs. Edna Simpson's School for Girls. As you probably have heard, Miss Jordan will be leaving for Washington next week to work with Alice Paul and other representatives of the National Woman's Party. Before she leaves, we thought you might like to hear her thoughts on the plight of women in America."

Sarah acknowledged the announcement and the audience's applause with a smile and a nod of her head. Then she turned her attention to the first speaker who was taking his place behind the podium. Alex tried to concentrate on the panelists as they came one after another to stand before the group, but all he could do was stare at Sarah.

Then he heard her name called from the podium. She stood, smoothed the satin dress with her hands, and stepped forward. Alex sat up straighter and gripped the chair arms as he studied her every movement. She glided to the lectern, took her place behind it, and let her gaze travel slowly across the people seated in the auditorium.

"Good evening." She paused as if waiting for an answer.

After she'd swept the group with her gaze, she reversed it and backtracked over the assembly. No one in the audience moved. As if she realized the hypnotic effect she'd had on the group, she leaned closer to the podium, a somber expression on her face. "I hesitate to add more to my greeting than to say good evening. Proper etiquette decrees that I acknowledge those in attendance and address you as ladies and gentlemen. However, I didn't come here tonight to charm you with empty words. I came in hopes of stirring your souls in protest of the injustice that is taking place in this land. The greeting I long to give you burns within me as I face you."

A hushed silence met her statement. "I prefer to greet you as fellow citizens, but I find that impossible. The voices of early suffrage leaders like Susan B. Anthony, Belva Lockwood, and Elizabeth Cady Stanton ring out to tell women we cannot be called citizens. We are not citizens of this country because our government has never afforded us that distinction."

"Government demands that we, as female members of American society, follow laws made by men and work for wages determined by men. In factories where men and women work side by side, men's wages often triple those of women. Those who seek justification for unequal pay tell us that women provide a supplementary income."

She paused and curled her lip into a sneer. "Tell that to the widow who must feed and provide for her children. Tell that to the young girl taking care of elderly parents, and tell that to women who labor ten to twelve hours a day and care for their families after work."

Applause rang out through the auditorium, and Alex glanced at the people near him. They nodded and clapped as they stared at Sarah. Near the front a few women stood to their feet and held their hands high in the air as they clapped.

Sarah waited until the applause had died before she smiled and swept the auditorium with her gaze again. "Now I'm not naïve enough to think that any of the women here tonight spent ten hours in a factory today. Oh, no. I look around and I see women dressed in the latest fashions, and I know those gathered here represent the privileged of our city. Some of you are blessed to live in comfort while others live in luxury." She paused for a moment as if a sudden thought had popped into her head. "Perhaps some of the ladies here tonight own houses, land, or businesses. You pay taxes according to the law, but you have no voice in making laws that dictate what must be paid."

Alex sensed a rippling of movement in the audience. "Some of you own businesses with male employees. Does justice prevail when your earnings pay wages to men eligible to vote, and the government denies you, the company owner, that same basic freedom?"

"No!" The shouted word seemed to erupt from every corner of the theater.

Sarah leaned forward, her hands gripping either side of the podium, and frowned. "How long must we wait for liberty? How long must we labor for justice? How long will we tolerate a government that delegates women to the lowest level of society? We must unite and press our legislators to raise us to the level of citizenship we deserve. Until they do, we remain as servants to this nation, not citizens."

Sarah raised her fist in defiance. "I say to you, fellow servants, how long must we wait before Washington listens? How long must we wait?"

Sarah stepped back from the podium, and the audience bounded to their feet. Alex rose with them. A woman to the left of the stage cried out, "How long must we wait?"

The hall vibrated with shouts as one after another voices joined the chant. "How long must we wait? How long must we wait?"

Sarah stepped to the side of the podium and bowed. The cries rose to the balcony, and the crowd clapped in rhythm with the words, the cries growing louder.

Alex clapped along with the crowd as Sarah walked back to her seat. She glanced down to where Roger Thorne sat and smiled. The acknowledgement sent a chill down his spine. If he had been hoping he could change the situation between Sarah and him, he now knew the truth.

Sarah had a new love in her life, and it was the cause she served. Whether or not her life included Roger Thorne, he didn't know. But after hearing her speak, Alex realized she was lost to him forever. And he had no one to blame but himself.

He stepped into the aisle and walked from the theater with the applause for Sarah's speech still ringing in his ears. Sarah had moved on. Maybe it was time he did, too.

Chapter 17

On Sunday afternoon Sarah wandered through the house trying to find something to occupy her time. Her notes to the teacher taking her class on Monday were completed, her trunks were packed, and the letter was written telling Uncle Charlie and Aunt Clara where she would be over the next few months. With nothing to do and Mrs. Simpson and Roger away for the afternoon, maybe a Sunday afternoon nap would be in order.

She walked to the staircase, but before she mounted the first step, a knock sounded at the door. Dora came hurrying into the entry, but Sarah held up her hand. "I'll get it, Dora." The maid nodded and retreated.

Sarah smoothed her hair into place and put a smile on her face before she opened the door. The smile slowly dissolved as she stared up at the towering figure of Alex Taylor filling the doorway. His eyes lit up with a smile that reminded her of the day he'd tipped his baseball cap at her.

"Alex." His name tasted sweet on her lips, and a thrill coursed through her veins.

Alex's eyes devoured her. "Hello, Sarah. I'm afraid I've given you quite a start. Maybe I should have called first, but I was afraid you wouldn't want to see me. May I come in?"

She stared back at him and took in every detail of his appearance. His hair, so unruly the day of the ballgame, lay neatly combed, and he held a hat in his hand. His brown suit with vest and matching tie accented his dark eyes, and the smile that curved his lips reminded her of a long ago encounter. The pulse in her neck beat like a drum, and she put a hand to her throat to still the pumping.

"C-come in, Alex."

He took a hesitant step towards her, and she moved aside to let him enter the house. He stopped in the hallway and surveyed the entry and parlor. He glanced up the stairway before he turned back to her. "I've ridden by here so many times in the past six months, and I've often tried to imagine what the inside was like. It really is a beautiful house."

Sarah shook her head to clear her senses. "You've driven by here?"

"Yes. Mr. Buckley's home isn't too far from here. I visit there quite often."

The truth behind his words penetrated her still foggy brain, and she flinched. "Of course. His daughter Larraine. I've seen your picture on the society page with her. She's very beautiful."

"Yes, she is, but you've been in the news quite a bit lately, too." As he said the words, he looked toward the parlor. "I hope I'm not interrupting your afternoon."

"Not at all. I was just wondering how I could entertain myself when you rang the doorbell. Please come into the parlor. Can I get you some tea?"

Alex's eyes twinkled. "I don't know. Can you cook now?"

She laughed as she remembered telling him of her lack of skills in the kitchen. "Well, they do let me boil water. I think I can handle a cup of tea."

He didn't take his eyes off her as he shook his head. "No, I don't want anything. Just to visit with you."

She led him to one of the fireplace chairs and motioned him to sit. When she sat down facing him, he leaned back and crossed his legs.

The old easiness in his presence overtook her, and the suppressed memories flooded back. This was so different than their last two meetings, and Sarah relaxed. She searched her mind for something they could talk about without a repeat of their Christmas encounter. Not suffrage and not the firm he worked for. She settled for a neutral subject. "Tell me all the news from Richland Creek. How is Ellen?"

"I suppose you haven't heard Ellen married last month. She has a husband to take care of now."

Sarah gaped at him. "A husband? Who did she marry?"

"Edmund Lancaster. I wasn't too happy about it at first, but I came to realize I was being selfish. Ellen deserves someone to love her, and I've never seen her happier. Edmund dotes on her, and she on him. I think theirs is a match made in heaven."

Sarah squealed in delight at the news. "I could tell when they came to see my mother that they liked each other. I told Ellen then she had an admirer, but she dismissed me. I couldn't be happier. Do they live at the farm?"

"Yes. Edmund still has his office across from Charlie's store, but he travels to house calls most of the day. Ellen helps him when he needs her."

Sarah blinked back tears of happiness at the thought of Ellen. "I wish I could see Ellen. I don't know what I would have done after my mother's death if it hadn't been for her."

Alex studied her face. "Ellen loves you, Sarah."

The words hung suspended in air between them. She wanted him to say that he did, too, but he just smiled at her and said nothing more. "She'll always be very special to me."

173

Alex uncrossed his legs and leaned forward with his elbows on his thighs. "I came here today because I feel I need to apologize to you."

She blinked. "For what?"

"For the way I acted the last two times we were together. I was hurt and angry, but I should have been more understanding of your feelings. I'm sorry if my words hurt you. I hope you can find it in your heart to forgive me."

"We both said some terrible things, and I need to ask your forgiveness for lashing out at you. At times I've thought you probably hate me for the things I said about your working for Mr. Buckley and your views on suffrage. My father always cautioned me about the way I talked to people. I hope you'll forgive me, too."

"Of course I will. I've done quite a bit of soul searching since I saw you at Christmas. I'm beginning to understand how important your cause is to you. I'm sorry I didn't before, and I apologize for belittling your dreams. I hope you can forgive me for that."

"I do, Alex, but what brought about this change in your attitude?"

He rubbed the back of his neck and shook his head. "Edmund had a talk with me and helped me understand how blind I'd been about the injustice of not allowing women to vote. I've prayed about it a lot, and God led me to a new way of thinking where women are concerned. If I hadn't already been convinced that I needed to rethink my position, you certainly made me with your speech at the Orpheum last night."

She sat up straight and gasped. "You were there?"

He nodded. "I was, and I stood and clapped right along with the rest of the crowd." His eyes softened, and a sad smile pulled at his lips. "You were wonderful, Sarah. I only wish I'd listened to you sooner. Things might have been different between us."

The regret she heard in his voice sliced through her like a knife, and she clasped her shaking hands together. His tone told her all she needed to know. Once he had said he loved her, but he didn't anymore. Now he talked of how things had once been between them. But what could she expect? He had a new life now, and it included a beautiful woman who happened to be very rich. Sarah pressed her lips together and swallowed. "It means more to me than you'll ever know that you came to hear me speak. I'm sorry I didn't see you afterwards."

He shook his head. "I knew you were with your friends, and I suspect you were swamped with well-wishers about your trip to Washington."

"I was. The members of our group have been very supportive. I can't believe I'm really going to volunteer with Alice Paul."

He scooted to the edge of his seat and frowned. "That's one of the reasons I decided to come here today. I want you to be careful in Washington. Up to this point Alice Paul and her followers have been tolerated, but I'm afraid it may change soon."

"How do you mean?"

"America is going to be at war any day now. I don't know why we're not in the fight already. President Wilson has been patient with Miss Paul's demands, but that may change when he has a war to worry about. I don't want to see you get hurt."

"It's kind of you to be concerned about me," she said, "but you don't have anything to worry about. How can I get hurt just working in an office? I'll probably be stuffing envelopes and mailing fliers out to supporters. I don't think I'll come in contact with anyone who might cause me problems."

"You never can tell. Summer is on its way, and Washington will probably be a hot city. If we are in the war as I predict, tempers may also be hot. Stay out of situations that may get you in trouble. Of course knowing how feisty you are, I'm probably not doing a bit of good with my warnings."

Her eyebrows arched, and she couldn't help but smile. "Whatever makes you think I'm feisty?"

He smiled, and again she could see the sadness in his eyes. He tried to mask it, but it probably reflected what was in hers. He reached for her hand and wrapped his fingers around it. "I knew you were a spunky girl the day I saw you with your skirt lifted. Later I came to know how strong-willed you are when you're passionate about a cause. All I'm saying is remember to use common sense, and don't get yourself in a situation you can't control."

Her chin trembled, and she tightened her grip on his fingers. There was so much she wanted to say to him—to remind him of their time together by the pond at her home, to thank him for all he did for her and her mother, and to tell him she would always love him—but she couldn't. He'd begged her to try and find some common ground with him, but she had refused. In so doing, she had ruined any chance they might have had.

Instead of the words she wanted to speak she said what she knew she must. "I'll be careful, Alex. Take care of yourself, and I hope you have a happy life."

The muscle in his jaw twitched, and he squeezed her hand. "Don't forget my promise."

She nodded. "If I ever need you, you'll come no matter where I am."

"Yes. Don't ever forget. . ."

Before he could finish what he was saying, Roger's voice from the doorway interrupted. "Well, well, I didn't know we had company."

Sarah jerked her hand away from Alex and sprang to her feet. Alex stood slowly and turned to face Roger. "I came to tell Sarah goodbye and wish her luck in Washington."

Roger strode forward, his hand outstretched. "I don't think we've met. I'm Roger Thorne, and I suppose you must be Alex Taylor. Sarah has told us so much about you I feel I already know you."

Alex's eyebrows arched, but he reached for Roger's hand and shook it. "I feel I know you, too."

Roger smiled. "I would have spent the afternoon here if I'd known you were coming."

Sarah darted an angry glance toward Roger for his subtle insinuation that Alex had come uninvited to his aunt's home. If Alex noticed the slight, he gave no indication. He picked up his hat from the table at the end of the sofa and smiled. "It was a spur of the moment visit so I could wish Sarah well in Washington. Now I think I'll be going." He turned back to Sarah. "Goodbye, and try to remember what I told you."

She tried to smile, but she wasn't sure how successful she was. Her mouth didn't want to cooperate. "Goodbye, Alex. It was good to see you again and give Ellen my best."

"I will."

Before Sarah could take a step to show Alex out, Roger turned to her. "Sarah, would you mind checking on the kitchen staff? I told them we wanted dinner early tonight. I'd appreciate it if you'd see what time it will be ready."

She glanced at Alex. "But I was going to. . ."

Roger waved his hand in dismissal. "No need for you to show Alex to the door. I'll do that." He gestured toward the door. "After you, Mr. Taylor."

Alex cast one more glance at her before he turned and headed toward the door. Sarah rammed her fist against her lips to keep from crying out as she stared at his retreating figure. When she heard the front door close, she turned and ran for the staircase. If Roger wanted to check on dinner, he could do it himself. All she could think about at the moment was that the man she loved had just walked out of her life. And this time she knew he would never walk back in.

Alex stopped on the front porch at the top of the steps and turned to stare at Roger Thorne who had followed him outside. The friendly attitude he'd displayed inside the house had disappeared, and in its place a sneer covered the man's face. His chest heaved, and he clenched his hands at his side. He stepped closer to Alex.

"Don't ever come into my home again without being invited."

Alex didn't think he'd ever seen such rage in a person's face. Had Sarah ever seen this side of Roger's personality? He hoped not. Without breaking eye contact with the man, Alex reached up, set his hat on his head, and pulled the brim down on his forehead.

"Oh?" he said with an eyebrow arched. "I didn't realize this is your home. I thought it belonged to your aunt and that you live somewhere else."

Roger's face mottled, and a speck of spittle hung in the corner of his mouth. "Don't be funny, Taylor. You know what I mean. You're to stay away from Sarah."

Alex shook his head. "I think that's Sarah's decision, not yours. But it probably won't be too hard for you to keep me away since you're taking her to Washington."

Roger exhaled, and his shoulders relaxed. An arrogant smile pulled at his lips. "She didn't tell you, did she?"

"Tell me what?"

"That she's going to marry me."

Alex almost doubled over in pain. He struggled to breathe, but his chest felt like something was squeezing the life from his body. He gulped a big breath of air and tried to steady his shaking legs.

"Marry you?" He could barely gasp the words.

Roger smiled, but it didn't reach to his cold eyes. "I see she didn't. Well, now you know. We'll be married this summer in Washington. I hope you won't feel left out, but we thought it best not to invite you to the wedding."

Alex searched for some clue that would tell him Roger was lying, but he could see nothing beneath the cool façade of his stony expression. "I-I don't believe you."

"Oh, believe it. That's been my plan for years. I was just waiting until Sarah was old enough. Now she is, and she wants a life of ease. But most of all, she loves me. I suppose she didn't tell you because she didn't want to hurt you." He grinned and took a step closer. "I have to thank you for helping my case, though. If you hadn't been so opposed to suffrage, you might be the one marrying her. Too bad for you."

Alex reeled from Roger's words. How could Sarah marry this contemptible man? His lack of character showed in every action and word. Alex longed to storm the house, throw Sarah over his shoulder, and carry her from this place, but good judgment prevailed.

After a moment he took a deep breath. "Tell Sarah I wish her every happiness."

Before Roger could respond, Alex descended the steps and hurried to his new car he'd parked in front of the house. As he cranked the engine and pulled away from the house, he heaved a sigh of regret. He wished he could have last summer over, maybe he could have made the situation different.

His stubbornness had helped drive Sarah away, and now she was lost to him. But what could she be thinking? Roger Thorne would never make her happy. In fact there was something rather sinister about the man, and he feared for her in a marriage to him.

At the corner he pulled to a stop and pounded the steering wheel. In the past when he and Sarah had argued, he'd been left with some hope that she still loved him. Where there was a tiny shred of love there was a possibility they would eventually work out their differences. Today that hope had ended. They would never be together. She would be married to Roger Thorne.

He thought of Larraine and how they had first met and how different things were between them now. He knew she was in love with him. It showed in her eyes, but she'd never spoken of it. Perhaps because she sensed he'd suffered a great loss in love. But she'd been a friend to him and had never pushed him in their relationship since that first day.

As he'd gotten to know her, he found her not to be the flirtatious girl he at first thought, but an intelligent young woman who wanted the attention of her father. She'd learned early in life she could only get it by outrageous behavior, and she had capitalized on that. Since Alex had known her, she had broken ties with all her old saloon-hopping friends and become more focused on her painting.

A car horn honked, and Alex realized he sat lost in thought at the corner. He pulled across the intersection and headed down the street to the house he'd visited many times in the past seven months. As he drove, he couldn't quit thinking about Roger Thorne's words.

If Sarah was lost to him, maybe it was time he got on with his life. He pulled to a stop in front of the Buckley house and jumped out. He only had to wait a moment before a maid answered the door. She smiled when she saw him.

"Good afternoon, Mr. Taylor. Come in."

"Thank you, Greta." He stepped inside the huge Victorian house and stopped in the entry. "Is Miss Buckley in?"

She nodded. "Yes, sir. If you'll wait in the parlor, I'll get her for you."

Greta disappeared, and minutes later Larraine hurried into the room. He rose from sitting on the sofa when she entered, but she stopped at the door. A look of uncertainty crossed her face, and she didn't come closer.

"Alex, I didn't expect you this afternoon. In fact I haven't heard from you in nearly a week."

He nodded. "I know. I'm sorry about that, Larraine. I've been busy, but I know that's not an excuse. I should have been more thoughtful of you."

She frowned as if she didn't understand what he was talking about and walked closer. When she stood in front of him, she stared up with a questioning look on her face. "There's no need for an apology. I know how busy my father is. He spends more time at the office than he does at home."

Alex swallowed. "I know he does, but I don't want to be like that. I want to have people in my life, and I want to be important in other people's lives."

Her eyes searched his face as if she wanted to understand his words. "What are you saying, Alex?"

He took her hand and wrapped his fingers around hers. "We've known each other for seven months now. We've gone to dinner, to the theater, to parties—all the things young couples do when they're trying to get to know each other, but we haven't tried to know each other better, to discover what makes the other one happy."

Tears glistened in her eyes. "I've tried, Alex, but you always shut down and push me away when I try to get to know you better."

He nodded. "I know. It's my fault, not yours. You're a wonderful woman, Larraine, and I've enjoyed the times we've been together. But I've reached the point I need to know if there can be more between us."

She sucked in her breath, and her lips trembled. "What about the woman you haven't been able to forget?"

His eyebrows arched in surprise. "How did you know there had been someone?"

A sad smile pulled at her lips. "A woman always knows when a man's thinking about someone else. Before we go any further, you need to know one thing. I can't be her."

He nodded. "I know that, and I would never try to make you into her. You have your own special qualities that make you Larraine. I'm sorry it's taken me so long to say this to you."

"What made you come here today and say these things?"

He could tell she still hadn't accepted what he was saying, and he struggled to put it into words so she would know he was sincere. "Today I have put my past behind me. I want to look to the future, and I want to see if that includes a relationship between the two of us. Will you meet me halfway?"

Tears ran from the corners of her eyes, but she smiled. "Yes, I will. I'm already at the halfway mark. I've just been waiting for you to join me."

He reached up and ran his index finger down the side of her face. "You really are a beautiful woman, Larraine, on the inside as well as the outside."

She wrapped her hands around his neck and stared up at him. "That's the best compliment anyone has ever given me."

He pulled her closer. "You deserve more, and I intend to give them to you."

He bent his head, and her lips came up to meet his. He searched for the excitement and pleasure he'd experience when he'd kissed Sarah, but he couldn't find it. Maybe it was too soon to expect the same feeling. He would in time. Don't be in a hurry, his battered heart whispered. You will love again. You will. You will.

Chapter 18

The rustling of her skirt and the staccato of her tapping footsteps vibrated through the small sitting room. Sarah paced back and forth in an effort to calm her excitement but found it impossible. She stopped as Dora entered the room carrying a tray.

Dora clucked her tongue at Sarah and set her load on the table by the window. "Miss Sarah, I know you're right carried away with the idea of gittin' down to that office today, but you gotta eat. You didn't hardly touch nothin' I fixed for you earlier."

Sarah smiled at the young girl who fussed over her. "Dora, I don't know what I'd do without you. I'm so glad Mrs. Simpson decided to bring you with us. You take care of this house so well, and you seem to know everything I need."

"Yes'm, I watch out for you." Her glance swept the small parlor. "This house sure ain't as big as the one in Memphis, and I ain't havin' no trouble keepin' up with the work."

A picture of the big house in Memphis flashed into Sarah's mind, and she compared it to the rented house they occupied in Washington. Sarah picked up the cup from the tray, held it to her lips, and peered at Dora over its top.

"I remember how your eyes almost popped out of your head when the taxi turned the corner onto this street and you saw all those magnificent rowhouses. But I have to say I was impressed, too. The houses with their stone masonry, conical roofs, and round towers remind me of English castles."

Dora laughed and propped her hands on her hips. "I reckon Mr. Roger was right when he said some of the wealthiest people in Washington live in the Dupont Circle area, and now we do, too. But I have to say, the people ain't the friendliest in the world. Of course I wouldn't expect them to be friends with me, but the maids even got their noses stuck up in the air. I heard the lady next door tell her maid not to have nothing to do with those suffragists who'd moved in to the neighborhood." Dora gave a chuckle. "As if I cared. I reckon I got better things to do than talk to any stuck up maids."

Sarah set the cup down and smiled at Dora. "Don't pay any attention to them. I'm your friend, and you're mine. We don't need anybody else in Dupont Circle."

Dora frowned and shook her head. "Oh, no, Miss Sarah. I thank you for saying that, but our places are too different for us to be friends."

Sarah took Dora's hand in hers and stared into her eyes. "Dora, what do you think enfranchisement is all about? It's about more than getting the vote. It's about giving a voice to all women so we can make our lives better. You have become very important to me while I've been at Mrs. Simpson's school, and I want you to think of me as your friend. We're in this fight together."

Dora clasped her hands and smiled. A look of awe covered her face. "I sure hope we can win. I can't begin to imagine what it would feel like to get to vote."

Sarah nodded. "I know, Dora. I feel the same way. You see, we're not different at all. We have the same desires. And someday we'll go to the voting precinct together and cast our votes."

Tears sparkled in Dora's eyes. "Thank you, Miss Sarah."

Sarah set the cup back on the tray and took a deep breath. "Now I need to get ready for my meeting with Alice Paul today. I've got to convince her to let me take on some added responsibility."

"But I thought you were satisfied working in the office and doing whatever they needed."

Sarah's eyes grew wide. "Oh, I've loved every minute of it, but things are changing in Washington, Dora. How much do you know about Miss Paul?"

Dora shrugged. "I know she's a Quaker, and she was active in the suffrage movement in England when she lived there for a while."

Sarah nodded. "She earned a reputation there as an activist and antagonist. In fact she was imprisoned three times in England."

"Lands sakes," Dora exclaimed, "I didn't know she had to go to prison."

"She did, but she knew we needed a constitutional amendment in America so women could vote. So she came home and began her crusade." Sarah grew more excited as she talked about Alice Paul. "Oh, Dora, I wish you could see her headquarters. It's near the White House, and there are women there from all walks of life. We're working together for a common goal, and I believe we're going to be successful."

"But, Miss Sarah, I heard you telling Mrs. Simpson that things are getting a little tense down there now that Miss Paul has women picketing at the White House gates."

Sarah grabbed Dora's hand. "You mustn't worry about that. The women are only standing there with signs. They don't say a word. We call them silent sentinels. All they're doing is trying to get the President to take notice of us."

"Well, I'm glad you're not one of them. I'd be worried about you."

Sarah smiled. "I don't want you to worry. But I suppose I should tell you. My meeting today with Miss Paul is to ask her to let me picket with the women."

Dora's eyes grew large, and she shook her head. "Oh, no, Miss Sarah, please don't."

Sarah laughed. "It's all right, Dora. She may not even let me. After all, I am the youngest volunteer." She sighed. "Everybody keeps reminding me of that."

Dora started to reply, but before she could the front door opened, and Roger's voice rang out. "Sarah, where are you?"

Dora jumped at the sound of his voice and scampered past him as he entered the room. Sarah frowned as Dora disappeared into the kitchen. She didn't understand why Roger's presence intimidated Dora so, but she had noticed it when she first came to Mrs. Simpson's school.

"Good morning, Roger. You seem happy this morning."

With quick strides he crossed the room and grabbed her hands. "I have a surprise for you."

"A surprise? Where is it?"

"Outside. Come and see." He drew her towards the door and to the front porch.

Sarah's eyes widened at the sight of a black automobile sitting in front of the house. "It's a Packard, and it looks very much like the one you have in Memphis. Where did you get it?"

"I bought it. I'm tired of us having to depend on taxis and public transportation to get around. Besides you need to arrive in style at headquarters each day, and I intend to drive you there."

"But what will you do with it when we leave Washington?"

"Sell it maybe. Or hire someone to drive it back to Memphis for me. I don't know yet."

Sarah turned towards Roger. "It really is a beautiful car, Roger. You've been so thoughtful of our comfort since we moved to Washington. The house is beautiful, you had a telephone installed, and now you've bought a car to transport your aunt and me. I hope you're not spending too much money on us."

Roger reached out and grasped her hand. His eyes studied her. "Sarah, money is the least of my worries. When my parents died, they left me a fortune. It could be yours, too. When you marry me, everything I have will be yours. I'm a rich man, and I can give you anything you want. All you have to do is say the word."

Sarah pulled her hand free and shook her head. "We've talked about this, and you know my answer. When are you going to accept it?"

His eyes narrowed, and he grabbed her arm and pulled her closer. "I always get what I want, Sarah, and I want you. I will never give up, so you might as well give in."

Sarah tried to pull free, but his fingers tightened on her arm. "Roger, please, you're hurting me."

His fingers eased, but he didn't release her. "Then maybe you know how I feel. I've done everything for you, Sarah, and yet you have no consideration for my feelings."

Tears sprang to her eyes. "That's not true."

He didn't answer, but still holding onto her arm, Roger guided Sarah down the steps to the waiting automobile and opened the door. She sank into the seat and rubbed her arm where his fingers had gripped her. Why did he have to bring up the subject of marriage today when she was so tense about her meeting with Miss Paul? She closed her eyes and tried to calm her racing heart.

As Roger guided the car through the Washington traffic, she studied the shining interior of the car and breathed in the pungent aromas of polished leather, oil, and gasoline. It really was a beautiful car, and Roger was right. As his wife, she could have anything she wanted, but she couldn't think about marriage. She had a mission in Washington to accomplish.

She turned her head and stared out the open window as they rode toward headquarters. A hot wind blew through the open window and ruffled her hair. When she'd first come to Washington, she'd tried to memorize the names of all the sites. Now the landmarks had become so familiar it seemed like the nation's capital had always been a part of her life.

When the White House came in sight, Sarah swiveled in her seat to get a better view of the women at the gates. The crowd partially obscured the signs they held, but some stuck up over their heads. She pointed to the sign that read MR. PRESIDENT, HOW LONG MUST WOMEN WAIT FOR LIBERTY. "Look, Roger, I helped make that sign yesterday. What do you think?"

He glanced at it and smiled before he stopped the car in front of the house in Lafayette Park right across from the White House. "Here we are. You're delivered safely, and I shall pick you up this afternoon. Good luck with your meeting with Miss Paul."

Sarah glanced at the sign on the porch that said Cameron House. "Miss Paul was very smart to set up headquarters right across from the White House. Surely the President is going to give in to her demands for his support of a constitutional amendment when he sees these protestors every day."

"You would think so, but so far he hasn't budged."

Sarah started to get out of the car, but she hesitated with her hand on the door. "Roger, I'm sorry if I upset you this morning. Please try to understand. I have a lot on my mind with the work here, and I don't want to think about marriage."

He nodded, but she could see the pain in his eyes. "I understand. Just remember that I love you, Sarah."

She nodded and tried to smile, but her lips only twitched. "I know you do."

His eyes narrowed. "And one day you're going to look at me the way you look at that farmer."

Her anger flared, and she whirled in her seat to face him. "I've told you he's a lawyer."

"Well, he still looks like a farmer to me," he sneered.

Seething with anger, Sarah climbed from the car and hurried into the house. She stopped inside the front door and took a deep breath to calm herself. The volunteers were already hard at work on their assignments at their desks scattered about the room. Some made signs, some worked at typewriters, and others bustled about carrying stacks of paper. No one seemed to notice her angry entrance.

"Good morning, Sarah."

Sarah turned and smiled at Marian Douglas who headed toward her. The young woman who supervised the volunteers had worked as a secretary before joining Alice Paul and exuded competence and professionalism. Her auburn hair lay pinned to the top of her head, and wire rimmed glasses perched on her pointed nose. Her simple shirtwaist dress fell in straight lines to her ankles, and its sleeves tapered to fit tightly around her small wrists.

"Good morning, Marian. It seems like everybody's gotten off to a quick start this morning."

"Some of the volunteers have been here for hours." She motioned for Sarah to follow, and they headed toward the back of the room. "Are you ready for your meeting with Miss Paul?"

"I'm a little nervous, but I'm ready."

Marian smiled and squeezed her hand. "Just tell her how you feel. She won't bite."

Sarah laughed. "I know that."

Marian led her to the back of the room where a door led into a small office. She knocked on the door, opened it, and stuck her head in. "Sarah Jordan is here to see you."

"Show her in." Sarah recognized Alice's soft voice.

Sarah stepped into the small office and stopped as Alice Paul rose from her chair behind an oak desk. During the two months Sarah had been volunteering at Cameron House, Alice had lost weight. Today she appeared frailer than usual. Although she was in her early thirties, there was a quality in her fierce commitment to their cause that made her appear older.

Sarah extended her hand. "Good morning, Miss Paul, I appreciate your taking time out from your busy schedule to see me today."

Alice smoothed her dark hair in place and smiled at Sarah. Fatigue lined her face. Did the woman ever sleep? She was at Cameron House at all hours of the day and night and was always ready to encourage those who needed it.

Alice took Sarah's offered hand and grasped it in both of hers. "How are you this morning, Sarah?"

"I'm fine." She reached in her purse and pulled out an envelope. "Mrs. Simpson, the lady who came with me to Washington hasn't felt well since we arrived. Since she hasn't been able to volunteer lately, she asked me to give you this."

Alice took the envelope and peered inside. Her surprised expression caused Sarah to smile. She looked at the envelope again before she spoke. "How very kind of Mrs. Simpson. I'm sure we can use the money."

"She wants to feel like she's a part of the movement and wants you to have the supplies you need."

Sarah felt uncertain whether she should sit or continue to stand. Alice motioned Sarah into a chair, sat down behind her desk, and placed the envelope in a drawer before settling into her chair.

"Now what did you want to speak to me about?"

Sarah swallowed and folded her hands in her lap. "I've been volunteering in this office for two months, and I love what I'm doing. But I want to do more. I want to join the silent sentinels at the White House."

Alice picked up a pencil and tapped it on the desk as she studied Sarah's face. "You're asking for something that you may not want once you get it. We're taking a risk by being there. Some people think we are openly defying the President. Tempers have flared over the past few weeks, and we may encounter some resistance. I'd hate to see a young girl like you involved in that."

Sarah straightened her shoulders and lifted her chin. "You were probably about my age when you first began your protests in England. But you believed in your cause and were strong enough to withstand three arrests. I doubt if I would be called on to face anything like that."

"You certainly have the commitment that's required of someone to experience such treatment, but I only want to spare you the possibility of a confrontation."

Sarah leaned forward. "I've been committed to suffrage for as long as I can remember. My father and mother admired you so much. They're both dead now, and I have to make my own decisions about where I should be in the suffrage movement. I admire Mrs. Catt and her belief that our best hope lies in our elected officials, but I feel like my heart is with the National Woman's Party. The only way we're ever going to get the vote is through an amendment to the constitution. I'm willing to take my place on the forefront of the fight as a picket."

Alice chewed on her lip and nodded. "You're right that Mrs. Catt isn't as militant as I am. For instance, take our suffrage parade in March of 1913, the day before President Wilson was inaugurated. Five thousand women marched down Pennsylvania Avenue to let the new president know how we felt about the vote. An angry mob attacked the marchers, and many of them had to be taken to hospitals. The police stood by and watched without doing anything."

A chill ran down Sarah's spin. "I know. I was still in school at the time, but I read about it in the paper. I don't think Mrs. Catt would have approved of that."

Alice laughed. "No, she wouldn't. It seems you've re-searched your argument well, Sarah."

"It's not research, Miss Paul. It comes from discussing the issues with my parents from the time I was a child. It's made me who I am today, and I want to join the pickets."

Alice leaned back in her chair and placed her finger-tips together in front of her. She seemed lost in thought for a moment before she looked back at Sarah. "Two weeks after that march I took a group of women with me to call on the president. We asked for his support of suffrage, but he would do nothing. That happened four years ago, and he still does nothing and refuses to even receive any suffrage delegations. That's why we began to picket outside the White House in January of this year. But the situation is tense and becomes more so every day. I don't want to involve you in it yet. In time if you still feel this way, I will."

Sarah felt her heart stir at Miss Paul's promise. "Thank you. Until that time I will do anything I can to help. I want to be a part of this great campaign you've started here."

Alice rose from behind her desk. "Good. Now let's see what we can find for you to do today."

As Sarah followed Alice into the outer office, she studied the woman's slight stature and marveled at how it masked the fighting spirit for which she was renowned. Her words had lifted Sarah's spirits and renewed her commitment to the fight ahead.

Alice stopped to say something to Marian, and Sarah let her gaze drift over the woman she had come to Washington to join with in a fight they both supported. She had read about Alice Paul, but the flesh and blood woman was so much more than Sarah could ever have imagined. She had taken the suffrage fight to a new level. With her militant attitude she had brought the injustices women suffered in their nation to the forefront and made it a topic of conversation all across the land.

In that moment Sarah realized more clearly than she had before that she stood in the presence of greatness, a woman determined to change a nation. Sarah closed her eyes and mentally pledged her life to help that cause. She would never give up until every woman in America had the right to vote.

Chapter 19

Alex stood up from behind his desk, walked to the window, and stared out at the sky. A flicker of light in the clouds and a far off rumble signaled a storm to the west. He wondered if the storm would move across the Mississippi River or would skirt Memphis. As he stared at the black clouds rolling in the distance, he thought of another storm on the day of the funeral for Sarah's mother and their conversation afterwards.

He wished many times he could go back to the days before that when their relationship had been sweeter and they were at ease with each other. If he had understood her then like he did now, he would have approached her differently. He sighed at the impossibility.

She was probably married to Roger Thorne by now. The thought made him sick to his stomach. He shouldn't be thinking about her. Not when he and Larraine were getting along so well. If things continued this well, he'd probably ask her to marry him on her birthday in October.

Maybe then he would quit thinking about Sarah. He raked his hand through his hair and groaned. Why were some days more difficult than others? Today everywhere he turned something reminded him of her. But the most troubling of all was the thought that niggled at his mind constantly that he needed to pray for her.

A knock on his office door caught his attention, and he turned. "Come in."

The door opened, and Lydia walked in. "Mr. Taylor, I'm about to go to lunch and wanted to ask if there is anything you need before I go."

He opened his mouth to say no. Instead words he hardly recognized came out. "Yes, Lydia, I'd like for you to put through a long distance call for me."

"Certainly, sir. Who are you calling?"

"I want to speak with Ben Cooper in Washington, D.C. He's a law school friend, and he's practicing in a firm with Dudley Malone and Matthew O'Brien."

Her eyebrows arched, and her back stiffened. "Yes, sir."

She turned to leave, but Alex held out his hand. "Wait a minute. Do I detect some misgivings in your attitude?"

Lydia turned and faced him. "No, sir, it's just that I've heard of these lawyers. They are very active in the suffrage movement. I'm not sure Mr. Buckley would like you associating with anyone in that firm."

Alex narrowed his eyes and glared at her. "Let me remind you, Lydia, that you work for me. It's not the other way around. Until Mr. Buckley removes you or me, it is not your place to comment on who I do or don't speak with. Now please get my friend on the phone without any more delay."

Lydia's face flamed bright red, and Alex swallowed back his regret at how he'd spoken to her. She lifted her chin and nodded. "Yes, sir. I'll get him right away."

It was only a few minutes before Lydia let him know the call had been completed. He smiled when Ben's voice echoed on the line. "Hello."

"Hey, Ben, this is Alex Taylor down in Memphis. How're things going in Washington?"

"Alex." Ben's greeting reminded Alex of how his good-natured friend had seen him through a lot of long night study sessions. "I've been wondering how you were doing. Is there any special reason you're calling?"

"Will and I are attending the same church in Memphis, and we talk about you a lot. He told me where you were working. I understand your firm has an interest in the suffrage movement."

"Yeah. The two senior partners are supporters of Alice Paul, and they're monitoring the situation with her supporters."

Alex sat up straight in his chair and frowned. "Do you think there may be some problems?"

"We're not really sure. Her silent sentinels are demonstrating outside the White House every day, and they're attracting big crowds. Some of those folks are quite vocal to the women. We hope it doesn't turn into something bad."

Alex swallowed his fear. "Look, Ben. I want to ask a favor of you."

"Sure. What do you need?"

"There's a young woman in Washington working with Alice Paul. Her name is Sarah Jordan. Or if she's gotten married, it could be Thorne. No matter what her name is, would you mind keeping an eye on her for me? She doesn't have any family, and I want to know if she gets sick or hurt."

Ben chuckled. "Is this girl close to you?"

Alex exhaled. "Yeah, but it's complicated. I just want to make sure she's all right."

"I'll do what I can, Alex. I'm going to be out of town for a while later this summer. I'm getting married, and my wife and I are taking an extended honeymoon in Europe."

Alex laughed. "It sounds like you must be making a lot of money."

"I'm doing all right, but my future father-in-law is the one with the money. He's paying for the honeymoon. I'll think about you when I'm in Paris."

"Yeah, you do that. It's good to talk to you, and I wish you well in your marriage."

"Thanks, Alex. I'll keep an ear open for anything you need to know about your girl."

"Goodbye, Ben."

Alex hung up and sat there thinking about Sarah. Why did he have this feeling that something wasn't right in Washington? He pushed up from his desk and walked back to the window.

The storm had passed by, and the dark clouds now traveled to the east. The bright sunshine, however, didn't relieve the dark fog that had hung in his mind for days. He feared the murky shadows that clouded his mind might be a premonition of bad things yet to come.

Sarah pecked at the keys on the typewriter with her index fingers and muttered under her breath at her lack of skills which many of the other girls possessed. Her tongue protruded from the corner of her mouth, and her teeth clamped down in concentration of the handwritten list of today's demonstrators she tried to type.

"Your willingness to try anything impresses me."

Sarah turned in her chair and smiled at Marian Douglas who stood there. "I never did learn how to type, so I have to use the hunt and peck method."

Marian sat down opposite her and crossed her legs. "You're doing an excellent job, and everyone appreciates the effort you're making to fit in here."

"Thank you. That means a lot to me."

Sarah noted a small frown wrinkle Marian's forehead. "Sarah, Alice asked me to talk to you about Roger. He comes here every day to drop you off and pick you up, and he's begun to spend a lot of time here in the office. I'm afraid he's becoming something of a nuisance with his bragging about how much money he's given our cause. Somehow his words don't sound sincere, and he's coming to sound like a braggart. It's almost as if he's trying to impress all of us about his commitment to our cause."

Sarah quaked at the Marian's words. "I'm sorry. I didn't realize he was in the way. Maybe I could ask him not to come inside."

Marian shook her head. "It's not just that he's in the way. It's his manner with everyone. He tells everybody he meets about all the money he's spent to get you in the movement and tells everyone how he rescued you from obscurity and made you an activist in Memphis."

"Well, he and his aunt have done a lot for me. I owe them more than I can ever repay."

Marian leaned forward and took Sarah's hand. "He's beginning to pester Alice to let you picket at the White House. He's offered her a lot of money for the campaign if she will let you go with the others. It appears he thinks his money can buy him anything he wants."

Sarah's mouth dropped open, and she frowned. "Oh, Marian, I'm so sorry. I don't want Miss Paul to be angry with me. I knew nothing about this. Roger knew I asked Miss Paul about joining the pickets. I'm sure he only wants to give me what he thinks I want."

Marian looked into her eyes. "Does he want it for you, or does he have some selfish reason for himself? Why did he really bring you to Washington?"

The question surprised Sarah, and she searched for an answer. "W-well, he says he's in love with me and wants to marry me, but I've told him repeatedly that I won't marry him."

"Did he think by bringing you to Washington you might be so grateful that you would marry him?"

Sarah shook her head. "But he didn't bring me here. Our group in Memphis sent Mrs. Simpson and me. Roger only came along to make sure we were safe."

"You think your suffrage group sent you here?"

"I don't think. I know. Roger is on the executive committee of our group in Memphis. When he came home from one of the meetings, he said they wanted me to represent them since no one else could get away at that time of year."

"But if I understood correctly, you were teaching school. How did you manage that?"

Marian's questions were beginning to cause Sarah some concern, and she fidgeted in her chair. "Mrs. Simpson owns the school. She hired a substitute for my classes."

"I see." Marian sighed, took off her glasses, and rubbed her eyes. "Sarah, there's something you need to know. Alice had a phone call from Mrs. Windsor in Memphis. She had called to check on you and see how you were making it since she hadn't heard from Mrs. Simpson or Roger. In the course of the conversation she mentioned that she and another lady were making plans to come to Washington, but Roger persuaded them to let you come in their places. In fact he donated a large sum of money to the Memphis group in exchange for him to bring you and his aunt."

"What?" Sarah stared at Marion in disbelief. "There must be some mistake."

"It's true. When Alice told Mrs. Windsor that Mrs. Simpson has done very little since she's been here, Mrs. Windsor said that didn't surprise her. Evidently she does very little in their group, too."

Sarah jumped to her feet and began to wring her hands. "Oh, this is terrible, but I assure you I knew nothing about this. I thought I had the whole-hearted endorsement of the group." Another thought hit her, and she placed her hands on her burning cheeks. "Oh, what Miss Paul must think."

Marian shook her head. "She thinks you're a very dedicated worker, but she's concerned about your involvement with Mrs. Simpson and Mr. Thorne. I know you don't have any family, but surely someone else must have warned you to be careful in your association with them."

The memory of Alex questioning her about the letter she received from them before her mother's death popped into her mind. "Someone tried to, but I wouldn't listen." She swallowed and asked the question she feared to ask. "Does Miss Paul want me to leave?"

Marian shook her head. "Of course not. She's very fond of you, and she thinks you do a good job. We felt you needed to know this."

"I did need to know. I must do something, but I don't know what. I can't give up the work here."

"What are you going to do about Roger's proposal?"

"The same thing I've been doing since he first spoke of it, tell him no. I don't want. . ."

Before Sarah could finish her sentence, the front door burst open. Henrietta Morris, a new volunteer from the Boston area, ran into the room. She stopped just inside the door and bent forward, her hair disheveled and her arms crossed at her waist. She panted for breath, and tears streamed down the girl's pudgy cheeks.

"Miss Paul! Miss Paul! Come quick!" she cried.

Alice came running from her office. "What is it?"

Sarah and Marian ran to the girl who was struggling to speak. Between sobs she gulped out her message. "They've been arrested! The pickets have been arrested and taken to police headquarters."

Unable to move or speak, Sarah glanced at Marian who appeared just as shocked as she. Alice grabbed Henrietta's shoulders and gave the girl a gentle shake. "Arrested? Who arrested them?"

"The police. They took them away in a police wagon. They said they were obstructing sidewalk traffic and arrested all of them."

Alice turned to Sarah and Marian. "I'm going to police headquarters. You stay here and see if you can calm Henrietta. I'll be back as soon as I know anything."

With that Alice charged from the office into the street. Sarah put her arms around the girl and led her to a room in the back that housed two cots. She settled Henrietta on one of the cots and went to the kitchen where Marian had already poured water from the kettle for a cup of tea.

Marian raised anguished eyes to Sarah. "I knew this would happen. It was only a matter of time."

Together they took Henrietta the tea and then left her to rest. Sarah walked back to the desk and sat down at the typewriter. She picked up her list of today's demonstrators and with a heavy heart read their names.

Chapter 20

A week had passed since Marian had told Sarah about Roger's deception, but she still hadn't confronted him. She wanted to, but she had mixed feelings about the matter. As angry as she was that he had paid the Memphis group to sponsor her, she was still glad she had been given the opportunity.

Every night she had tossed and turned trying to decide what to do. Tell him she knew the truth, or ignore the situation? Deciding hadn't been easy, but now she knew what she must do, and it couldn't be put off any longer.

She took a sip from her second cup of coffee and rose from the dining room table just as Dora appeared at the kitchen door. "Are you through with your breakfast, Miss Sarah?"

"I am, Dora. Thank you."

Dora stacked Sarah's dishes and picked them up. "When are you leaving for headquarters?"

"I'm not sure. Mr. Thorne will be here any time now, but I'm not sure I'm going today."

Dora's mouth dropped open, and she frowned. "You're not sick, are you?"

"No, it's nothing like that. I just may take the day off."

Dora narrowed her eyes, and cast a suspicious look in Sarah's direction. "Are you sure you ain't sick? It's not like you to miss a day."

"No, I'm not sick. I'm going in the parlor to wait for Mr. Thorne. I'll talk with you later."

Dora backed toward the kitchen door, but she didn't take her eyes off Sarah. "I have to go to the market to pick up some things for Mrs. Simpson, but I won't be gone long. I'll check on you when I get back."

"All right, Dora."

Sarah walked to the parlor and sank down on the brocade sofa that faced the fireplace. She clasped her hands in her lap and waited for Roger to arrive. It should be any minute for he was never late. As if she'd conjured him up, the door opened, and he walked into the house.

His eyes lit up when he spotted her on the sofa, and he eased down beside her. "Aren't you ready to go?"

Sarah nodded and let her gaze drift over him. Since they'd been in Washington, Roger had appeared to relax, and he'd acted happier and looked healthier than he had in months. Perhaps it was being away from the stress of his business in Memphis and the hours he'd spent on the golf course since arriving in Washington that had brought about the change. Whatever it was, he seemed to have benefited, and she hoped he didn't get too upset over what she was about to say.

She sat up straight on the sofa and cleared her throat. "I need to talk to you."

He nodded. "All right." Then he frowned and glanced around. "Where is Aunt Edna?"

"A friend picked her up early this morning. They're spending the day out at Mount Vernon."

"Oh, yes, I forgot." He shifted on the sofa to face her. "I think I'd like to have a cup of coffee while we're talking. Is Dora in the kitchen?"

"No, she had to go to the market, but there may be some left in the pot on the stove."

He shrugged. "I'll get some at the golf course after I drop you at headquarters. Now what did you want to talk to me about?"

She took a deep breath. "I learned something last week that really upset me." His eyes narrowed, but he didn't move as she told him what Marion had revealed to her. When she'd finished, she waited for him to say something, but he didn't move. "Aren't you going to explain yourself, Roger? Why did you lead me to believe the Memphis group wanted me to represent them when you had really bribed them to let me take someone else's place?"

He stood up, walked to the fireplace, and then turned to face her. His face was void of any emotion, and that frightened Sarah more than if she'd seen anger. He stared at her as if she was some insect he was studying under a microscope. "You disappoint me, Sarah. Surely you can't be stupid enough to believe an organization as large as our group would want to send a girl who's lived the pampered life you have."

Sarah rose to her feet and bit down on her tongue to keep from giving a heated retort. Making him angry wasn't the answer. He needed to understand how betrayed she felt. "I wouldn't call my life pampered, Roger. I've lost both my parents, and I'm working so I can take care of my needs."

He took a step toward her, and his mouth curled into a sneer. "Your needs are being very well taken care of, my dear. You've been furnished a place to live, given all your meals, and paid a salary, too. I think that sounds rather pampered."

"I understood I was given room and board as part of my salary."

Roger threw back his head and laughed. "Do any of the other teachers get anything extra? They can barely make ends meet on what my aunt pays them."

Sarah closed her eyes for a moment to digest the things Roger had said. When she opened them, he was staring at her, one eyebrow cocked. "I suppose I am a foolish girl. I can see now I was given special treatment, and it makes me ashamed. The other teachers must hate me."

Roger shrugged. "Who cares what they think? I'm sure they suspected your special treatment was because you're going to marry me."

Sarah gasped and shook her head. "Roger, I have told you repeatedly I don't want to marry you. When are you going to believe me?"

His eyes narrowed, and he took a menacing step toward her. "And when are you going to understand you have no choice? I have given you a comfortable life, and I've arranged for you to get to do what you've dreamed about. You owe me, and I intend for you to repay your debt."

She heard the words, but she couldn't believe what he was saying. Tears ran down her face, and she shook her head. "You have done some wonderful things for me, and I was naïve enough to think you did it out of friendship. Now I understand it was your way of manipulating me into marriage. But it's not going to work, Roger." She took a deep breath and pulled herself up to her full height. "Now I think I must leave this house. I have money my parents left me, and I will repay you every penny you've spent on me in the past year. I'm just sorry we have to part on such bad terms."

She turned to leave the room, but he caught her by the arm and whirled her around to face him. "Where do you think you're going?"

"Upstairs to pack. Then I'm going to call a taxi to take me to Cameron House. Maybe Alice will let me stay there for a few days until I can find a place to live."

His faced turned pale, and he shook his head. "No, you can't leave. I'm sorry if I made you angry. I'll do anything if you'll just stay."

"I can't stay, Roger. I'm sorry." She pulled loose from his grip and strode to the staircase. She had just put her foot on the first step when he called out to her.

"Don't leave me, Sarah. Please."

Sarah glanced back at him, and for a moment was almost persuaded to go to him. His shoulders drooped, and tears stood in his eyes. He reminded her of a little lost boy with nowhere to turn. She couldn't let him manipulate her again.

"I'm sorry, Roger. I'm leaving."

She left him standing alone in the parlor as she rushed up the stairs and to her room. There was no need to pack all her clothes at the moment. She could take only what she needed and get one of the volunteers to come back with her later for the rest.

Her small valise sat in the corner of the room, and she grabbed it. Within minutes she had stuffed three dresses inside. She opened the top drawer of her dresser and pulled out a nightgown. She was just closing the bag when Roger's quiet voice interrupted her. "What do you think you're doing?"

She turned to face the door, and a shiver raced up her spine. He leaned against the door jamb, his body filling the opening. The anger burning in his eyes made her breath hitch in her throat.

Sarah's heart pounded like a drum at his imposing figure. "I-I'm packing. I told you I was leaving."

Roger's cool stare bored into her and sent an icy surge through her veins. She stepped to the far side of her bed to put some distance between them. He straightened before he walked closer. "You're not going anywhere, Sarah. Not until I say you can."

Fear radiated through her, and she swallowed. "Roger, please. Let's not argue. I just want to go."

He shook his head. "But you can't because I'm not going to let you."

She frowned and shook her head. "Please don't make this more difficult."

He sighed and stepped closer. "Oh, Sarah, when your parents brought you to the school, I thought you were the most beautiful child I'd ever seen, but I waited until you were eighteen before I let anyone know how much I cared for you. Then you left with your mother, but I knew you'd be back. So I waited." He paused a moment and frowned. "But when you came back, you were different."

Sarah's stomach roiled, and she wrapped her arms around her waist. "H-how was I different?"

He tilted his head to one side and studied her face. "You weren't the happy girl I remembered. There was a sadness about you that I couldn't understand. I knew something had happened to you while you were gone."

Sarah shook her head. "You're mistaken. Nothing happened to me."

His face contorted into a mask of rage, and he moved around the end of the bed. She took a step away from him and felt her back pressed against the wall. She looked for an escape route, but he blocked her way. His lips curled downward, and his chest heaved. "It was that farmer, wasn't it? You wanted him, and now you want to run back to him."

Sarah forced her voice to speak. "No, it's not Alex. I just want to leave."

Roger took two steps toward her and clamped a hand around her throat. The chain of her mother's locket dug into her neck. "You're not going anywhere."

She drew her hand back and swung with all her might. His grip loosened as her palm cracked across his face. His stunned expression reflected surprise at her action. "Let me go!"

The words barely left Sarah's mouth before his fist crashed into her jaw. Her head reeled from the punch, and she fought to remain conscious. Her body sagged and slid down the wall, but he caught her before she hit the floor.

Through a painful haze she saw Roger's fingers close around her locket, and the chain snapped. He hurled the necklace across the room where it bounced off the wall.

"My locket!"

Roger's body shook with rage. "I'm sick of seeing you wear that cheap piece of jewelry."

His fingers tightened on her throat again, and a new fear overtook her. She was about to die. With a surge of energy, she curled her fingers and scratched at his face. She tried to speak, but he was slowly blocking her airways.

He raised his hand again, and Sarah threw her hands in front of her face to deflect further blows. In one quick move he released her throat, grabbed both of her wrists with one of his, and held them in a grip like a vise. With his free hand he slapped her repeatedly across the face.

Blood poured into her mouth, and she struggled to free herself from his hold. He pushed her towards the bed, his body pressed to her. The more she fought, the tighter his hands held her prisoner.

Through her blurred vision she looked into his crazed eyes. She toppled onto the bed, and he fell on her. His weight pinned her to the bed, and a new fear dawned on Sarah. She fought like a caged animal as his free hand fumbled at the opening of her dress.

Roger abandoned his efforts with the unyielding buttons and grabbed the front of her dress. He muttered and yanked the material. A swishing sound split the air, and his head jerked toward the side. A choking sound escaped his lips.

Suddenly he released her and toppled to the bed beside her. Sarah propped up on her elbows, her eyes wide in astonishment. Dora, holding a frying pan, stood over her. Terror masked her face. "Did I kill him?"

Sarah felt for a pulse in his neck and shook her head. "No."

Dora grabbed Sarah's arm and pulled her into a sitting position. "Miss Sarah, are you all right?"

Her chest heaved, and she glanced down at Roger unconscious beside her. "Oh, Dora, I thought you weren't here. Thank you for coming to my rescue."

Dora shook her head. "I was about to leave when I heard you and Mr. Roger in the parlor. I couldn't tell what you was saying, but it sounded like you was real mad. I thought I'd better stay around for a while. I'm real glad I did."

"So am I." She pushed to her feet. "But we need something to tie him up with, and we need to call the police."

Dora handed Sarah the frying pan. "There's some rope in that shed out back. I'll go get it. If he moves before I get back, hit him again." Sarah's hands shook, but she wrapped her fingers around the skillet.

"Hurry, Dora."

Roger didn't move until Dora returned, and within minutes they had him tied up and the police called. He had just begun to stir when the police arrived, and Sarah surrendered the frying pan to the first policeman in the door.

Then she collapsed in a chair and sobbed. Dora sat down beside her and hugged her. "Don't cry, Miss Sarah. It's all right now."

But Sarah knew it wasn't. She'd trusted Roger, and that choice had almost gotten her killed. A memory of sitting underneath a willow tree on a summer day returned, and a tear trickled from the corner of her eye.

She wished she could go back to last summer and change the choices she'd made, but that was impossible. Now all she could do was try to face a future of uncertainty. She had no idea where she would go or what she would do, but for now she still had the cause she'd sacrificed everything for. That's what would get her through the days to come. Taking a deep breath, she pushed to her feet and looked at Dora who hadn't moved from her side.

"Let's go, Dora."

Dora's eyes grew wide. "Where we gonna go, Miss Sarah?"

"To Cameron House. That's all I have right now."

Chapter 21

After a week of tending her battered face, Sarah felt like she could rejoin the human race. It was still hard to believe what had happened with Roger. She had trusted him, and now the very thought of him sent shivers down her spine. Yesterday she'd learned that the police had dropped the assault charges against him, and he and Mrs. Simpson had returned to Memphis. Apparently his wealth had been a factor in his release as well as the fact that he'd painted her as one of those crazy suffragists who were stirring up trouble. All that mattered to her, however, was that he was out of her life for good.

With a sigh, she stepped into the room in Cameron House she and Dora had shared for the last two days. The rustle of a skirt captured her attention, and she turned to see Dora enter.

Dora stepped close, leaned over, and examined Sarah's face. "It looks a heap better today. I reckon you're gonna heal nicely."

Sarah sat down on the cot and patted the mattress beside her. When Dora dropped down beside her, Sarah grasped her hand. "I don't know what I would have done without you. When I look more presentable, I'm going to the bank and have some of my funds from Memphis transferred here. I want us to look for a house where we can be comfortable."

Dora's eyes sparkled. "A house? You mean you're gonna let me be a maid at your house?"

Sarah took Dora's hand in hers. "No, you'll not be my maid. We'll live together as sisters, and we'll take care of each other. After what we've been through, we have a bond for life."

Tears spilled from Dora's eyes. "Sisters? I ain't never had no family, and you say we're gonna be sisters. Why would you do something like that for me? I'm just a servant."

Sarah bit down on her trembling lip as she remembered the faces of all the people who had helped when her mother was sick. Most of all she thought of the first one who had be-friended her at a baseball game. "A person helped me a long time ago. She gave me the strength to face the dark days when my mother was ill. In fact everybody in that little community did."

Dora frowned and gazed at Sarah. "And you left to go back to Mrs. Simpson's? Why?"

That was a question Sarah had asked herself many times in the last few days. "The main reason was that I wanted to be a part of the suffrage movement. Besides, if I hadn't left, I would never have met you. Now let's have none of that crying. We're facing a new life together, and we must be strong. I'm going now and ask Miss Paul when I can picket."

Sarah got up from the bed and marched to Alice's office. She knocked on the door and entered to find the leader en-grossed in the morning paper. Alice looked up from the paper, and Sarah detected sorrow in her eyes.

"Are you reading the account of the latest arrests?"

Alice folded the paper and lay it aside. "Each day seems to bring a new threat. What can I do for you this morning?"

Sarah sat in the chair facing Alice's desk and took a deep breath. "I wanted to ask again when I'll be able to join the picket line."

Alice leaned forward with her elbows resting on her desk. "The picket line becomes more dangerous each day and more of our volunteers are being arrested. When you go out there, you must be prepared for whatever happens. Right now the sentences are running two or three days, but I predict that will be lengthened."

"I've thought about that, but I feel like I need to join the other women."

Alice stared at her for a few seconds. "Give your face another week to heal, and then you can go."

Sarah jumped up. "Thank you, Miss Paul. That should give me enough time to find a house for Dora and me."

Alice held out a hand in caution. "Wait before you get a house. I think you and Dora should continue to stay here until we know what the next few weeks bring."

A ripple of fear tightened Sarah's chest. "You're really concerned about the pickets, aren't you?"

Alice nodded. "The crowds are becoming unrulier each day, and the police do nothing. I fear for all our women out there, but we can't give up now."

Sarah studied the woman whose shoulders carried the weight of their movement. The sagging dress on Alice's small frame hinted at a loss of weight in the last few weeks. Sarah resolved to do everything in her power to help this woman who carried so much responsibility.

"We'll stay here for the time being, and I'll be ready next week to join the other women."

Alice nodded, picked up the newspaper from her desk, and began to read the account of the arrests again. She glanced up at Sarah. "What more can we do?"

Sarah had no answer for her.

★ ★ ★ ★ ★

Alex was in the middle of dictating a letter when the phone on his desk rang. He reached for it, but Lydia's hand grabbed it first. She smiled at him as she placed the receiver to her ear.

"Mr. Taylor's office. May I help you?" She frowned and then handed the phone to him. "It's long distance from Washington."

His eyes grew wide, and he held the receiver to his chest before he spoke. "Thank you, Lydia. You can go back to your desk. We'll finish this letter later."

He waited until she had closed the door behind her before he spoke. "Hello."

"Alex, this is Ben. In case you haven't heard the news about your friend Miss Jordan I wanted to let you know."

Alex's fingers tightened on the phone. "Wh-what news?"

"It happened a week ago, but I just found out about it today."

Alex bounded to his feet. "Tell me what happened."

Ben chuckled. "Oh, I'm sorry. Well, it seems the man who's responsible for her being in Washington attacked her and tried to rape her. He and his aunt have left Washington, and she's now living at Alice Paul's headquarters."

Alex's mouth dropped open. "What?"

For the next few minutes Alex listened as Ben related how Sarah and her maid had fought Roger Thorne to keep him from attacking Sarah.

Alex sank back down in his chair and shook his head. "How did you find out about this?"

"I have a friend at the police department. He knows things are getting tense with the demonstrators at the White House, and I'd asked him to keep a lookout for the girl you'd told me about."

Alex clenched his fist at the thought of what Sarah had endured. "I appreciate it, Ben. Do you know how she is?"

"From all reports she's fine. She's moved into Cameron House which isn't the safest place in Washington, but she's not spending time with a man who tried to kill her."

"That's for sure. So, Sara hadn't married Thorne?"

"From what my friend said, Thorne became violent with her because she kept refusing to marry him."

"Thanks, Ben, and let me know if anything else happens."

"I will. But don't forget I'm leaving on my honeymoon trip to Europe in a few days. I won't be back until the middle of November. I'll ask one of the other lawyers in the office to call you if anything new happens with your friend."

"Have a great trip."

Alex hung up the phone and sat there thinking about his conversation. Then he jumped to his feet and began to pace back and forth across the room. So Roger Thorne had lied to him. Sarah had never agreed to marry him. How could he have accepted what Thorne said without asking Sarah? But he had accepted it, and now he had moved his relationship with Larraine ahead. He knew she was expecting a proposal on her birthday. Maybe he would put it off until Christmas.

He stopped at the window and stared out. His new spacious office, a benefit of keeping company with the boss's daughter no doubt, had one of the best views in the firm. From here he could see the river beyond Front Street and the bluff. He watched the water roll by, but his thoughts weren't of Larraine. They were about all the time he'd wasted arguing with Sarah about things that could have been solved if he had just given an inch. But he'd been determined to stand firm, and it had cost him the only woman he would ever love.

Sarah had finally gotten her wish. Miss Paul had let her join the pickets a week after she came to stay at Cameron

House, and now she'd been on the picket line for weeks. Each day proved more troubling than the one before. With the heat and the unruly crowds that harassed them, Sarah had been exhausted by the time she returned to Cameron House each day.

Today was no different. The September sun reflected off the sidewalk sending heat waves radiating upward. Perspiration rolled down Sarah's forehead and dripped onto her cheeks. Even with a hint of autumn in the air, the temperature climbed higher with each passing hour. The shade of an overhanging tree at the White House gates tempted her to step into its coolness, but she stood still and silent.

The restless crowd milled about in the street and muttered among themselves. Sarah held her sign, DEMOCRACY SHOULD BEGIN AT HOME, high but said nothing. Remaining silent had been one of the most difficult things for her, especially when she heard the taunts of men who stood close by.

As if he could read her thoughts, a man at the edge of the curb pointed to her and laughed. "Look at that young one there. Do you think it's a she-male?"

His friends roared in response and punched each other in the ribs. The young man stepped onto the curb in front of Sarah and sauntered to where she stood. When his friends laughed, he turned and winked at them. "I'll go have a look."

He took off his flat brimmed straw hat and bowed from the waist. When he straightened and looked into her eyes, Sarah could see the smile on his face didn't extend to the blazing anger of his stare. His gaze traveled up and down her body before he spoke.

"Honey, why aren't you home where you belong? You don't have to vote to be able to clean out your kitchen sink."

His friends roared at the insult, and he swaggered back into the street. They patted him on the back and laughed at his bravery.

Sarah refused to acknowledge the crude comments and stared straight ahead. She had endured the insults and taunts for the last month, but each day proved harder than the one before. She longed to charge forward and bring her sign down on the head of the young man, but she knew the foolishness of such an act.

The newspapers portrayed them as Silent Sentinels of Liberty, and she would do nothing to endanger the image of the demonstrators. The hecklers they faced each day had strengthened the bond of the women who picketed at the gates on Pennsylvania Avenue.

She blinked from the perspiration that rolled into her eyes and grasped her sign tighter. How had her group escaped the wrath of the police over the past few weeks? The erratic arrests and sentences of the demonstrators followed no logic. Some women were given two to three days in jail while others had charges dismissed. Many of those arrested were still detained at the Washington jail awaiting their fate, but some had even been sentenced to short stays at Occoquan Workhouse.

Sarah looked at the other five women who picketed with her today. Henrietta stood next to her and held a sign which proclaimed in bold letters KAISER WILSON. She wondered if the President had seen that one.

A hot wind blew across the sidewalk, and Sarah sensed a change in her surroundings. The taunts grew louder as the size of the crowd increased, and her heart pumped at the warning flitting through her mind. Within minutes a mob had filled the wide street, and angry voices shouted at them from all sides. From her spot on the sidewalk, she couldn't see the back of the group.

Fear rose in her throat at the change she sensed taking place in the gathering. She reached up to touch her mother's locket and smiled at the gesture, for it did not hang there. The pendant, from which she drew strength, had been taken to the jeweler's for repair after Roger's attack had left the catch damaged. She was supposed to pick it up later today.

She focused her attention back on the angry crowd that faced her. The young man at the front, encouraged by his friends, continued to strut about and shout. "They're all mentally deranged. Are we going to put up with women telling men what to do?"

"No!" An angry chorus rang out from the crowd.

Sarah glanced at her friends and saw fright in their eyes at the restless tension rumbling through the atmosphere. She pulled herself to her full height and pushed her sign upward as a signal for them to do the same.

Without warning, the young man ran forward again, grabbed Sarah's sign, and pushed her backwards. In one swift movement he cracked it across his knee, splintering the handle, and threw it to the ground.

Sarah staggered to her feet in time to see five other men grab her friends and pin their arms to their sides. Henrietta fought against the man holding her, and he threw her to the ground.

"Stop this! We're not hurting anyone!" She cast a panicked look around for a policeman and saw two standing with their arms crossed observing the altercation. She screamed at them. "Please, do something!"

At the sound of her voice, the policemen stepped forward, grabbed two of the men, and pushed them toward the curb. Then they motioned the men to release the women. "That's enough. You men get on back out to the street."

Sarah bent to help Henrietta. Before she could offer any aid, one of the officers spun her around and pushed her face against the fence. Strong hands gripped her arms and pulled them behind her. Cold metal encircled her wrists, and Sarah heard the snap of locking handcuffs. She glanced around to see her friends with their arms behind them also. With a sick feeling she realized they had just been arrested.

Fear rose in her throat, and she struggled to remember the words she'd memorized to use in this situation. *Stay calm. Don't resist arrest. Nothing is going to happen to you.*

The crowd cheered as the officers herded them toward the street where a police wagon sat. An officer opened the door and motioned them to climb inside. "Ladies, you are under arrest for obstructing sidewalk traffic. Just do as you're told, and no one'll get hurt."

With her head held high, Sarah followed the other demonstrators to the wagon where the man who had attacked her stood beside the vehicle. He stepped closer when she approached and leaned over for one last taunt. "You're off to jail." He leaned closer and whispered in a loud voice. "I hear they have rats in the cells."

Sarah glared at him, lifted her foot, and kicked him in the shin with all her strength. The man bent over in pain, and Sarah scrambled aboard before he could recover. Henrietta huddled on the bench, and Sarah took a seat next to her. The girl shook with sobs, and Sarah's heart sank at her friend's distress.

She scooted closer to her in an effort to comfort her. "Henrietta, it'll be all right. We may have to stay two or three days, but we'll be back soon."

Henrietta raised a tear-stained face to stare at Sarah. "Do you really think so?"

Sarah swallowed her own fear and summoned some confidence before she replied. "I'll wager we'll be back at headquarters within three days."

As the wagon rolled down the street, Sarah hoped her prediction proved true. Would they be fortunate enough to have the charges dropped as some had been, or would they have to stay in jail a few days? Whatever happened, her course was set, and she had to follow it.

Chapter 22

Sarah jerked into a sitting position in her bed and opened her eyes. The unfamiliar surroundings puzzled her. Where was she? One glance around the small room, and the cell bars across one side of it answered her question. Her shoulders slumped and a shiver rippled through her body. Her prediction of three days had lengthened to seven in the Washington jail, but they were scheduled for police court tomorrow.

She'd slept little in the last week. She needed some rest before that ordeal, but she doubted that would be possible. She lay back down and turned to face the wall. Even in this position the light that burned in the hallway all night lit the wall next to her bed. There was no way to escape its probing rays. She covered her head with her thin pillow and wondered what tomorrow would bring.

Eight hours later when she and her friends were ushered into the courtroom, she wished she had been able to sleep the night before. Her eyelids drooped, and her legs wobbled as she walked to the bench where they would sit. As she bent her knees to sit, a dizziness swept over her, and she pressed her hand to the seat to balance herself.

After a few seconds the dizziness eased, and Sarah glanced over her shoulder. A ray of hope blossomed as she stared into the faces of Alice and Marian seated in the court-room. They waved and smiled in encouragement, and Sarah nodded in their direction before she turned back to face the front of the room.

She'd barely had time to get settled, when the door to the judge's chambers opened, and a man in a black robe entered the room. The bailiff who seconds before had been propped against the front of the judge's bench flirting with the court stenographer straightened at the sound.

"All rise." A hush settled on the courtroom as the judge took his seat.

Sarah and her friends, dressed in the same clothes they had worn seven days ago when they were arrested, rose from their bench and waited until the judge sat down. The bailiff paused before addressing the room again. "Police court is now in session. The Honorable Judge Mullowny presiding. Please be seated."

Sarah sank back to her seat. She heard a soft sob and glanced at Henrietta who sat next to her. She reached for Henrietta's hand and squeezed. Henrietta pressed her hand in return but didn't take her eyes off the judge whose penetrating gaze swept across the prisoners.

The judge uttered a disgusted grunt before he turned his attention to papers lying in front of him. He adjusted his glasses and flipped through the pages before he looked up at the packed courtroom.

"Today we'll hear charges against Henrietta Morris, Sarah Jordan, Ernestine Stevens, Rose Wainscott, Laura Barnes, and Helen Mitchell. The accused are being brought before this court for obstructing sidewalk traffic at the White House." He peered over the top of his glasses. "Is Chief of Police Major Pullman here?"

A tall man dressed in a police uniform stood. The decorations on his jacket identified him as the chief of police. "Yes, sir. I'm here."

The judge stared at him. "Please explain the charges against these women."

The chief straightened his back and pulled his shoulders back. "Your Honor, after repeated warnings the militant demonstrators of the National Woman's Party have blocked the sidewalk traffic at the White House each day. The police have been patient with these people, but they return to stir up more trouble. They incite bystanders with their slogans and demonstrations, and their presence on the sidewalk is a hindrance to those citizens wishing to walk there. The police have exhausted their options with dealing with this nuisance and ask for help from this court with this problem."

The judge turned his attention back to the women and leaned forward as he spoke. "I've seen your fellow violators of the law in here for weeks. Your display of unpatriotic behavior begins to try my patience."

Sarah wanted to protest, but Chief Pullman's menacing stance struck terror in her heart. With his hands behind his back, he shot a sinister look at the women. "Your Honor, the short sentences these women have received haven't deterred them. If it pleases the court, I would suggest lengthening the sentences of convicted demonstrators in hopes of discouraging their supporters."

The judge shuffled the papers before him and stacked them before he looked up at the women. "I agree with Chief Pullman. With America at war and our young men fighting in Europe, I find your total disregard of support for the President and your unpatriotic actions reprehensible. Since you violate the law day after day on the streets of Washington, D.C., I feel a harsher sentence is in order. Therefore, I sentence each of you to sixty days in the Occoquan Workhouse in Fairfax, Virginia."

Having spoken, he banged his gavel, stood, and exited the room. The bailiff called out to the stunned crowd in the courtroom. "All rise. Court is adjourned."

Henrietta wailed and threw her hands over her face. Sarah placed her arm around her shoulders to comfort her and looked over her shoulder at Alice and Marian. Their stunned faces registered shock.

Before she could speak, a guard stepped in front of her, grabbed her arm, and pulled her to her feet. As he pushed her toward the side door, she called out to Alice and Marian. "Don't worry about us. We'll be all right, but please take care of Dora for me."

She saw Marian nod before the guard shoved her through the door. Outside a police wagon sat next to the building, and the guards hustled them toward it. Two women in front of her climbed inside, but Sarah stopped and faced one of the guards. "Are we on our way to Occoquan now?"

The man grabbed her arm and attempted to push her aboard. "Get in."

Sarah twisted away from his grip and planted her feet in a wide stance. "Tell us where you're taking us. I demand to know."

The officer raised the nightstick in his hand and stepped closer to her. "You're a prisoner, and I don't have to tell you anything. Now get inside before I pick you up and throw you in."

Sarah raised her trembling chin in defiance and jumped into the back of the wagon next to Henrietta. Muffled sobs from the other women surrounded her. Her heart pounded like a drum, but she had to calm the other women. She took a deep breath and sat up straight.

"Ladies, do you realize we have an opportunity to make a bold statement about our commitment? We're going to jail for a cause we believe in passionately. Let's make a pact that we won't let them get the best of us."

A wail erupted from Henrietta. "But what do you think they'll do to us?"

Sarah put her arm around Henrietta's shoulders and drew her close. "They won't hurt us. Surely the President wouldn't let that happen to women who are political prisoners. And that's what we are. Keep saying it to yourself until you believe it. We are political prisoners, and we're fighting to become citizens of this country. What we're facing may be difficult, but let's make the choice not to give up no matter what they do to us."

The women wiped tears from their eyes, and Henrietta managed a small grin. Sarah threw her head back and laughed. The sobs stopped, but Sarah knew that uncertainty of the unknown frightened all of them, including herself. She twisted in her seat, threw back her head, and yelled. "Occoquan, get ready for us. Here we come."

The women giggled then, and Sarah laughed all the harder. She hoped she'd convinced them of her courage. Now she had to keep telling herself not to give up. So far none of the suffragists had spent sixty days at the workhouse, but there was always a first time.

The officers climbed in the front of the police wagon and started the motor. Sarah, who knew little about the city, had no idea how far they would travel before reaching their destination.

The prisoners faced each other on benches bolted to the sides of the windowless vehicle and swayed with the movement of the vehicle as they bumped over the streets of Washington.

After a period of perhaps an hour, the crunch of tires on gravel announced their arrival. The back doors opened, flooding the dim interior of the wagon with sunlight. Sarah blinked and shrank from the blinding light, but the bang of the officer's billy club on the side of the door demanded they exit.

As Sarah climbed out of the wagon, she surveyed her surroundings. Rolling farmland spread in every direction, and an orchard dotted the landscape in the distance. The similarity of the land to Richland Creek struck her, but her present circumstances didn't resemble that long ago life.

The guard nudged Sarah with his nightstick. "Welcome to your new home. Move on inside."

Her legs cramped from the ride, and she shuffled toward the large frame building before her. This didn't look like a prison. She imagined all prisons had high walls and fences, but this rambling structure didn't. It stood alone beside the road surrounded with fields. The women's skirts rustled on the walkway as they shuffled to the door that would open to what was to be their home for the next sixty days.

"Delivering prisoners. Open up!" The guard's loud bark delivered with three loud bangs on the door sent an impending feeling of doom flowing through Sarah. This was no longer a warning issued to the pickets at Cameron House. This was reality, and she suddenly realized all the discussions there hadn't really prepared her for this moment.

The door opened, and Sarah took a deep breath before she stepped inside. The others clustered behind her as they followed her. The door clanged shut behind her, and with it came the sobering fact that they were now shut off from the outside world and at the mercy of people who considered them criminals.

Sarah's head jerked around at the sound of a door opening across the room. A man and woman entered, stopped in front of the prisoners, and studied each one. The woman's lips curled in disgust, and she directed an angry glare at her before her gaze sliced to the each of the other prisoners. The cold, dead look on man's face sucked the breath from her, and her knees trembled.

After a moment the man stepped forward, hands clasped behind his back. The sinister look in his eyes darkened, and a mocking smile radiated fear in Sarah that could only be described as impending evil. He scrutinized each one of them carefully before speaking. "Let me introduce myself. I am Warden Whittaker, and you have just entered my world. We each have a job to do while you're here. Mine is to make the laws, and yours is to obey them. If you fail to do what I say, then, you'll suffer the consequences. Do you understand?"

Sarah's eyes widened, and he glared at her. "Don't look me in the face, prisoner. Did you hear my question?"

Sarah dropped her gaze and nodded.

He took a step closer, and Sarah could feel his breath on her face. "Prisoner, I asked you a question. I expect an answer. Do you understand?" he thundered.

Terror seized her. "Yes."

He leaned even closer and yelled into her face. "You will address me by saying 'yes, sir' when you answer. Do that now."

Sarah's stomach churned, and she fought to keep from becoming sick. "Yes, sir." The words were soft, but at least she'd been able to respond.

The warden took a step back from her. "That's better." He waited a moment before he began to speak again. "This is Matron Herndon. She'll be in charge of you during your sentence. Do what she says, or you'll deal with me."

He turned and strode from the room. Sarah glanced up and stared at the woman who stood in his place. Her rumpled uniform fit loosely on her thin frame, and her hair dangled from the tight bun behind her head. The grim line of her clenched lips and the menacing glare directed towards them caused Sarah to cringe.

With a sharp sweep of her hand Matron Herndon motioned the women to stand beside each other in a line. Quickly they repositioned themselves. Then she walked slowly in front of them, scrutinizing the faces of each prisoner with an icy glare that seemed to make the room go cold. When she reached the end, she jerked her head in the direction of the doors.

The male guards who had brought them in exited, leaving them with the matron and several uniformed women who Sarah supposed to be other prison employees. She glanced back at Matron Herndon who held a nightstick in one hand. A slight frown wrinkled the woman's forehead as she quietly tapped the stick in the palm of her opposite hand. An eerie silence filled the room at the slapping sound that seemed to vibrate off the walls.

"You're in my care now, and if you know what's good for you, my orders will be obeyed." Matron Herndon's harsh tone made the hair on the back of Sarah's neck stand up. "You are about to enter the prison population but before you do you will shower and be given a uniform. Take off all your clothes, and drop them where you stand."

A sob escaped Henrietta who stood next to Sarah as she clutched at her arm. A gasp of disbelief rippled over the women as they clustered closer together. Sarah looked toward the matron. She needed to make the matron understand these women were modest and not used to revealing themselves to others. "Please, Matron Herndon," she begged, "we're not accustomed to undressing in front of anyone. Would you please allow each of us to take our clothes off after we enter the shower?"

The matron opened her mouth to speak but didn't say anything. With a shake of her head she walked behind the women toward Sarah instead. Sarah dared not turn her head, but she knew when the woman stopped behind her. She heard the swish of the nightstick before an agonizing blow struck the back of her legs. She toppled forward and tumbled to the floor. In pain she looked up at the fierce expression on the matron's face.

"Who do you think you are?" she yelled as she raised the nightstick above her head ready to strike again. "You don't tell me what to do. Now get up off the floor, drop your clothes, and walk to that shower."

Grimacing from the pain in her legs, Sarah pulled herself to her feet. Her fingers shook as she began to unbutton her dress. One after another her garments hit the floor until she stood naked in front of everyone. Out of the corner of her eye she saw the other women had their eyes averted, but the matron chuckled.

"Now that wasn't so hard, was it?" One of the attendants stepped forward and handed Sarah a bar of soap. The matron motioned toward the door leading to the shower. "Now get in there and wash."

Sarah looked at the half used bar of soap in her hand. She wondered who last used it but knew better than to ask that question. With head held high, she walked across the floor and into the shower.

As she stepped back into the room afterwards, she averted her gaze at the sight of the women standing naked together. Humiliation burned in their red faces that were wet with tears. The matron motioned her towards a table stacked with clothing. "Pick up your underwear off the floor, and come get your workhouse uniform here."

Sarah walked to the table and looked at the sack dresses lying there. Dirt smudged the fronts of all of them, and the smell of perspiration made her stomach roil. Nausea rose in her throat.

"These clothes not good enough for a fancy lady like you? Well, that's all you'll get here." The matron, her arms crossed and a smirk on her face, stood next to the table.

Sarah struggled to control the sick taste that now poured into her mouth. She feared what would happen if she threw up at the matron's feet. She swallowed the bile in her mouth and concentrated on getting dressed, then pulled on her underwear. Knowing she couldn't delay the moment any longer, she picked up one of the dresses and slipped it over her head. Once again the stale odor of perspiration engulfed her. For a moment all she could do was wonder who the last unfortunate woman was to wear this rough garment that enveloped her figure and drooped from the shoulders. As if she could read her mind, Matron Herndon laughed and pushed Sarah back to the center of the room.

When all the prisoners completed their showers, the two women guards ushered them from the room into a hallway. Silently they climbed a stairway to the upper level and entered a long corridor with cells on each side.

Two by two they entered cells with Sarah and Henrietta being last. As she stepped inside, she flinched at yet another foul odor assaulting her nostrils. Unable to determine the source, she looked around until her gaze rested on the toilet against one wall, and she retched when she realized the smell was coming from the unflushed toilet.

Henrietta began to gag and stuffed her fist in her mouth. Sarah whirled and took a step toward the door just as the guard slammed it in her face. to face the guard. "Please," she begged, "tell me how to flush this toilet."

The woman turned a somber face toward her. "All the toilets flush from the outside. The guards have to do it."

"Then would you please flush it for us?"

The guard smiled and turned the key in the lock. "I will whenever I get time."

With a mocking smile on her face, the guard turned and marched down toward the door at the end of the hallway. Sarah turned to Henrietta, and the girl's wide eyes reflected terror. Sarah felt her resolve crumbling, too, but if they were to survive their ordeal, she couldn't give in to her own fears. At the moment sixty days loomed before her like eternity.

Sarah awoke and lay there a moment remembering where she was and the events of the day before. She closed her eyes and willed it all to be a bad dream, but it wasn't. She and her friends were prisoners at Occoquan Workhouse and at the mercy of Matron Herndon and her guards.

Fighting back the tears, Sarah threw the thin blanket back and swung her legs over the side of the bed. She pushed into a standing position and flinched at the pain in her wobbly legs, a reminder of the matron's stick. After regaining her balance, she walked to the toilet in the corner of the cell.

The guards had flushed it sometime during the night. How long would it take for it to be emptied this time? When she finished, she rearranged the dirty dress she still wore and walked over to Henrietta's cot. The girl's eyes looked swollen from the muffled sobs Sarah had heard throughout the long night.

Sarah bent to shake Henrietta awake but jumped at the sudden sound of a shouting voice and metal clanging. "Get up, prisoners. Breakfast in fifteen minutes."

Sarah ran to the bars of the cell and pressed her face against them in an effort to see down the hallway. Two female guards stood at the far end of the detention area. One had a wooden rod in her hand and struck it against the door of the first cell.

Henrietta sprang out of bed. "What is it?"

In one swift movement Sarah turned and gathered the terrified girl into her arms. Henrietta's teeth chattered in Sarah's ear, and she stroked the girl's hair to calm her. "Sh-h, it's all right. They're only waking us up."

Henrietta's shaking subsided some, and Sarah held her at arm's length. "Now that's better. I declare, Henrietta, you look a fright this morning. If we had a brush, I would get those tangles out of your hair, but I didn't seem to have one in my welcome basket last night."

Henrietta's mouth gaped open, and she stared at Sarah a moment before her frightened expressions eased, and she burst out laughing. "Sarah, welcome basket, indeed. I think we're lucky just to have these filthy dresses."

"All right, cut out the talking, and get yourselves out here," a voice called from the hall.

They turned to see a large, uniformed woman holding a ring with keys on it standing in the hall. She unlocked the door, stepped back, and motioned for them to move toward the exit.

Sarah and Henrietta moved to line up with the women pouring from the cells along the corridor. Sarah's heart leapt when Laura Barnes who'd been sentenced with them stepped out into the hall. She started to speak to her, but a quick frown and shake of Laura's head silenced her.

Without speaking, they shuffled down the stairs and proceeded to a large room at the back of the building. Long tables with benches on either side lined the room, and a serving area stretched across one end. A guard waved her nightstick, indicating that they were to line up for their breakfast. A growl from Sarah's stomach reminded her that they'd had nothing to eat after their arrival yesterday.

She watched as the women in front of her picked up their trays and walked to the tables in the room. When it was her turn, she stopped and waited for one of the women in white uniforms to offer her some food. One of them pushed a bowl of thin gruel at her. "Move on," she growled without ever looking up.

Sarah grabbed a piece of bread from a wooden bowl and moved into the dining hall. She spotted Laura at a table and hurried over. Laura jumped up and gave her a quick hug. "Sarah, how did you make it last night?" she whispered.

Sarah cast a nervous look at the frowning guards who were watching them. She slid into her seat as Laura sat down. "We made it okay. How about you?"

"I'm all right, but sixty days seems like a long time."

A woman sitting next to Laura looked up from eating, her eyes wide. "Sixty days? Oh, you're going to have to be brave to endure in this place."

"From what I've seen so far, I believe you're right." Sarah looked around for Henrietta and motioned her over. "You remember Henrietta. She came with us."

Laura nodded and pointed to the other two at the table. "Rose and Ernestine are here. So we have most of our group together."

Sarah smiled at the group. "It's good to see you this morning. I'm starved. Have you tasted your breakfast yet?"

Ernestine grunted in disgust. "It's awful, but we have to eat something if we don't want to starve."

Sarah picked up a spoonful of the watery liquid in her bowl. "I'm so hungry I think I could eat anything this morning."

She shoved the spoon toward her mouth but stopped, her eyes widening. "There's a worm in my food."

She threw the spoon down, and it rattled on the tray. Two guards who'd been involved in a conversation jerked their heads in her direction and stared at her before they walked toward the table. Anger lined their faces. The two stopped beside Sarah and looked down at her. "Is something wrong?"

Sarah swallowed the fear in her throat at the sight of the guards' angry faces. "T-there's a w-worm in my food."

"Where?"

"Right here." Sarah's voice quivered even more as the guard's menacing face hovered near her.

The woman looked at the bowl, straightened, and stared back at Sarah. "Yeah, that's a worm all right. So what do you want me to do?"

"I can't eat this."

"Are you saying you don't want this?"

"Y-yes."

One of the guards picked up the bowl and turned to the other one. "She can't eat this. Take it back to the kitchen."

Sarah watched as the women walked toward what she supposed was the kitchen.. "Will she bring me another bowl?"

The guard arched her eyebrows. "Another bowl? This is a prison, not a restaurant where you place an order. You just refused your breakfast. Maybe the noon meal will be more to your liking, Princess."

She started to walk away but turned to the other women at the table. "If I see anyone sharing their food with her, you'll end up in solitary."

Sarah's body tingled from head to toe, and she fought to hold back the tears. Henrietta pushed her bowl forward, but Sarah shook her head. "I'll share with you," she whispered.

"Thank you, Henrietta, but I won't have anyone getting in trouble because of me. Eat your breakfast. My mouth has gotten me in lots of trouble before. I suppose I'd better watch it in here."

Laura reached for Sarah's hand and held it for a moment. "We're all in this together. We'll take care of each other while we're here."

Sarah eyebrows arched, but she said nothing. She curled her fingers around the bread Laura had slipped into her palm and stowed it in her pocket. She kept her hand on the bread and from time to time when the guards weren't watching she pinched off bits and slipped them into her mouth.

After about thirty minutes a whistle blew, and all the prisoners stood. Sarah thought they would be returned to their cells, but instead they were led into another room. Chairs sat scattered at one end of the room near a table that was piled with fabric, thread, and other sewing supplies.

One of the guards stopped in the middle of the room and faced them. "Prisoners, file by the table and pick up your work for the day."

Sarah joined the group and picked up a large piece of material, a needle, and some thread. The coarse texture of the fabric which was the same as the dress she wore chafed her fingertips. "Are we supposed to make prison uniforms like those we're wearing?" she whispered to Rose.

Rose looked over her shoulder. "I guess so."

Sarah took her seat between Laura and Henrietta and gazed at the dress lengths in her lap. She had a sudden thought that she should have listened when her mother tried to teach her to sew. At that she'd dismissed her mother's efforts saying that she never intended to sew and didn't want to learn. There were many things she'd done in the past she wished she could change, but it was too late. If only she could do it all again.

Chapter 23

Sarah sat on her cot, her back against the wall, and listened to the muffled sobs coming from Henrietta's bunk. Even though she loved her friend dearly, the constant tears were beginning to grate on her nerves. The close quarters in the cell made it impossible to escape the whimpers, and after three weeks at Occoquan she yearned for just one night of quiet.

Suddenly a voice pierced the quiet. "Prisoners, we have a treat for you tonight. We're gonna give you some time out of lockup so you can visit with each other. You'll have one hour, so enjoy your time."

Sarah jumped up and pushed her face against the bars. Guards were opening doors up and down the hallway, and some of the women now stood in the small hallway. "Henrietta, dry those eyes. We're going to get out of here for a while."

Henrietta sat up, wiped at her tears, and stared at Sarah. "I'm hungry. The food tonight tasted spoiled."

"It probably was, but for the first time in three weeks we have a chance to talk with the others. So come on and join the fun."

The female guard sidled up to their cell and inserted the key in the lock. "You have to stay in the cellblock, but you can spend some time talking with each other."

The woman's stern face bore the look of authority, but Sarah detected some compassion in the nasal twang of her

236

words. Sarah stared into her gray eyes, and they softened, sending a secret message of hope.

Sarah slipped past her and into the passage. "Thank you, for allowing us to visit tonight."

"One hour. That's all, so make the most of it."

Sarah grabbed Henrietta by the hand and hurried toward where Laura stood. Several women formed a circle, and Sarah eased into the group. Ernestine, her voice lowered, held the attention of those gathered. "This place is a disgrace. We've got to let people outside these walls know what the conditions here are."

All the women nodded their agreement. Sarah glanced toward the guards who had sat down in chairs at the other end of the cellblock. Their nightsticks lay across their laps, and they laughed and talked with each other.

Rose leaned closer to the group, and everyone crowded closer together. "I thought the food and the filthy clothes were bad, but I wasn't prepared for what I saw today." She held up her bandaged left hand. "You know I had to go to the infirmary this morning because I cut my hand on the sharp edge of my cot. I couldn't believe what's down there."

Concern lined the faces of all in the circle, and Sarah cast one more glance at the guards. "Tell us what it's like, but talk quietly. We don't want to alert them that we're talking about the conditions here."

Rose closed her eyes, her brow furrowed. When she opened them, a tiny tear clung to her bottom lash. "There's a woman who's a prisoner here, and she's in one of the beds. The guards told me she has syphilis, and they'd cut off one of her legs because it had rotted. It was alive with maggots when they finally brought her to the doctor, and now her other one's almost as bad."

Sarah shuddered at the thought of the woman's suffering, but Henrietta's face had a green tint to it. The expressions on the faces around the circle told her she wasn't alone in her compassion. "But that's not the worst. They're short of nurses, and a little girl about twelve years old waits on her. They told me the little girl is from a very poor home, and she's here to have her tonsils removed because her family can't afford to have it done elsewhere."

Sarah's stomach retched at the thought of a child being subjected to such. She leaned against the cell bars behind her and bit down on her lip. A child shouldn't have to be subjected to something like that. She needed the comfort of a mother when she was ill. A lump formed in Sarah's throat, and she pressed her fingers against her chest to keep from gasping at the sudden ache in her heart. She, too, was alone and would never feel her mother's soft embrace again.

She glanced around at the snort of disgust that came from Laura. "It seems we've been sentenced into a place where there's no thought for individuals' rights or needs. I agree with Rose and Ernestine. We've got to focus attention on the plight of everyone here."

A thought struck Sarah, and she looked around at her friends. "This is a workhouse. I wonder what they would do if we refused to work."

Henrietta eyes widened, and she grabbed Sarah's arm. "What do you mean not work? There's no telling what they'd do to us if we didn't work."

Sarah patted Henrietta's hand. "Think of it this way, ladies. We've done nothing illegal, but the court has sentenced us to this horrible place. Why should we sew dresses that other unfortunate women will be forced to wear?"

The women looked from one to another. Laura smiled at Sarah, respect written on her face. "I think Sarah may have something here. What can they do to us besides feed us less of the slop we're already having to eat?"

Sarah nodded. "Tomorrow let's take our seats in the sewing room and refuse to take even one stitch. We haven't broken any laws, and we are being held as political prisoners. Why should we respect the false charges and abuse they we're having to endure?"

"I agree." Laura stuck her arm forward, her finger spread and her palm facing downward. "If you agree, join your hand with mine. We'll show these people how determined we can be."

Sarah thrust her hand forward and laid it on top of Laura's. One by one the others did the same, Henrietta last of all. They stood there a few minutes with their heads down. Slowly each looked up, and smiles lit their faces. They laughed and moved their arms up and down in a symbol of unity.

As their giggles became louder, one of the guards at the end of the hall jumped up from her seat. "You're getting too loud, prisoners. Just keep it up, and you'll go back into lockup early."

The women stepped back in the circle, their fingers clasping at each other as their contact broke. They sat down on the floor and scooted close together. Laura spoke first. "Why don't we tell about ourselves and what brought us to work in the suffrage movement."

Rose nodded. "That's a good idea. I'll go first. I grew up in a little town in Pennsylvania. The textile mill provided the only way of making a living, and both my parents worked there. My mother came home at night bone tired, and she had to take care of our family—my father, four brothers, and myself. She received very little pay for her long day, and I knew I didn't want to end up the same way."

Several of the women nodded. Rose pulled her knees up under chin and wrapped her arms around them. "I hired out as a kitchen helper in a wealthy woman's home when I turned twelve. She had friends who would come to her house, and I dreamed of being like them with fancy dresses and servants. I worked there until my seventeenth birthday, and then I cast myself into the world."

Rose smiled at some memory before continuing. "I came to Washington and found a job in a hotel cleaning rooms. When I heard about Alice Paul's demonstrations, I joined and helped out in my free time from the hotel. I don't suppose I'll have a job when I get out, but it'll all be worth it."

Ernestine spoke up. "That's a lot like my story except I grew up on a farm in Texas. I came to Washington when I read about the demonstrations at the White House, and I knew I wanted to be a part of it."

Henrietta gulped and looked at Sarah. "Well, my story's not very exciting. I grew up in Boston in a wealthy family. My mother's always supported the right of women to vote, and she insisted I come here. I really didn't want to at the time, but I'm glad now that I did. I've learned a lot about life, and I think this prison sentence will teach me how to take care of myself in the world."

Laura glanced over at Sarah. "Sarah? Tell us about yourself."

Sarah breathed in deeply before beginning. "I grew up in Tennessee. My parents died, and I ended up teaching at a girls' school in Memphis. I'd been involved with the suffrage movement on the local level, but I came to Washington with the school owner and his aunt who was the head mistress. When he attacked me, my friend Dora and I escaped to Cameron House. They went back to Tennessee without a word to me, and I stayed at Alice Paul's headquarters." She sighed. "But I didn't realize I'd end up here."

Sarah blinked back tears when she thought of what she'd left out. She couldn't bring herself to speak the most troubling thing of all—that her heart belonged to a young lawyer in Tennessee. Those memories she couldn't share with anyone.

The guards stood up and walked toward them. "All right, prisoners, that's enough for tonight. File back into your cells."

Sarah pulled Henrietta to her feet, and they moved into their cell. Sarah turned to face the guard as she locked the door. Her gray eyes stared into Sarah's, and a half-smile curled her lips. A flicker of kindness flashed across her face, and Sarah realized it was the first time she'd seen compassion in anyone since arriving at Occoquan.

Just as the guard turned the lock, Sarah stepped back to the cell door and wrapped her fingers around the bars. "I'm Sarah Jordan. Please tell me your name."

The guard hesitated and looked over her shoulder. Satisfied that none of the other guards were listening, she leaned closer and pulled the key from the lock. "My name is Ruth Cochran," she whispered.

Sarah smiled at her. "Good-night, Ruth Cochran. Sleep well."

Ruth stood still for a few seconds, her brows drawn into a slight frown. "I will, Sarah Jordan, and you do the same."

She turned and walked down the hallway to where the other guards stood. One of them flicked off the switch that controlled the lights in the cells and left, closing the door behind them.

The lights in the cells might be out, but those in the hall burned brightly, their beams scattering across the cell floor. Sarah slipped out of her dirty dress, lay down, and stretched beneath the thin blanket on the cot. Her thoughts drifted to the part of her story she hadn't told her friends tonight. She wondered where Alex was and what he was doing. But most of all she wondered if he still thought about her.

She pulled the cover over her head and gagged at the blanket's stench of body odor. She folded it back from her face and turned toward the wall in an attempt to block the light.

Henrietta stirred on her cot. "Good-night, Sarah. Thanks for all your help. I promise I'll be stronger, and I'm not going to cry again."

Sarah smiled. "That's good. We've all got to stick together if we're to survive this place."

Sarah lay awake for hours listening. Snores rattled the walls of some cells, while muffled cries crept from others. The words of someone talking in their sleep reached Sarah's ears. "Take care of my baby," it begged.

Everyone here had a story, different from all others, but they all had one thing in common—their determination to make lawmakers finally give them the liberties promised to all citizens under the constitution. Sarah knew the long struggle still lay before them. Maybe their imprisonment would help reach the final conclusion.

★ ★ ★ ★ ★

Thirty days—halfway through the sentence, but each day grew more difficult. Sarah stared at the tree barely visible through the small window of the sewing room. She ignored the hunger pangs in her stomach and focused on the change in the color of the leaves. For the last thirty days the tree had been her one link to the outside world, and she watched each day to detect the slightest hint of autumn in the foliage.

"Attention, prisoners!"

The booming voice startled Sarah from her daydreams, and she pulled her attention to the matron who had just entered the sewing room. The menacing scowl on the woman's face alerted everyone that they were about to be chastised. "I'm tired of this ridiculous display. You've come in here for weeks now and refused to sew. I can't let this insubordination continue. You will sew, or you will suffer the consequences."

Sarah braced her hand on the back of her chair and pushed to her feet. She fought the dizziness from hunger that swirled through her body and struggled to keep from swaying. "We're political prisoners. We have broken no laws, and we refuse to be bound by your work rules."

The guard, her face mottled with red splotches, walked toward Sarah,. She opened her mouth to speak and tiny flecks of saliva lined her lips. "Well, if it isn't our little princess." She practically spat the words. "You've given us trouble since the day you came. You watch your step, or you'll end up with your great leader down in solitary."

A ripple of surprise vibrated throughout the room. Sarah frowned and tried to concentrate on the words but couldn't comprehend their meaning. She frowned. "What are you talking about?"

The guard smiled and licked her lips. "I guess you ladies don't know that none other than Alice Paul joined us last night. She got herself arrested, and now she's downstairs locked up in solitary confinement."

Sarah lurched and grabbed the chair to keep from falling. She lowered herself back into the seat and looked at her friends scattered around the room. Disbelief etched their faces, and tears streamed down their cheeks.

The guard laughed and walked back to the front. "Well, I guess that surprised you a bit. Now it's time for the noon meal, so line up without talking."

The women walked slowly across the floor and formed a line to march to the dining room. Sarah still reeled at the news of Alice's imprisonment in this very building. How could this have happened? The plan had been to protect Alice from the authorities since she plotted the strategies and directed all the activities. With Alice in jail, who was leading the movement now?

The silent group trudged to the serving area and picked up their half-filled bowls. Since their refusal to work, their food had been cut in half. Sarah sat at her assigned table and watched her friends pick at their food. Henrietta shot looks of despair at her from time to time, and Laura appeared lost in thought.

Sarah glanced up at the kitchen worker who stood by their table with a pitcher of water. She leaned forward to fill their glasses and glanced over her shoulder before she spoke. "I took Alice Paul's food to her, and she refused to eat it," she whispered. "She said she's a political prisoner and she won't eat a bite until all the women are released from this place."

Sarah clutched at the girl's skirt to keep her from leaving. "How is she?"

A look of fear flashed on the girl's face, and she brushed Sarah's hand off her dress. "She said to tell everyone to take care. She's planning a hunger strike in hopes the news will leak out and all of you will be released."

One of the guards looked their way, and the girl moved on to the next table. Sarah pondered what the girl had told them. A hunger strike? Maybe that was the way to focus attention on their plight. If word got out that prisoners were staging a hunger strike, the authorities might release them.

Sarah pushed her bowl to the center of the table and folded her hands in her lap. "I'm going on a hunger strike in support of Alice. I don't think any of you should join me unless you're prepared for possibly the worst time of your life."

Laura, Ernestine, Rose, and Henrietta stared at her and down at their uneaten food. Slowly Laura pushed hers away and placed her hands in her lap.

Henrietta burst into tears. "Sarah, I don't think I can do this. Please don't do anything that will get you hurt."

Sarah thought of her parents who had encouraged her to stand up for her rights. She thought about Alex and how she'd lost his love. Then she thought of Roger Thorne and the evil things he'd done. She had endured much in her journey toward enfranchisement. Nothing could be as bad as what she'd already experienced.

She took a deep breath and let her gaze drift over her friends. "I've come a long way from home and lost too much for this cause. I have to do everything I can to win this fight."

"Win what fight?"

The cruel sneer startled Sarah, and she turned her head to see Matron Herndon standing behind her. Sarah raised her chin and looked into the woman's eyes. "We have done nothing wrong. All we want are our rights as citizens under the constitution. We still insist we are political prisoners."

Matron Herndon bent over and glowered at Sarah, their eyes only inches apart. "Princess, when are you going to realize that you're mine now and you'll do as you're told or suffer the consequences? Now quit your smart talk and finish your meal."

Sarah glanced down at the bowl in front of her and with a swift shove toppled it onto the floor. The crash of the utensil startled the inmates at other tables, and they looked down in horror at Matron Herndon's shoes covered with the thin gruel that had been Sarah's meal.

The woman stared down at her shoes for a few moments and then back up at Sarah. A red flush started at the base of her neck and flowed upward until her face appeared crimson and her eyes flashed fire. "You little demon!" she screamed. "You'll be sorry you ever crossed me."

Sarah reeled as the matron's fist connected with the side of her face. With a groan she toppled to the floor and landed on her knees. Two guards towered over her, and each grabbed one of her arms and pressed her face toward the floor. Sarah struggled to raise her head and looked into raw hatred etched into the matron's face.

The matron lifted her foot toward Sarah's mouth which nearly touched the floor. "Now lick it off! You made the mess now lick it off!"

Sarah clenched her lips and twisted her head away from the shoe which inched closer to her. The guards bent her forward again until her mouth touched the tip of the matron's foot, but she twisted her head to the side, crushing her cheek against the shoe.

All around her the inmates screamed as they yelled for the guards to quit, but the pressure on her head increased. Strong hands pushed her face until it scraped the floor. With back and forth motions they smeared her mouth across the shoe and through the gruel covering the floor.

They relaxed their grip, and Sarah, her face streaked with the remains of her meal, peered up at Matron Herndon. A cruel smile curled the woman's lips. "What do you have to say now, Princess?"

Sarah stiffened her body and looked into the face before her. "I have done nothing wrong. I am a political prisoner."

"Get her out of my sight," the matron snarled. "We'll see how hungry she gets before morning."

The guards pulled her to her feet, and Sarah stood and wiped her face with her hand. "I don't intend to eat anything else in this prison until I'm rightfully freed from here."

The guards grabbed her and turned toward the door. Sarah looked over her shoulder as they led her away and smiled at Laura in hopes of gaining some courage and strength from her friend. Her heart pounded, and energy coursed through her body. If they wanted a fight, they'd get one.

It was time to become an adversary.

Chapter 24

Sarah blinked and tried to focus her eyes on the familiar tree outside the window of the sewing room. With her blurred vision, she could barely make out the outline of the tree limbs, bare now of their leaves, waving in the early November wind.

She tried to remember how long it had been since she had eaten, but she found it difficult to hold onto any thoughts. She shivered and rubbed her arms. Her skin prickled from the icy coldness that filled her body. She glanced at the other women sitting in the room. Everyone seemed lost in thought, their faces devoid of any expression. She wondered if their arms and legs felt weak like hers.

Her hair hadn't been combed in days, and she reached up to brush some from her eyes. She frowned and stared in unbelief at her hand as she pulled it away. Her fingers grasped long blonde hairs. With a gasp she spread her fingers, and the hairs fell to her lap.

Panic struck her as she reached up and tugged at the locks that tumbled over her forehead. A tangled clump pulled from her head. She was losing her hair. Buy why?

She looked up, and Ruth Cochran stood in front of her. Without speaking, Sarah held out her fingers for Ruth to see. The guard knelt beside Sarah's chair and touched her arm. "Hair loss is a symptom of starvation, Sarah. You haven't eaten in weeks, and you were already malnourished before you began this hunger strike. Give up this ridiculous rebellion before it kills you."

Sarah clenched her teeth and shook her head. "If I die, it'll be for something I believe."

Ruth shook her head sadly. "I don't want to see you get hurt more."

"What more could you possibly do to me?" Sarah averted her gaze from the woman.

Ruth stood and moved back to the front of the sewing room with the other guard. The door opened, and Sarah looked up to see two men enter the room with Matron Herndon. She spoke softly to the guards. Ruth frowned and cast a quick glance in Sarah's direction.

Matron Herndon walked to where Sarah sat and bent over her. "Will you give up this hunger strike and eat some food?"

Sarah tried to swallow, but her mouth was too dry. "I am a political prisoner. I have broken no laws. I will eat when I'm released from this workhouse."

Matron Herndon grabbed her arm and jerked her out of her chair. "I think you may change your tune, Princess."

She pushed Sarah to the front of the room where the group stood. A middle-aged man dressed in a wrinkled black suit peered at her through wire rimmed spectacles. His loosely knotted tie bulged upward from the vest that fit snugly across his midriff.

"I'm Dr. Gannon, the prison physician, and I'm here to help you." His soothing voice contradicted the look of anger Sarah detected in his eyes.

Sarah struggled to straighten her shoulders and push to her full height. She gritted her teeth and bent double when sudden stomach cramps attacked her. She inhaled a deep breath, "H-how can you help me?"

The doctor placed his finger under her chin and tilted her face up until she stared into his eyes. "You're suffering from malnutrition. The guards tell me you haven't eaten in over two weeks. That's a long time to go without food."

Sarah crossed her arms over her stomach and shook her head. "I-I'm f-fine. I'm a political prisoner who has broken no laws. I refuse to eat until we are released from this horrible place."

Dr. Gannon shook his head sadly. "We can't allow you to die because you won't eat, so we're going to help you."

Sarah hobbled a step back from the group and surveyed the faces watching her. These people had no desire to make things better for her. Her gaze darted around the room for an escape route, but none existed.

The guards took a step toward her, and Sarah frowned. She raised her arms to fight them off, but her hand flopped like the wings of a wounded bird. "D-Don't t-touch me. I've done nothing wrong."

Ruth Cochran moved in front of the other guards. An expression of regret shadowed her eyes, and she clenched her lips. She reached for Sarah's arm. "We just want to help you, Sarah."

"No." What she had intended as a scream released more like a moan.

The two men pushed past Ruth, grabbed Sarah's arms, and pulled her toward the door. Despite her weakness, Sarah willed her feet to kick at her attackers. The man who entered with Dr. Gannon cried out in pain. "Ow, you little hellion, you nearly broke my leg."

The cries of the women in the sewing room bounced off the walls. "Let her go! She's done nothing wrong!"

Sarah turned her face toward the hand that gripped her arm and clamped her teeth into the soft flesh.

He let out a cry of pain, and his hand slapped her so hard she was afraid it had loosened a tooth. "Let go, or you'll be sorry!"

Sarah increased the pressure until she felt the hand release her arm. She looked up into the angry eyes of Matron Herndon.

Sarah quaked at the sight of the woman raising her nightstick into the air. This attack had now become a matter of survival, and Sarah threw her released arm over her head to ward off the blow. The nightstick crashed down on her arm, and Sarah sank to the floor in pain. Dizziness overtook her, and she struggled to stand but could not. She felt her body being lifted and carried from the room.

Dr. Gannon's assistant, who supported her weight as if she were light as a feather, walked quickly through the halls and descended the stairway into the basement. Sarah tried to wriggle free, but he held her tightly. "Be still. You're making this worse for yourself."

Where were they taking her? She felt the dizziness again and wished she could sleep and never wake. A face flashed before her eyes. "Alex," she whispered.

Welcoming darkness closed over her.

Sarah blinked her eyes open and lay still for a moment as she tried to figure out where she was. She winced at the piercing beam of a bright light shining into her face and realized she sat upright in a chair. People moved about the room and spoke in soft whispers, but she couldn't make out what they were saying. She wanted to rub her eyes to clear her blurred vision, but her arms wouldn't move.

Slowly her surroundings came into focus, and she turned her head to stare about the room. Shelves containing medical utensils and bottles of various liquids lined the white walls. Footsteps approached her bed, and she looked up into the face of Dr. Gannon. He held a long tube in his hand.

"Sarah, you must be fed for your own good. We don't want you to die."

Understanding of her situation flashed in her mind, and terror rose in her throat. "No." She hardly recognized the feeble voice that protested the coming assault. Again she tried to raise her arms, but something restrained them.

Dr. Gannon leaned closer. "This will go a lot easier if you don't fight us."

Sarah turned her head to the side and gritted her teeth.

Dr. Gannon sighed. "Have it your way." He hesitated a moment before he spoke to someone nearby. "I've got to begin. Hold her down."

Strong hands pinned her arms and legs to the chair. Another person held her head. Dr. Gannon bent over her again. "Open your mouth, Sarah."

She tried to twist from the grip of those holding her, but it was no use. Determined the tube would not slip between her lips, she gritted her teeth and clamped her mouth shut..

"Stubborn, huh? Well, I can be, too."

And then she felt it. The tube slipped into her left nostril and snaked its way toward her throat. As it scraped and gouged its way through the passageway, waves of nausea rolled through her, and she retched violently.

Something wet tickled her upper lip, and the taste of blood trickled into her mouth. She twisted in an attempt to escape, and her chest heaved as she gasped for air. The more she resisted, the harder the doctor pushed.

Sarah thought the assault would never end. After a few minutes Dr. Gannon released his hold on the tube. "It's in her stomach now."

Sarah panted in dread of what would come next. Dr. Gannon turned, picked up a container, and began to pour a liquid through the funnel at the protruding end of the tube. "This isn't moving fast enough," she heard someone say. "It's backing up in the tube."

Sarah gagged, and the contents spewed from her mouth. Her hope that it would end died when Dr. Gannon began to pour again. As the foul-smelling liquid continued to pour into her stomach, Sarah lost sense of time. It seemed hours before she heard Dr. Gannon speak again.

"We're just about finished."

She tried to relax, hoping that would speed up the end of her torment. At last, she felt the hose being withdrawn. She opened her eyes and watched the doctor pull it from her nostril. She shivered at the sight of the blood-covered tubing.

Ruth Cochran stepped forward. She released Sarah's arm, handed her a cloth, and guided it to her nose. "Here, Sarah. Use this to stop your nose bleed."

Blood rushed from her nostrils, and she pressed the handkerchief to her nose. Her stomach churned, and she felt bile rising in her throat.

She turned her head to the side of the chair and expelled the contents of her stomach all over the floor. When she had finished, she sat back exhausted.

Matron Herndon stepped up. "Take her back to her cell for now. We'll try again tonight."

The words penetrated Sarah's foggy mind, and she froze in fear. They were going to do this again? Soft whimpers drifted from her throat. "No. Please, no."

Ruth Cochran bent over her. "If you'll eat, they won't do this again. Please say you will."

She wanted to yes to anything that would keep her from having to endure again the torture she had just been through.

Before she could speak, she remembered telling her father she would be an adversary. Instead of yielding to the kindness she heard in Ruth's voice, she closed her eyes. "I'm a political prisoner. I have done nothing wrong. I'll eat when we're released from this workhouse."

Matron Herndon leaned over her and sneered. "Have it your way, Princess. We'll send you to your cell for now, but we'll see you later."

Without saying another word Sarah allowed herself to be lifted and stood upright. Ruth held onto her to keep her from falling and supported her as she stumbled from the room. Minutes later Ruth helped her into her cell and onto her cot.

Blood still oozed from Sarah's nostrils, her stomach cramped, and her head swam in dizziness, but it felt good to be in a familiar bed. She pulled the sour smelling cover over her shoulders and turned to the wall.

Ruth left the cell and returned a few minutes later. She pulled the dirty blanket from the bed and spread another over Sarah. The fresh scent of soap drifted up to Sarah, and she curled into the softness of the clean coverlet.

The memory of a baseball field and a woman with the kindest smile she'd ever encountered entered her foggy mind, and she smiled. "Thank you, Ellen, for being my friend."

Sarah jerked from the edge of sleep and looked up. Ruth Cochran, not Ellen, stood over her. This wasn't a baseball field. It was a prison, and she was more alone than she had ever been in her life. "I think I must have talked in my sleep. Thank you for the clean blanket."

Ruth knelt down beside the bed. "Sarah, do you have any family I need to notify? Maybe Ellen."

Sarah felt the tears well in her eyes. "Ellen is not my family. She's someone who was very kind to me when my mother was dying."

"Let me get in touch with her. Surely she would want to help you now."

"No, I've made lots of choices that makes that impossible."

"Isn't there anyone else?"

Words someone else had spoken drifted through her mind. *If you ever need me, let me know. I'll come for you wherever you are. That's my promise to you.*

But Alex had another life now and probably didn't remember. A tear rolled from the corner of her eye. "No, there's no one else."

Rush squeezed Sarah's arm before she pushed to her feet. "I'm sorry this is happening to you. Get some sleep. I think they'll be back for you before very long."

Sarah heard the key turn in the lock of the cell. They would be here for her again soon. Until then she would rest.

Chapter 25

Alex leaned back in his chair and stared around the kitchen where he'd spent so many happy times with Ellen when he was growing up. He patted his stomach and smiled at his sister, brother-in-law, and Augie who sat at the table with him. "I sure have missed this good cooking since I've been in Memphis. I may be taking the train here more often just to get a good meal."

Edmund directed a smile toward his wife. "Let me echo your compliments to the cook. I don't think I've had a better meal, unless it possibly could have been last night."

Ellen jumped up and began to clear the dishes. "No need to butter me up. I just fixed what I had, but I gotta admit you sure did eat it."

"I liked it, Miss Ellen." Augie stopped with his fork in mid-air before shoveling in another mouthful. "Mr. Alex, could you pass those beans back over here?"

Alex handed Augie the bowl and looked around the table at his family. For the first time it dawned on him that Edmund now sat in the chair where he had always eaten. He supposed that was only fitting since he was now officially the head of this household.

He thought of all the things he and Ellen had talked about in this room, and now he was no longer a part of it. It saddened him, but at the same time he felt thankful Ellen had someone with her who truly loved her and would take care of her. He would always be a part of this family, and to him this would always be home.

Ellen glanced at him and smiled. "You sure are lost in thought. What's on your mind tonight?"

He chuckled and drank the last sip of coffee from his cup. "I'm thinking how happy I am for you and Edmund." He grinned at Ellen. "And I'm thinking how lucky he is to have a meal like this every night. It sure does get lonely eating by myself."

Ellen stood and began to stack their plates. "Well, I imagine that's going to end soon. When you going to ask your boss's daughter to marry you?"

Alex picked his cup up again but set it down when he saw there was nothing in it. "I think maybe at Christmas. I thought I would do it on her birthday in October, but I was busy that week and didn't get around to doing it."

Ellen cocked an eyebrow. "Didn't get around to it, huh? Sounds like you might be trying to put off doing something you really don't want to do."

Alex shook his head and frowned. "No, it's not that. She's really a nice girl with lots of good qualities. She can't help it because she's been raised to have everything she wants."

"Does she expect you to give her everything she wants?"

Alex sighed. "I don't know, Ellen. I guess we'll find out."

Ellen sank back down in her chair and stared at him. "You better find out before you marry her. It's too late afterwards to do anything about it."

"I know."

Ellen glanced at Edmund before she continued. "We just want you to be sure about what you're doing. You ain't never told me how much you love her and how you want to spend the rest of your life with her. I think if you really loved her you wouldn't be able to wait another day without proposing."

He sighed and rubbed the back of his neck. "Ellen, you have to realize not everyone has a great love happen to them like it did to you and Edmund. Sometimes you have to settle for what you have."

Sadness flickered in Ellen's eyes, and she shook her head. "You had that chance one time, and you gave it up. Isn't there anything you can do to make things right with that?"

He shook his head. "I don't think so. Sarah is off in Washington, and apparently she's happy as she can be. She made her choice a long time ago."

Ellen stared at him without blinking. "It seems to me you had a lot to do with that choice. Maybe you could do something to help change it."

"I don't think so." He pushed his chair back from the table and started to stand. He froze at the thought thundering in his head—*pray for Sarah.*

He closed his eyes and rubbed his temples with his fingertips, but the thought persisted. *Pray for Sarah.*

"Alex, what is it?" Ellen came around the table and put her arm around him.

He dropped his hands to his side and shook his head. "Maybe it's because we've been talking about her, but I have this overwhelming need to pray for Sarah."

"We do – everyday."

Alex grabbed his sister's hand in his. "No, you don't understand. We have to pray for her now."

Ellen looked at her husband and Augie. "Alex, are you all right?"

"We have to pray for Sarah right this minute." He dropped to his knees and heard the scraping of chairs. He looked around to see Ellen, Edmund, and Augie on their knees beside him.

"God, I don't know what's happening, but I know Sarah needs you. Protect her from whatever she's facing. Keep Your hand on her, and let her find peace in You. Let her know that we love her and will always be there for her. Amen."

"Amen," the three voices echoed.

Alex rose from his knees and stumbled toward the back door. Ellen ran after him. "Alex, where are you goin'?"

"I'm going to the arbor. I'll be back in a little while."

He ran out the back door and down the path toward the place that had always offered him sanctuary when he needed to spend time with God. He ducked under the dried vines of the grape arbor, fell on his knees, and cried out to the Lord. How long he stayed he didn't know, for the moon shone brightly through the trees when he reentered the quiet house.

He walked to the window of his room and looked up at the stars. "Sarah, wherever you are, remember what I said."

★ ★ ★ ★ ★

Sarah felt a hand on her shoulder shaking her awake. Ruth Cochran's voice drifted into her sleep. "Sarah, it's time to go back to the infirmary."

Sarah groaned and threw the blanket back. She pushed up on her elbows and tried to move her legs, but they wouldn't respond. "Can you help me up, Ruth?"

Ruth reached down and pulled her into a standing position. Sarah tried to take a step, but her knees wobbled and threatened to buckle under her weight. "I don't think I can walk alone."

Ruth placed her arm around Sarah. "Lean on me. I'll help you."

Sarah looked into Ruth's eyes. "It gets worse each time I go. I don't know how much more I can take."

"You've held out for five days. Give it up. It's not worth what you're going through."

"I can't give up."

Uncontrollable coughs shook Sarah's body, and she turned to the toilet to spit out the phlegm which rose from her throat. Her skin burned like fire, but she shivered with cold.

Ruth felt of Sarah's brow. "I think you have fever."

She shook her head. "It's nothing. Let's go get this over."

They stepped from the cell, and Sarah saw Laura Barnes being led back to her cell. Two guards supported her, and Laura smiled as they passed in the hallway.

After the ordeal, Ruth helped Sarah back to her bed. She covered her with the blanket and left the cell. She returned minutes later with another blanket. "I know you have fever."

Sarah felt like she watched a play being performed. She knew that Ruth and Henrietta were there, for she heard their voices. She knew what they said, but she couldn't respond.

Henrietta knelt beside Sarah and looked up at Ruth. "What do you think is the matter with her?"

"Forced feeding can cause pneumonia if the liquid gets in the lungs. The way she's fought it, I don't doubt that's what happened."

"Pneumonia? Oh, no. What will we do?"

There was silence for a moment and then Ruth replied. "We'll watch until tomorrow and see what happens. Do you know if she has any family?"

Sarah reached for Ruth and grabbed her arm. She tried to suck in a deep breath, but the pain in her chest made her cringe. "I-I have to t-tell you something," she gasped.

Ruth's warm hand wrapped around her. "What do you want me to know?"

Sarah tried to swallow, but her mouth was dry. She didn't know if she could speak, but she had to tell Ruth. "I am dying, and I want you to know about me." She hesitated at the coughing which seized her. When it passed, she continued. "I have an uncle and aunt, Charlie and Clara Weston. They live in Richland Creek, Tennessee. Tell them I want to be buried by my mother."

Henrietta dissolved into tears and threw herself face down on her bunk. Ruth patted Sarah's arm. "Nobody's gonna die, Sarah. But I'm glad you told me."

Sarah closed her eyes and succumbed to the swirling darkness pulling her downward.

Sarah sank back on the pillow and pressed her hands over her pounding head. Cramps gripped her stomach, and her body shivered with cold. Sounds of movement came from the other cells, and she knew another morning had arrived.

"Sarah, how are you feeling?" Henrietta's anxious face peered down at her.

"Horrible. I don't think I can get out of bed."

Henrietta felt of her forehead. "You still have fever. I'll tell the guards you need to go to the infirmary."

"No." Sarah reached up and grabbed Henrietta's hand. "I go to that place enough without having to be sick there. They don't have medicine, so I'm better off right here in my bed."

The key turned in the lock, and one of the guards walked into the small cell. "You gonna get up today and eat, or are you waiting for the servants to bring it to you?"

Henrietta stepped in front of the woman, her fists clenched at her sides. "She's sick. Can't you leave her alone? You've all done quite enough to her without coming in here and taunting her more. She's staying in bed today."

Sarah's eyes widened at the force with which Henrietta spoke. The guard glanced down at Sarah and back at the young woman blocking the bed. "Have it your way, but you'd better get yourself down the hall before all the food's gone."

The woman turned and walked from the cell. Henrietta swallowed and turned toward Sarah. "I can't believe I stood up to her. Maybe you're a good influence on me."

Sarah flashed a weak smile at her friend. "You be strong on your own. You're a kind, gentle girl, but you must stand up for yourself in this world."

"Maybe I'm on my way to doing that. I have to go to breakfast now, but I'll check on you later."

Sarah reached for Henrietta's arm. "What month is it? I can't seem to remember how much time has passed since we came here."

"It's the second week in November. We have about ten days left of our sentence. We're going to make it."

Henrietta stepped into the hallway, leaving Sarah alone with her thoughts. Ten days and her ordeal would be over. All she had to do was stay alive. Choking coughs shook her body, and her breath wheezed in her lungs. Ten days seemed like a lifetime.

"Are you ready?" The sinister voice chilled her blood, and she cringed at the sight of Matron Herndon. An ominous smile curled her lips, and her nostrils flared as she advanced toward her. She stopped beside the bed, threw the covers back, and jerked Sarah upright. "Let's go have something to eat."

★ ★ ★ ★ ★

The morning feeding had been horrible, but the second one of the day proved more of an ordeal. Sarah stumbled to the toilet and braced herself to keep from falling. Her body heaved and retched the thick liquid from the feeding. A sour smell floated up from the mixture floating in the bowl, and she wondered what they combined to make such a distasteful substance.

When she expelled the last bit, she doubled over in pain at the coughing spasms which attacked. She gasped for breath and tried to control the hacking which shook her body, but it only caused her to cough harder. Henrietta would return soon from supper, and she didn't want the girl to think her illness worse. She staggered to the bed and tumbled onto the cot just as the cellblock doors opened.

Henrietta rushed in and sat on the floor by Sarah's cot, her brows pulled across the top of her nose in a tiny frown. She looked over her shoulder and waited for the guard to lock the door before she spoke.

"Sarah. Are you awake?"

"Yes."

"I have some news, and I want to make sure you understand what I say. Can you hear me?"

Sarah tried to focus on Henrietta's face, but it kept floating before her eyes. "I can hear you. What is it?"

"At supper one of the kitchen workers told us there was an attack on the women picketing at the White House today. Agnes Morey, you know the one from Boston, was assaulted by two soldiers, and they jabbed her broken banner pole between her eyes. Dora Lewis, that sweet little grandmother from Philadelphia, was mauled by three young boys."

Sarah tried to prop up on her elbows. "Are they all right?"

"I don't know. They were arrested, and the rumor is that they'll arrive here tonight."

"Sarah and Henrietta." They jumped at the intrusion of the voice and turned to see Ruth standing outside the bars. "Watch yourselves tonight. I'm off duty, but some of the guards are upset over the day's events. Get in your bunks and stay there."

Ruth cast a furtive glance down the hallway and moved toward the exit. Sarah lay back, her head a jumble of unanswered questions. Why would the guards be angry at them?

She watched Henrietta slip into her bed and smiled at her. She closed her eyes and waited for morning.

Sarah hadn't been asleep long when frenzied cries awakened her. Screams poured from the cells down the hallway, and the thud of crashing nightsticks echoed in the passage. Hurried footsteps approached their door, and a key turned in the lock.

Sarah tried to focus on the guard at the door, but she could only tell it was a man. His voice thundered again. "Get up, prisoners."

Two other guards, their faces masked in rage, pushed past him and reached for her. Sarah shrank from the figures standing over her and scooted against the wall, but they grabbed her by the arms and pulled her from the bed. She tried to wrench free of the men's grasps, but in her feverish condition she could only offer a feeble resistance.

Henrietta's scream bounced off the cell walls. "No! Leave her alone. She's sick." Out of the corner of her eye Sarah saw Henrietta spring from her bed and throw herself against the two attackers. One of them turned, picked up the girl, and hurled her against the wall. Henrietta's body crumpled at the impact, and her lifeless body toppled in a heap on the floor.

"No, no. Help her." Sarah tried once again to wiggle free from her captors, but they tightened their grip.

Someone leaned close to her, and a menacing voice whispered in her ear. "You'd better worry about helping yourself. You've given us nothing but trouble since the day you came. It's about time you got what you deserve."

The two men drug her, twisting and turning, toward the door. She summoned all the saliva she could in her dry mouth and spat the small ball at one of the guards.

He stopped and wiped his face with his free hand. He stared at the wetness between his fingers before he looked into her eyes. He stood there, a snarl curling his lower lip, before he raised his hand and slapped her with a force that snapped her head back. He grabbed her hands and raised her arms above her head.

"Let's let her cool off some."

Cold metal encircled her wrists, and Sarah felt her body being lifted. She heard a snap and felt the guards release her. Her full weight dropped toward the floor, and she hung suspended, her body pressed against the bars.

Sharp pains shot through her body at the pressure being exerted on her joints. She looked at her arms stretched above her head and the shackles that cut into her wrists. She stretched her legs downward in an effort to stand, but her feet dangled above the floor. Her toes barely brushed the surface.

She twisted and turned her head in an attempt to glimpse Henrietta, but she couldn't. "Henrietta, are you all right? Henrietta, wake up."

No answer came from the still form, and Sarah sobbed in fear for her friend. Screams still echoed through the hallway. Sarah pressed her face into the bars and tried to see where the sounds came from.

Two guards at the end of the passage held a woman down, her back bent across an iron bench. The hand of one encircled her throat while he beat her about the face with his other. Another man held and twisted her wrists over her head.

Other uniformed officers raced in and out of the small cells, and cries of pain and fear rang out each time they entered a new area. Had they gone mad? Why were they doing this to the prisoners?

Sarah pulled at her shackles, but they wouldn't budge.

"Going somewhere?"

She jerked her head up and stared through the bars into the menacing eyes of a guard. "Why are you doing this? We've done nothing to deserve this."

The man glanced over her shackled form and smirked. "I thought in your work you could stand anything. Sweet dreams."

Without speaking again, the officers pushed the woman who had been beaten in the hall into her small room and banged shut all the doors they had entered. They walked from the cellblock and turned off all lights on the way out.

For the first time since coming to Occoquan, no light shone through the darkness. The black night crept across the floor and obscured everything from sight. Wails drifted from the cells through the murky hallway.

"Why, oh, why?" a woman's shrill voice wailed.

From the other end of the hall someone groaned in agony. "Sweet Jesus, help us."

Sarah pressed her head between her arms to block the pitiful cries, but the weeping surrounded her from every direction.

Suddenly a voice rose above all the others, a soothing one lifted in song. "Amazing grace, how sweet the sound," it sang.

A hush fell over the area, crying ceased, and voices joined in. The song, a familiar one from her days of attending church with her mother, engulfed her. The voices sang on and on, reaching a crescendo with the final words, "We've no less days to sing God's praise than when we've just begun."

The cellblock quieted, and sobs no longer could be heard. Soon sounds of sleep filled the night, but Sarah's aching and feverish body still hung from the bars.

The minutes turned to hours. Her arms felt like they were being pulled from their sockets by her weight, and any attempt to change her position added extra pain. Coughing bouts wracked her chest, and her skin grew hotter by the minute. She shivered from the cold and wondered at her temperature.

"Henrietta." She called out to her friend from time to time, but no answer came.

The clock from the sewing room downstairs chimed midnight, and she realized six more hours had to pass before the new shift of guards would arrive. Would they release her, or would they leave her hanging as a warning to others?

She felt herself slipping toward unconsciousness and fought to stay awake. She could barely breathe now, and she knew her lungs were filling with fluid. If she slept, she might drown in the mucous filling her body.

Her head lolled against her shoulder, and she tried to straighten to relieve her labored breathing. Her chest hurt, and she felt as if she was drowning. She opened her mouth to scream for help, but she only succeeded in producing a soft moan. Was there nobody to help? Was she to die alone hanging with her arms suspended above her head?

Then the words of the song the women had sung earlier drifted into her fevered mind, and she thought of her mother. She had always received such pleasure from attending church, singing hymns, and praying. Sarah had enjoyed it once, too, until her father's death. Her faith had waned when he died and had disappeared with the passing of her mother. She hadn't prayed in years.

In her mind she could see the church at Richland Creek and the faces of the people who worshiped there. She hadn't intended to like them, but she had come to know their kindness and their concern for her and her mother. Uncle Charlie and Aunt Clara had supplied them a house to live in, and Ellen had welcomed her from the first.

Then there'd been the most important one of all—Alex. She would never forget how he had looked the day he rode through the rain after her mother's funeral to tell her how much he loved her. He had begged her not to leave, and she had walked away from him and the love he offered.

266

The truth flashed into her head, and her body jerked against her bonds. God hadn't forsaken her during the days when she felt so alone. He had taken her to a community of people who offered her love and support, but she had been so filled with self-pity she couldn't see what He'd given her. She had made the choice to turn her back on Him and everyone else who loved her. Instead she had chosen the false friendship of Roger Thorne and his aunt.

Tonight she hung shackled to the bars of her cell and had listened to the voices around her sing of God's amazing grace. It suddenly became clear to her that God had never deserted her. He was only waiting for her to come back to Him. She wasn't alone. She had never been alone. All she had to do was reach out to Him.

She closed her eyes and prayed for the first time in years. "Forgive me, Lord, for the years I've wasted, and the hurt I've given to others. Thank you for loving me and dying for my sins. Take care of Alex and give him a good life. I give myself into Your hands."

"Alex, I love you," she whispered. "Bury me by my mother."

Her head dipped, her body sagged, and she welcomed the blackness overtaking her.

Chapter 26

Sarah opened her eyes and turned her nose into her pillow. The smell of disinfectant hovered in the air, and she knew she wasn't lying on her cot. She could make out the forms of several people beside her bed, but she couldn't tell who they were. She lay very still and tried to make out the words above her that were being spoken in hushed tones.

"How is she, doctor?" The voice came from far away and sounded like someone calling into the depths of a well.

"She's very ill. The malnutrition coupled with the pneumonia has caused serious infection throughout her body."

"Will she live?"

"I don't know."

"You must save her. She doesn't deserve this."

Sarah blinked again and stared at the figure standing by her bed. "Ruth? Is that you? How's Henrietta?"

A warm hand touched her cheek, and she turned her face toward the voice. "Yes, I'm here. Henrietta's fine. She just had a bad bump on the head. How're you feeling?"

Her muscles contracted as another coughing spasm shook her body. She tried to raise her head, but it was no use. When the spell had subsided, the reality of her situation became clear. A tear rolled from her eye. "I don't think I'll make it, Ruth."

"Don't say that. Of course you'll be all right."

The memory of what had happened in the cell returned, and she smiled. "It doesn't matter now. Everything's fine with me. I'm ready."

"Sarah, don't talk that way. Do you want me to call your uncle and aunt?"

She lay back against the pillow, her eyes closed. Alex's face drifted into her mind, and she smiled. "Not my family. Someone else. Call Alex Taylor."

Ruth leaned closer. "How can I reach him?"

"Telephone. He's a lawyer at Buckley, Anderson, and Pike law firm in Memphis. Tell him I remembered his promise. It's important for him to know that."

"I'll call him."

Ruth turned to leave, but Sarah grabbed her skirt. Ruth bent over her. "What is it?"

"You must tell him I remembered his promise, and I need him to do something for me."

Ruth's hand covered hers. "What do you want him to do, Sarah?"

She gasped, her ragged breath stressing each word. "I want him to bury me beside my mother."

Ruth patted Sarah's hand before she slipped it back underneath the cover. "I'll tell him. Now you get some rest."

Sarah smiled, sank back on the pillow, and surrendered to sleep again.

★ ★ ★ ★ ★

Alex wrote his signature on the last document in the stack Lydia had brought him and handed it to her. "That's the last one. Do you have anything else for me before I leave for the day?"

Lydia took the last paper, laid it on the stack in her arms, and shook her head. "No, sir. That's all I have for you today. I'll take care of these so you and Larraine can be on your way."

269

She glanced at Larraine who sat with her legs crossed and her elbows resting on the arms of the chair in front of Alex's desk. Larraine straightened and smiled at Lydia. "Are you sure you're through with him now?"

Lydia gave a curt nod, but Alex didn't miss the affectionate gleam in her eye. "He's all yours, Miss Larraine. I hope you have a wonderful dinner tonight."

Larraine rose, walked to the middle of the room, and struck a pose worthy of a stage actress as she turned in a small circle. "Alex and I are having dinner with his sister and brother-in-law who are in town. Do you think I'll pass inspection?"

Lydia smiled and nodded. "I know they will love you just like everybody else at the firm does."

Larraine crossed her arms and arched an eyebrow in Alex's direction. "I hope so. It's certainly taken Alex long enough to decide he wanted to introduce me to his family."

Alex's face grew warm, and he pushed to his feet. "Edmund's practice keeps him busy. They don't get to Memphis often. But there's no need to worry. They'll enjoy meeting you."

"I hope so." Larraine tilted her head to one side and smiled at him. "Like Lydia said, I want them to love me like everybody else here at the firm does."

"I'm sure they will." Alex dropped his gaze back to his desk, picked up the pen he'd used, and placed it in the top desk drawer. Taking a deep breath, he walked to the coat rack where Larraine had hung her coat when she walked in. He removed it and held it up for her. "Ready to go?"

He swallowed hard at the momentary look of disappointment that flashed on her face. She wanted him to reassure her that he loved her and would make sure his sister liked her, but the words stuck in his throat. Words like love and affection were no longer a part of his vocabulary. He had substituted companionship and friendship for them. Larraine knew this, but at times she appeared to want more.

She tilted her chin up and smiled as she walked toward him. "I can't wait to meet your family."

He held the coat as she slipped her arms into it and then reached for his topcoat and hat. Lydia crossed the office and opened the door. "Have a good time tonight."

Alex nodded. "We will, Lydia. I'll see you tomorrow."

Larraine had just stepped out of the door when the phone on his desk rang. Lydia frowned and turned toward his desk. "I'll take that, Mr. Taylor, and leave a message for you."

He shook his head. "No need for that, Lydia. Officially I'm still at work. I'll get it." He tossed his coat and hat on a chair, strode toward his desk, and picked up the phone. "Hello."

"I have a long distance call for Mr. Alex Taylor."

Alex frowned at the voice of the operator. Which of his clients would be calling him long distance at this time of the day? "This is Alex Taylor."

"Caller, I have your party on the line. You may go ahead now."

"Mister Taylor, my name is Ruth Cochran. I'm calling from Fairfax, Virginia."

He searched his mind for a client who had ties to anyone in Virginia, but he could think of no one. "I'm sorry. Have we met?"

"No, we haven't. I'm a friend of Sarah's."

The breath left his body, and he grabbed the edge of his desk to steady himself. "S-Sarah? H-how do you know her?"

"I'm a guard at Occoquan Workhouse in Fairfax, Virginia. Sarah asked me to call you."

Alex's fingers tightened on the telephone receiver. "She did? Why?"

"Mr. Taylor, are you aware that Sarah came to Washington to work with Alice Paul and the National Woman's Party?"

"Yes."

"She began demonstrating with the group in front of the White House nearly two months ago, and she was arrested for picketing. She's been a prisoner here ever since."

"What?" Alex exploded. "A prisoner? How is she?"

"That's why I'm calling. She's very ill, and I thought her family needed to be called. She told me she had an aunt and uncle, but she wanted me to call you. She needs someone here for her."

Visions of Sarah in prison swam before his eyes. Why hadn't Ben let him know? The answer popped into his mind right away. Ben was probably still on his honeymoon. But someone else in the office was supposed to call him. All this time he had assumed she was all right, and she was locked up in a prison cell.

He closed his eyes and rubbed his hand across his forehead. "What's the matter with her?"

"She's suffering from malnutrition because she went on a hunger strike, and now she has pneumonia. The doctor says there is so much infection he's not sure she'll live."

Alex's heart raced at the words he heard. "Not live? It's that serious."

"Mr. Taylor, I could lose my job for telling you this, but I think someone needs to know. After Sarah went on a hunger strike, the warden ordered her to be force fed. They pushed a tube through her nostril and down her throat and fed her with a liquid. The doctor thinks some of that got into her lungs and caused the pneumonia." A soft sob came over the line. "Mr. Taylor, when she was so sick, they shackled her to the bars of her cell and left her there all night. If she dies, it's because they've killed her. Can you get word to her uncle that he needs to come?"

Alex's heart pounded in his ears, and he shook his head. "There's no need for that. I'll leave on the first train to Washington. Will you tell her I'm coming?"

"I'll tell her, and one more thing. She insisted I tell you something else. Let me see if I can remember the words correctly." Ruth paused before she spoke again. "She said—tell him I remembered his promise, and I want him to bury me beside my mother."

Alex bent over as if he'd been punched in the stomach, tears filled his eyes. "Please tell her I remember, too, and I'm on my way. Thank you for calling, Miss Cochran. I'll be in Washington as fast as the train can get me there. And thank you for taking care of Sarah."

He hung up the phone and turned toward Larraine and Lydia. Tears stood in Larraine's eyes, and she glanced at Lydia. "Would you excuse us for a few minutes, please?"

Lydia dropped her gaze and nodded. "Of course."

Larraine waited until the door closed behind Lydia before she walked over and stopped in front of him. She threw her purse into the chair where she'd sat a few minutes earlier. "I suppose that was about Sarah Jordan."

Alex's eyes grew wide. "How did you know her name?"

Larraine's eyes darkened, and she clenched her teeth before responding. "My father told me about your little suffrage friend when you first came to the firm. I have to admit I was glad when she went to Washington. I thought with her out of the way things would work out for us. I guess I was wrong."

Alex raked his hand through his hair and frowned. "Larraine, I'm sorry. I made her a promise that if she ever needed me I would come for her. That was a guard from Occoquan Workhouse on the phone. Sarah is a prisoner there and is dying of pneumonia. I can't abandon her. I have to go."

Larraine shook her head. "No, you don't. Any promise you made to her is no longer valid. I know you're going to ask me to marry you, and I don't want my future husband running off to help out some old love. In fact I forbid you to go."

Alex narrowed his eyes and stared at Larraine. "I can't believe I heard you correctly. You forbid me to go?"

She squared her shoulders and nodded. "I do. I'm sure my father would agree. Your place is here." She turned toward the chair, picked up her purse, and smiled. "Now let's have no more of this nonsense. Your sister and brother-in-law are waiting for us to pick them up so we can go to the club for dinner. Get your hat and let's go."

Alex stared at her, and in that moment he saw what the rest of his life would be like if he married Larraine. How could he have been so blind to think he could marry a woman he didn't love? His failure to support Sarah's dream didn't mean he had to sentence himself to such a life.

He picked up his hat and coat from the chair and took a deep breath. "Larraine, I think we should cancel our dinner to-night. I'll make your excuses to my sister. Right now I need to go home and pack so I can be on the first train to Washington in the morning."

Her face turned crimson, and her mouth pulled into a straight line. She advanced toward him, and jabbed her index finger into his chest. "Didn't you hear me? You're not going to Washington."

He pushed her finger away. "Didn't you hear me?" he hissed. "Sarah is dying. I have to go."

"Call her family. Let them take care of her." Suddenly the anger on her face disappeared, and fear replaced it. She lunged at him, wrapped her arms around him, and pressed her cheek to his chest. "Please don't go, Alex. I love you. I don't want that woman to come between us. Please stay with me."

Alex grasped her shoulders and pushed her back until he could stare into her face. "I'm sorry, Larraine. I tried to make it work with us, but I couldn't. I love her, and I can't turn my back on her. Now I've got to go."

Her palm cracked across his face, and he staggered backwards from the blow. She gritted her teeth and glared at him. "If you walk out that door, don't expect to come back. Your job won't be waiting for you."

He nodded. "Somehow that doesn't seem too important at the moment. Tell your father I appreciate the opportunity of working here, but it just hasn't been a match. Maybe we'll meet in court some time."

Before she could respond, he strode across the floor and jerked the door open. Lydia stood in the hallway. "Mr. Taylor, I overheard part of your conversation, and I checked with the depot. There is a train leaving at seven in the morning headed toward Washington."

He smiled and nodded. "Thank you, Lydia. I'll miss you."

"I'll miss you, too, sir."

Alex turned and hurried from the office. For the first time since coming to Memphis, peace washed over him, and joy filled his soul. He had no idea what he would find in Washington, but Sarah had remembered to call for him. Now all he could do was pray that God would spare her so he could try to make her love him again.

Chapter 27

Alex's fingers, white from gripping the brim of the hat he held, trembled at his surroundings. The stark walls and the sparse furniture of the Occoquan Workhouse receiving area where he stood with Ellen and Edmund offered a depressing entrance into the facility. Smells of cooking food, perspiration, and human waste mingled in the air to produce a pungent odor that burned his nose and throat.

A door opened and a middle-aged woman entered the room. The corners of her mouth drew down in a scowl, and her gaze darted over each of them. She stopped in front of them and crossed her arms. "I'm Matron Herndon. I understand you're here to see one of our inmates."

Alex stepped forward and studied the woman's face. "Yes, we want to see Sarah Jordan."

The woman waved her hand in dismissal. "I'm afraid that's impossible. She's in solitary right now. Good day."

She turned to leave, but Alex raised his voice. "Just a minute. I don't think you understand. We've come a great distance, and it's important we see her."

The matron turned slowly and frowned. She glanced over her shoulder at two guards who entered from a door behind her. "I've told you it's not possible, and that's final."

Alex took a step toward her. "We understand Sarah is very ill. If that's the case, we insist on seeing her."

She pointed to the two officers who moved closer to her. "I'm telling you for the last time, you can't see her. Now get out of here before I have you thrown out."

Alex moved closer to her and shook his finger in her face. "Have us thrown out, and we'll go straight to the newspapers and every judge in this city. If we find out you've harmed Sarah in any way, we'll press charges against you for assault. If she should die, it'll be murder."

Matron Herndon's eyes flared, and she took a step backward. Alex pressed on, his finger wagging. "We know she's here, so you'd better take us to your infirmary. I want my brother-in-law to examine her, or I'm going to tear this place apart!"

"Matron, why don't you let them see her? It would be better than having newspaper reporters all over the place."

Alex glanced in the direction of the sound and saw another guard entering. Her voice was identical to the one on the telephone. She moved beside the matron and placed her hand on her superior's shaking shoulder.

"Let me take them to the infirmary, and you just go on with whatever you were doing. I won't let them stay long."

Matron Herndon frowned. "I don't know. Warden Whittaker doesn't want any visitors."

The guard smiled. "I know. But you may be saving him more trouble than he needs right now. The newspapers are already questioning his administration of this place, and we don't want to give them anything else to hound him about."

The matron hesitated for a few seconds and nodded her head. "Maybe you're right. I suppose it wouldn't hurt just to let them see the girl. All right, take them to the infirmary." With that she motioned for the guards behind her to follow, and they disappeared through one of the doors.

Alex started to thank her, but the woman raised her fingers to her lips to signal silence. She walked to the door, placed her ear against, and turned back to face Alex. "I'm Ruth Cochran. Follow me."

Alex breathed a sigh of relief. "I'm so glad you came along. I don't know if I could have bluffed her much longer. Thanks for persuading her."

Ruth nodded. "Matron Herndon's not very smart. She just follows orders. You're lucky the warden's not here right now, or you'd never have gotten inside."

Alex, Ellen, and Edmund hurried behind Ruth down a long corridor and descended a narrow stairway into the basement. The smell of antiseptic drifted through the air of the hallway. Doors on either side opened into rooms filled with beds, and groans rose from the crowded quarters. Alex sensed the suffering humanity he passed, but he stared straight ahead. His thoughts today centered on Sarah and her nearness.

Ruth stopped before a closed door and turned to face them. "You don't have very long so make it quick."

Alex nodded. "We don't want to get you into any trouble, so we'll hurry."

Ruth stepped aside for them to enter. "I told her you were coming, but I don't know if she understood. Please brace yourself before you see her. She's very ill."

Alex reached for the doorknob, but his hand trembled so he couldn't turn it. He looked over his shoulder at Ellen and Edmund, swallowed, and tried again. The door creaked open, and they stepped into the room. Rays of light filtered through the tiny window over the bed and revealed a still figure lying there.

His legs buckled at the sight of Sarah's white face against the pillow, and he fell on his knees beside her. Ellen pressed a handkerchief to her nose, gasped, and walked to the other side of the bed. Edmund stood behind her, his hand on her shoulder.

Alex studied the still figure and looked for signs of his beloved Sarah in this pitiful creature before him. Her dry, white skin appeared thin, and bones protruded from her skeleton frame. Bald spots covered her head, and her chest rose slowly in shallow breaths. The inflamed area around her left nostril drew Alex's attention, and he looked up at Ruth. "What's the matter with her nose? It's crusted over with sores."

"That's from the tubing they used when they force fed her. Her nose would bleed for hours after each one."

Edmund stepped around Ellen and leaned over to study Sarah. "Force feeding? That's a form of torture. It has nothing to do with needed nutrition."

Ruth's eyes teared. "I know."

Alex glanced up at his brother-in-law. "Edmund, what do you think?"

Edmund felt of Sarah's forehead before he took a stethoscope from his coat pocket. He placed the ends in his ears and the other against Sarah's chest. Concern shadowed his face as he lifted her emaciated wrist to check her pulse.

"It's not good, Alex. We've got to get her some decent care."

Sarah stirred, and Alex grabbed her small hand. He leaned close to her. "Sarah, it's Alex. Can you hear me?" Her eyelids fluttered, and she stared upward. Alex pressed her hand tighter. "Look at me, Sarah. I'm here."

Slowly she turned her head, looked into his eyes, and smiled. "Alex, I'm so glad you're here." Her words were no more than a whisper, and he leaned closer to hear her.

Alex wiped at the tears filling his eyes. "I came as soon as I knew you needed me. I'm here to take care of you."

Sarah turned her head and looked to the other side of the bed. "Ellen, you're with me, too."

Ellen leaned closer. "Yes, child, we're all here. Edmund, too."

Sarah reached for Ellen's hand and pulled it and Alex's across her chest. "I'm glad you'll both be here when I die."

Terror ripped Alex's heart. "No! You're not going to die. We're going to get you out of here, and we're going home."

Sarah smiled. "I've come home, Alex. I came home to Jesus."

She closed her eyes, and her hands lay still. Alex jumped up from the floor. "Edmund, we've got to get her out of her so you can get her well. What should we do?"

Ruth had been quiet since they'd been in the room. She stepped up beside Alex. "I think you should go to Cameron House. Talk to the people there. You've seen what this place is like. Tell them they've got to get their friends out of here."

"What's Cameron House?" Alex demanded.

"It's the headquarters for the pickets. It's near the White House. Any taxi can get you there. Tell them these women can't stand another night of terror like they suffered last week."

"Night of terror?"

"The guards went on a rampage, beating and choking the inmates. Sarah had her arms shackled to bars above her head and hung there all night."

Alex shook his head in disbelief. "I can't believe any human being would treat someone that way. Thank you, Ruth, for all your help."

He started for door with Ellen and Edmund right behind. Nothing mattered at the moment but getting Sarah away from this place before it killed her. "We'll get her released. Please don't let her die before we do."

His mind raced as he rushed up the stairs from the infirmary and out the front door of the prison. They didn't have a moment to waste if they were to save Sarah's life. He hoped they hadn't arrived too late.

Sarah's head throbbed, and her body ached all over. She tried to find her way through the darkness around her, but it hurt to move. A weight crushed her chest, and she thought it might go away if she could just quit breathing.

She'd had a new dream while she was asleep, and she smiled at the memory of it. Alex and Ellen held her hands and told her they would take her home. She wanted to go home. Not back to Mrs. Simpson's school, but to the little house at Richland Creek where she and her mother had lived.

She wanted to sit under the willow tree with Alex and watch him skip stones across the pond. She wanted to go to baseball games and dinners after church on Sunday and run through the yard without wearing shoes. That's what she wanted, but she would only be going home to be buried next to her mother. Then they would both be with Jesus.

"Alex." Her hand reached up, and someone clasped it. But it wasn't Alex.

"It's Ruth, Sarah. I'm here with you."

Sarah smiled. "Thank you for being so kind to me, Ruth."

She felt the darkness washing over her again, but she felt no fear, only peace. She was ready for whatever was to come.

Cameron House hummed with activity. Alex had never seen anything like it, and the dismay on Ellen's face told him she agreed. Typewriters clicked, women darted about displaying signs on poles, and voices chattered throughout the room. The energy of the workers contrasted with the lines of fatigue on their faces and the weariness in their sagging shoulders.

Alex shook his head in bewilderment. "It's hard to imagine Sarah being a part of this."

Ellen nodded. "I know. When we saw those pickets at the White House before we came here, I wondered how she must have felt standing out there taking the insults like those women did today."

Alex shuddered at the thought. "She tried to tell me how she felt about suffrage, but I wouldn't listen. I was too caught up in my own feelings. I thought I could make her change and be like I wanted."

"You did what you thought best at the time. Now don't you go blaming yourself for any of this mess." Ellen grabbed his arm and gave it a shake.

"But if I had offered to help her go after her dream, she might never have left with Roger Thorne." Alex's pulse pounded at the mention of the man's name.

"But if, but if," Ellen echoed. "You can't go back and undo the past. We gotta figure out what to do about the present."

A young woman approached them from an office in the back. "Hello, my name is Marian Douglas. I'm sorry to keep you waiting. I was on the phone when you got here. Please come with me."

They wedged between the busy workers and followed her into a small room at the rear of the room. She motioned them to sit and closed the door behind her. "I understand you've been out to Occoquan. What were your impressions of the workhouse?"

"It's a disgrace and an abomination." The words exploded from Alex's mouth. "Sarah looked like a skeleton. One of the guards told us she had been force fed with a tube up her nose, and she hung shackled from her cell bars all one night last week."

Marian's elbows rested on the desk in front of her, and she pressed the tips of her fingers together. "We've heard about the night of terror, as its being called. We also know about the forced feedings, food with worms in it, and the filth of the place."

Alex shook his head in surprise. "Then why haven't you done anything?"

"Mr. Taylor, you must remember that our pickets were sent to Occoquan because we embarrassed the President of the United States. Everyone he's sent to investigate tell him all the reports of abuse in the facility are false."

"Well, I've seen the place, and there's a guard there who might be willing to testify. What can we do to get Sarah out of there?"

Marian sat back in her chair and stared at Alex for several seconds. "Since word leaked out about the night of terror, the newspapers have reported about the ordeal of the jailed pickets. We've engaged two lawyers, Dudley Field Malone and Matthew O'Brien, to represent the women at Occoquan. I'm going to their office this afternoon. I'll tell them what you've told me."

"I called their office before I left Memphis. One of my law school friends works there. He was supposed to keep me informed about Sarah, but he's away on his honeymoon. I know they're working to get the women released, but it's urgent we get Sarah out of there. She won't live much longer."

"We want to get all our friends out. Why don't you stay here while I'm gone? I should be back in about two hours."

Ellen stood and extended her hand. "Thank you for helpin' our Sarah. She means a lot to us."

The door to the room suddenly burst open, and a young girl rushed in. "Are you really Mr. Alex? Have you come to help Miss Sarah?"

Alex rose slowly from his chair. "Why, yes, I am. How did you know my name?"

The girl's cheeks flamed, and she ducked her head. "Oh, I beg your pardon for flyin' in here like this, but I just about burst when I heard you were here."

Marian walked over to the girl and hugged her. "This is Dora Lewis. She came here with Sarah, and she's been about to go out of her mind ever since Sarah's arrest. I'll leave her to tell you the story of how they came to be here."

Marian glanced at a watch pinned to the front of her dress and frowned. "I have to go, or I'm going to be late. Please make yourselves at home while I'm gone." She grabbed a coat from the rack near the door and hurried from the room.

Ellen rose and motioned the girl to sit in a chair next to her. "I'm Ellen, Alex's sister. Tell us how you came to be with Sarah."

Dora edged closer and opposite Ellen. "Miss Sarah told me all about how good you were to her when she and her mama moved to Richland Creek. She said. . ."

Ellen smiled and held up a hand. "Dora, tell us how you came to be with Sarah."

Dora grinned. "Oh, I'm sorry. I get carried away when I'm excited, and I'm just so glad you're here. Well, you see, I worked as a maid at Mrs. Simpson's school, and Miss Sarah was real good to me. When they decided to come to Washington, they brought me along, too."

The words poured from Dora's mouth, and Sarah's life in the sixteen months since leaving Richland Creek unfolded. Alex sat with his elbows on his knees and his hands covering his face. The more Dora talked, the lower his heart sank.

When she finally completed the story, Alex raised stricken eyes to his sister. "No wonder God kept telling me to pray for her. I knew she needed me, but I didn't know where she was."

Tears rolled down Ellen's cheeks, and she knelt in front of Alex. She cupped his face in her hands and looked into her eyes. "You didn't know, but God did. Your prayers have gotten her this far, and they're gonna git her home."

Edmund dropped to his knees by his wife. He encircled her shoulders with one arm and placed the other around Alex.

"I think we need to pray for the lawyers who'll meet this afternoon. Let's ask God to give them the wisdom to get these women out of that prison."

Dora joined the group, and the four bowed their heads as they petitioned God to spare Sarah and reunite the jailed pickets with their families.

Chapter 28

The hands on the clock above the desk moved slowly. Alex paced the floor, his hands jammed into his pockets. Marian had said two hours, but it had already been over three. Where could she be? He froze at the sounds of shouts rising in the outer office. The door flew open, and Marian stood there looking as if she had just finished a race. Red splotches covered her cheeks, and her breath came in short spurts.

She raised her arms in victory. "It's a miracle."

Ellen and Edmund who had dozed in their chairs jumped up, and Alex ran to Marian. "What happened?"

Marian struggled to catch her breath. "I'm sorry I've been gone so long, but I rushed back as quickly as I could. I didn't want to get your hopes up before I left, but I knew that Mr. Malone and Mr. O'Brien planned to meet with Judge Edmund Waddill in Alexandria today to request a habeas corpus hearing for the jailed pickets. I've been at their office waiting to hear from them."

"And?"

"Judge Waddill ordered the White House pickets be brought to his court for a hearing tomorrow, but he released all of them into Mr. Malone's custody. He's making arrangements now for their transportation here to Cameron House."

"Can we meet him there and take Sarah to a hospital?"

Marian nodded as another big smile lit her face. "The receptionist has called for a taxi. You're welcome to go."

286

Alex headed toward the door but stopped when Dora cried out. "Wait. Don't leave yet."

She ran from the room and returned in minutes. A locket dangled from her fingers, and she held it out to Alex. "Give this to Miss Sarah. I kept if safe for her."

Alex's fingers closed around the locket, and he clutched it in his hands. "Thank you, Dora."

Ellen put her arm around Dora and looked into her eyes. "Why don't you come with us and give it to her yourself?"

A smile lit Dora's face. "You mean I can come see Miss Sarah get released?"

"Well, you can do that, and then I 'spect you'll have to go to the hospital to help nurse her back to health. And then I guess you'll just have to come back to the farm in Tennessee and help me get her good as new."

Dora threw her arms around Ellen, and sobs shook her body. "Miss Sarah said nobody was kinder than you, and now I know it's true."

Alex looked over at Edmund as the two women exited the room. "Well, I guess Ellen's found someone to take over my empty bedroom."

Edmund threw back his head and laughed. "That's my Ellen. Lord love her, there'll never be another like her."

Tears filled Alex's eyes at the sight of his sister, brother-in-law, and a girl he'd never met before today. They all shared a bond. They loved Sarah and wanted to see her restored to health. He only hoped they weren't too late.

★ ★ ★ ★ ★

What was happening to her? She cried out and struggled to resist being pulled upward, but strong arms lifted her. "Wrap this blanket around her. She's burning up with fever."

287

A familiar voice sounded in her ear, and lips brushed her forehead. Soothing words drifted into her ear, and she snuggled closer to the warm body that cradled her and offered security.

Her nose nuzzled soft fabric and inhaled the familiar scent of homemade soap she remembered from long ago. She opened her mouth and tried to call out Ellen's name, but no sound emerged. The arms tightened around her. "It's Alex, Sarah. You're safe now." She relaxed and felt the darkness washing over her again.

Where was she, and what was happening to her? Sometimes she felt something cool wash across her face and heard voices speak words she didn't understand. "Fever. Cold water." Maybe they said more, but she felt too tired to listen.

Hot liquid poured into her mouth, and she cringed at the fire it ignited as it slithered over the rawness of her throat. More words drifted into her foggy mind. "Know it hurts. Good for you."

Gentle hands pushed and probed her body, and she winced in pain. She tried to fight off her attackers, but weakness prevented that. All she could do was lie still and endure whatever they did to her.

She had no idea how long she endured the torture, but it seemed to go on forever. All she wanted was to sleep, but they kept waking her. Finally she opened her eyes and blinked. She lay in a bed in a darkened room. She ran her fingers over the crisp sheet and blanket that covered her. These weren't the covers she was accustomed to at Occaquan. She inhaled, and a sweet smell of lilac rose to her nostrils.

Her eyes adjusted to the darkness, and she realized a small lamp burned on a table next to the bed. A chair with a sleeping figure slumped in it sat next to the table. She blinked to focus her eyes and rubbed them with her fingers.

She blinked again and concentrated on the person in the chair. Her heart thudded in her chest. Was it really him? Her hand reached toward him.

"Alex?" Her voice cracked, and her throat constricted in pain.

A snore drifted from the chair. Sarah swallowed and tried again, this time with more force. "Alex?"

His head jerked up, and he sprang toward the bed. Rumpled hair tumbled over his sleepy eyes, and the shadow of a beard darkened his tired face. He fell on his knees beside her and grabbed her hand. His gaze raked her face. "Sarah, you're awake!"

For a moment all she could do was stare into the face that had filled her dreams for months. Then her gaze traveled to the white walls of the room, and she frowned. "Where am I?" It took all her strength to mutter those three words.

"You're in a hospital," he said. "You've been very sick. How do you feel now?"

"Tired." She closed her eyes and sucked in a deep breath. Her mind was playing tricks on her. Alex couldn't really be here. Slowly she opened her eyes and frowned. "Am I dreaming, or are you really here?"

He pulled her hand to his mouth and kissed her knuckles. "You're not dreaming. I'm here and thankful that you're finally awake."

She swallowed and flinched at the raw soreness in her throat. "B-but how? I don't understand."

He smiled. "I'll tell you all about it later. But for now, you need to rest so you can get better."

She closed her eyes and gave a slight nod of her head. "I'm tired, but I don't want to go to sleep. I'm afraid you won't be here when I wake up."

His hand stroked her hair, and he leaned closer. "Sleep, sweet Sarah, and I promise you I'll be right here when you wake up."

She wanted to protest, but she was too tired. She wanted to be with Alex, but he promised he'd be here when she woke up. With a sigh she relaxed and let the darkness overtake her again.

Sarah slowly opened her eyes and frowned. She realized she was lying in a bed, but the blanket didn't have the smell she'd come to associate with the workhouse. Then she remembered. She was in a hospital. Alex had told her he would be here when she woke up, but that had to have been a dream. Alex was in Memphis, working at a law firm, and in love with another woman.

Her eyes burned from the tears that filled them, and she blinked. When her vision had cleared, she let her gaze drift around the room. She took in the stark white walls and tried to focus on the one window, but there was no sunlight coming in. It had to be night. Her body stiffened at the memory of another night and darkness surrounding her as she hung shackled to the bars in her cell.

"Ruth! Henrietta!" she rasped. "Where are you?"

She sucked in her breath at the sound of a quick movement beside her bed. "Sarah! You're awake again. I've been so worried."

She looked up at the figure hovering over her and let out a gasp. If she'd been dreaming earlier, she was again because Alex looked down at her. She licked her lips and forced herself to speak. "You really are here."

He smiled and clasped her hand. "Yes, I'm really here."

Her gaze raked his face, and she flinched at the tired look in his eyes and the stubble on his cheeks. He looked as if he hadn't shaved in days. "How long have you been here?"

"We brought you from the prison five days ago, but you've been very ill. We've been so worried." His voice quivered with the words, and his hand gripped hers like a vise.

She rubbed her forehead with her free hand. "I remember hanging in my cell, but not much after that. I heard voices sometimes, and I tried to talk to them. It hurt too much. I just wanted to sleep."

"You're going to be fine now. You're in a good hospital, not that excuse of an infirmary where we found you. The doctors here have been very cooperative and have let Edmund help treat you since we brought you here. Ellen and Dora have hardly left your side. I had to make them get some sleep tonight."

Her heart skipped a beat. "Ellen and Dora are both here?"

"You'll see them in the morning. Just rest now. You need to get your strength back."

She shivered and clutched Alex's hand at a sudden thought. "What about the other women?"

"After the night the guards went on their rampage, word leaked out to the newspapers about what was going on in Occoquan. Two lawyers took the story to a judge, and he released all the women into their custody." He smiled at her and rubbed her hand.

"Where are they now?"

"The day after their release, they went to court. You were too sick to be there, but the others went. The judge dropped all the charges and freed all the pickets."

"And Henrietta?"

He chuckled and shook his head. "Henrietta fine. She's been very worried about you. She told me that she couldn't have made it in the workhouse if it hadn't been for you."

Sarah smiled at the thought of her friend. "Where is she now?"

Alex's smile grew larger. "That's the interesting part. Her mother came from Boston to take her home, but Henrietta refused to go, even when her mother insisted. She said she meant to stay here until you recovered. I don't think she had ever defied her mother before, and she was really impressed that Henrietta stood up for herself. She's very proud of what she did for the suffrage cause."

Tears filled Sarah's eyes, and her heart soared at the words she heard. She placed her free hand on top of his which still held hers. "I'm glad they're all safe, but there's something I want you to know. That judge may have dropped the charges against me, but my real freedom came the night the guards shackled me to the bars."

He shook his head. "I don't want you to think about that night. What they did to you was unforgiveable, and I hope the court makes them pay for their cruelty."

"You don't understand," she said. "Being shackled in that cell made me take a good look at myself, and I didn't like what I saw. I knew then the only one that could help me was God, and I gave Him my life that night. I wish I could really explain what peace came over me, but I knew I was going to be all right no matter what happened." She paused for a moment before she continued. "And I prayed for you while I was hanging there."

Alex's eyebrows arched. "What did you pray about for me?"

Her eyes filled with tears again. "I prayed that you would have a good life, that you'd be happy. I knew I'd thrown away what we had, but I wanted you to find happiness somewhere else."

He didn't say anything for a moment, and then he smiled. "There is no happiness for me if it isn't with you, Sarah." Alex raised her hand to his lips and kissed her fingers. "I've prayed for you ever since you left. Some days I'd nearly go crazy worrying about you, but God would remind me He still controlled our lives."

"Thank you for praying and not giving up."

Alex looked into her eyes. "That last day when I saw you in Memphis, I told you I understood about your dream. I should have listened to you from the very beginning and supported you, but I didn't. I let the lure of a lucrative law practice and the prestige that went with it cloud my judgment. I soon found out, however, that the money at Mr. Buckley's firm could never take the place of having you in my life. I still love you, Sarah. I always will. Please come home with me and be my wife."

She studied his face for a moment. "But what about Larraine Buckley?"

A slight flush covered his face. "She's a very nice person, and I enjoyed her company. I thought I could trade love for companionship, but I couldn't. I never felt about her like I've felt about you since the day I saw you with your skirt pulled up at the pump behind Charlie's store."

A chuckle rumbled in her chest, and she frowned at the temporary pain. "I thought you were scandalous to talk to me like you did, but I couldn't deny the feelings I had for you, that I still have for you. But are you sure you still want me, Alex?" Her voice trembled, and a tear welled at the edge of her eye.

He grinned. "I want you more than ever, but you may not want to marry me. I don't have a job anymore."

A small gasp escaped her mouth. "You've left Mr. Buckley's firm?"

He nodded. "Well, I guess I was fired, but it's all right. I didn't fit in there. I'll find something else."

Her stomach clenched at the thought of the people she'd trusted at the school where she'd taught. "I guess I'm fired, too." Tears sprang to her eyes. "Alex. I'm so sorry I didn't listen to you about Roger Thorne. H-he t-tried to. . .he tried to. . ."

Alex pressed his finger to her lips. "I know. We don't have to talk about this until you're better. We both made the wrong choices, but now we have the chance to undo that and make the right one. What do you say, Sarah? I choose you, and I hope you'll choose me."

A tear trickled from her eye. "I do choose you, and I'm so sorry it's taken me so long to tell you that. I should have tried harder to work things out instead of accusing you of just wanting to make money. I was so happy to see you that day you came to the school, but I let you leave without telling you. Can you ever forgive me for being so selfish?"

Alex swallowed and took a deep breath. "That's all behind us now. All I want is to spend the rest of my life with you as my wife. I love you so much, Sarah."

Her heart pounded in her chest, and happiness bubbled from deep inside. "I love you, too. I want to go home and be married in the church at Richland Creek. Can we do that?"

Alex's tired face beamed. "We'll go just as soon as you can travel." He released her hand and fumbled in his pocket. "Oh, I almost forgot. Dora wanted me to give you this when you woke up."

Her mother's locket hung from his fingers. He gently raised her head and fastened the catch. She clasped the pendant in her hand and felt the indentions on the back. "Sometimes at the workhouse I would reach for this, and I'd remember how I'd lost it just like I lost everything else. I didn't think I'd ever regain anything I threw away."

"Well, you have the necklace and all of us back. We're going to have a grand life together, Sarah."

A sudden thought crossed her mind, and she frowned. "You do understand that I still intend to work for women's right to vote."

Alex reached behind him, drew a chair closer to the bed, and sat down. His eyes softened as his gaze raked her face, and he let out a deep sigh. "Sarah, you went on a hunger strike and defied all the guards at Occoquan Workhouse. I am in awe of your courage and determination. I've done a lot of soul searching since you left, and I don't like some of the things I found out about myself. So, I want to work with you in this campaign. There's a lot we can do back in Tennessee to help convince our legislators to support women's rights." He paused and cocked an eyebrow at her. "I just don't want to have to get you out of jail again."

Sarah studied his face to detect any signs of doubt, but all she could see was love shining there. "Alex, I may make your life miserable. Are you sure you want to tie yourself to a woman that's stubborn and opinionated and argues at the drop of a hat?"

He chuckled. "Do you remember the day Ellen and I came to visit and you'd been working in the garden?"

She nodded. "I looked a mess and didn't have any shoes on."

"And I said you were feisty."

"I remember."

He leaned closer. "Well, I liked feisty then, and I still do. We're going to have a wonderful life, Sarah."

They laughed together, and Sarah's heart reached to God in silent gratitude. When she had thought she was so alone, He'd been watching over her and reminding those who loved her to keep praying for her. God had seen her through a terrible time, and now a new life lay before her. She would never be alone again.

Epilogue

Tennessee State Capitol
Nashville, Tennessee
August 18, 1920

The day Sarah had waited years for had finally arrived. If all went well, the long struggle would soon be over. Only one more state was needed to ratify the 19th Amendment giving women the right to vote, and the nation's attention focused on the Tennessee legislature today. From her front row seat next to Alex in the public balcony above the Tennessee House of Representatives' floor, Sarah studied the men below. The legislators huddled in small groups and glanced up from time to time at the rapidly filling public balcony. Try as she might she couldn't make out anything they were saying to each other. She glanced down at the basket of yellow rose petals in her lap and gripped the handle of the container tighter.

The newspapers had sensationalized the governor's called session and dubbed it the War of the Roses. The delegates who supported suffrage wore yellow roses in their lapels, and those against wore red. From all appearances an equal division occupied the coats of the men.

A tug on her arm distracted her, and she turned to smile at her year-old daughter sitting in Alex's lap. She raised her daughter's chubby hand to her mouth and kissed it. "Do you

296

think we should have let Dora keep Catt at home instead of bringing her with us?"

Alex glanced down at the child and held her closer. "No, I want her to know she was in the legislature the day history was made. Besides Dora wanted to be here, too."

Sarah glanced at her family beside her. Edmund, Ellen, and Dora had joined Alex and her to witness what could be the end of a struggle that began many years before. Ellen smiled at her brother and leaned over to pat the silky blonde hair of the baby. "If you get tired of holding her, just pass my little angel over. Edmund and I don't mind taking our turn."

Edmund smiled his agreement. "That's right."

Sarah laughed. "You just want to spoil her and then give her back to me."

Ellen arched her eyebrows. "What's an aunt and uncle for if we can't spoil her when we're with her?"

Alex laughed and patted his sister's arm. "We're glad you came to Nashville with us. It means a lot that you're here supporting this vote today."

A rustling sound in the aisle next to her caught Sarah's attention, and she turned to see a woman who had become a close friend over the past few years. "Good morning, Sarah. Is this precious child the one I've heard so much about?" Carrie Chapman Catt leaned over and chucked the baby under the chin.

Sarah smiled up at the woman. "This is Catherine Ellen Taylor. But we call her Catt."

Mrs. Catt's eyes softened. "So you're my namesake. What a beautiful daughter you have. I'm honored you wanted to name her after me."

The manner in which Carrie addressed the child contradicted the take charge attitude Sarah had seen in the woman during the last three years. Her almost regal bearing and her white hair gave the appearance of a kindly grandmother, but Sarah had seen the woman in action and knew her ability to evaluate situations and make quick decisions.

Sarah grasped the woman's hand. "I'm honored to have worked with you these last three years. I know we're going to see the fruits of our labors today."

"I hope so. You and Alex have certainly gone way beyond the call of duty in traveling across your state and talking with the legislators. I hope your work didn't suffer because of taking time off."

Alex waved his hand in dismissal. "That's one of the good things about having your own firm. You can arrange your schedule like you want. Of course having a partner like Will Page who shares your beliefs helps a lot."

Sarah nodded and smiled. "And he's praying for us today. We know God's in control of what happens here today."

Mrs. Catt looked toward the men on the floor. "I see they're all wearing roses. Our last count on each one's position tells us we're deadlocked with forty-eight on each side of the issue. With thirty-five states having ratified the amendment so far, I had hoped when the voted passed in the Tennessee senate two days ago this state would be the final one in the needed thirty-six for ratification."

Sarah smiled. "But that just means we're only a half state away from ratification."

Mrs. Catt smiled at her. "Ever the optimist, Sarah."

"Where do you go from here if Tennessee fails today?" Alex asked as he jiggled his daughter on his knee.

Mrs. Catt sighed. "I don't know. The prospects aren't good in any of the remaining states. We'll just have to decide after today."

Sarah hugged her basket closer. "There's no need to go anywhere else. I know God has listened, and I've called on

Him for a victory. The Tennessee representatives will come through for us. I know it."

Mrs. Catt stared at her for a moment, and Sarah saw a hint of tears in her eyes. "I envy you the great faith you have." Then she turned and found her seat among the women who sat across the aisle from Sarah.

When the Speaker of the House finally called the assembly to order, Sarah clasped her hands in her lap and squeezed so tightly that her fingernails dug into her palms. She fidgeted through the opening of the session and waited impatiently for the question of the day to be called. Just as she thought it was about to happen, the Speaker pounded his gavel and addressed the group.

"Representatives of the Tennessee Legislature, I surrender my chair so that I may address the assembly."

Sarah scooted to the edge of her seat and held her breath as he walked from the podium and stood on the floor facing the delegates. "I move that the Tennessee House of Representatives table the vote on ratification of the amendment for enfranchisement for women."

A quick second to the motion rose from the seated assemblymen.

Waves of unrest rippled across the gallery. Alex swiveled in his seat and muttered under his breath. "I can't believe he would do a cheap trick like this. He knows if this is tabled, there's no chance of getting it back before the legislature, and the amendment along with the vote for women is dead."

Sarah reached over and patted her husband's arm. "It's all right."

The roll call began as names of the assemblymen rang out. One after another they voted. "Ayes," and "Nayes" echoed throughout the chamber until all had answered.

The temporary speaker turned to the recorder. "What is the vote?"

The man glanced at the totals. "Forty-eight ayes, for-ty-eight nayes."

The temporary Speaker pounded the gavel on the po-dium. "The motion is defeated. We will now proceed to the matter at hand. Please vote for or against ratification of the 19th amendment to the Constitution of the United States when your name is called."

The roll call began again. Sarah bowed her head and listened to the men who called out their vote one after anoth-er. She had memorized the names of the delegates and took mental note of each of their answers. Suddenly she jerked her head up and stared in disbelief at the floor below. She glanced across the aisle at Mrs. Catt who whispered excitedly to the woman next to her.

Alex frowned and leaned close to her. "What is it?"

"Harry Burn just voted for ratification. He's wearing a red rose." Her pulse began to race, and those seated in the gallery began to stir. An air of anticipation hovered over the listeners.

The minutes ticked by slowly with one after another responding to the question. A hush fell across the room as the Speaker asked for the results. The clerk rose to report the tal-ly. "The vote is as follows. Forty-nine Ayes, and Forty-seven Nayes. The motion to ratify the amendment passes."

Screams of joy rose from the gallery. Sarah jumped up with all the women who stood along the front row and scat-tered her yellow rose petals over the assemblymen below. She then turned to Alex who was on his feet and hugged him before running across the aisle to embrace Mrs. Catt. Tears of joy ran down their faces as they hugged.

Loud cries rang out from below. Sarah looked to the floor below where policemen formed a protective circle around Harry Burn. They pushed through the mob of angry legislators who screamed and shook their fists in Representative Burn's face.

Sarah turned to Alex. "I've got to find out why he changed his vote."

She ran from the gallery and raced down the steps to the lower level. Harry Burn, surrounded by policemen and reporters, stood outside the assembly room.

The reporters shouted questions, but the angry roars from inside the assembly room almost drowned them out. A reporter beside Harry called out. "Why did you do it, Harry?"

Sarah shoved her way through the crowd and wedged into the group as close to Representative Burn as she could get. He glanced over his shoulder as if expecting to be attacked any moment before he spoke. "I grew up on a farm that my mother still runs in East Tennessee. She gets mighty upset that the men who work for her can vote, and she can't. She wrote me a letter this week and told me she's been thinking about this ratification thing. She told me to help Mrs. Catt put the rat in ratification, and you know a boy needs to do what his mother says."

The reporters all laughed. "Is there more to the story?"

He hesitated before answering, and a somber expression covered his face. "I knew that I had an opportunity like few ever have to change history, and I wanted to do that."

He pushed from the reporters and walked quickly down the hall with his police escort. Sarah watched him go, his shoulders back and his head held high. Her eyes filled with tears at the courage it had taken for him to stand against his friends, and she closed her eyes. *Thank you, God, for using this man. Thank you for the victory for today's women and those yet to come.*

"Are you ready to go, Sarah?"

She opened her eyes and looked around at Alex standing beside her with their daughter in his arms, and her heart nearly burst with joy. Catt leaned over toward Sarah and grabbed the locket she wore.

Sarah smiled and pulled the pendant from Catt's hand just before the child stuck it in her mouth. A loud wail erupted from Catt's mouth, and Alex struggled to hold his daughter still.

Sarah looked into Alex's eyes and laughed. "My mother used to tell me I'd pay for my raising. I didn't understand then, but I can see this little girl is going to keep me on my knees."

Alex put his arm around Sarah, and they walked to the front entrance of the capitol and exited into the sunshine. She looked up at her husband and remembered a conversation they'd had years ago.

Alex had told her once that our lives are ruled by the choices we make. Today Harry Burn had made a choice that wasn't a popular one with many people, but it had been the right one. Because of him, women would now have the privilege of walking into a voting booth and casting a vote for a candidate. It never ceased to amaze her how God could take a situation doomed to failure and turn it into something for good.

God had taken the bad choices she made and turned them into a life filled with joy and a family who loved her. Today He had added another blessing that at times she thought might never come to be.

Sarah glanced down the steep steps to the street below where cars honked and people on foot rushed by without looking to the right or left. She reached over and took her daughter's small hand in hers. "Look, Catt. They don't realize this is a special day. Today we're citizens."

Dear Readers,

Thank you so much for reading The Right Choice. This story of the fight for women's suffrage in America is one that all women should be familiar with. Although the characters in the book are fictional, the facts presented about the suffrage movement are true. The fight to gain the right to vote for women took many years and there were many advocates who worked hard to make it happen.

It is difficult to believe in the twenty-first century that there could ever have been the belief by some that women should never have the right to vote. Today we enjoy the freedom that wasn't afforded our ancestors who struggled to see that their daughters, granddaughters, and generations to come would enjoy the opportunity they never had. This is a story that honors those who worked so hard to give us the choices that we have today.

If you enjoyed this book, I hope you will share it with a friend. I've found so many new authors that way. Also the more reviews a book gets the more likely readers are to find it. I would appreciate it if you would leave a review on Amazon or Goodreads.

Would you like to know more about my next book? You can sign up for my newsletter on my website http://sandrarobbins.net or become my friend on Facebook or follow me on Twitter. Titles of more books, both historical romance and romantic suspense, are also on my website, and I hope you will check it out.

Sandra Robbins

Other Books by Sandra Robbins

Angel of the Cove
Mountain Homecoming
Beyond These Hills

Igniting the Flame
Targeted
Hunted
Betrayed

Dangerous Reunion
Shattered Identity
Fatal Disclosure

Dangerous Waters
Yuletide Jeopardy
Trail of Secrets

Fugitive Trackdown
Fugitive at Large
Yuletide Fugitive Threat

In a Killer's Sights
Stalking Season
Ranch Hideout
Point Blank